Hook's Tale

Being the Account of an Unjustly Villainized Pirate Written by Himself

Emended and Edited by

John Leonard Pielmeier

SCRIBNER

New York   London   Toronto   Sydney   New Delhi

Scribner
An Imprint of Simon & Schuster, Inc.
1230 Avenue of the Americas
New York, NY 10020

First Scribner hardcover edition July 2017

SCRIBNER and design are registered trademarks of The Gale Group, Inc.,
used under license by Simon & Schuster, Inc., the publisher of this work.

For information about special discounts for bulk purchases,
please contact Simon & Schuster Special Sales at 1-866-506-1949
or business@simonandschuster.com.

The Simon & Schuster Speakers Bureau can bring authors to
your live event. For more information or to book an event, contact the
Simon & Schuster Speakers Bureau at 1-866-248-3049 or visit our
website at www.simonspeakers.com.

Interior design by Kyle Kabel

Manufactured in the United States of America

1   3   5   7   9   10   8   6   4   2

Library of Congress Cataloging-in-Publication Data is available.

ISBN 978-1-5011-6105-6
ISBN 978-1-5011-6107-0 (ebook)

For Tiger Lily and Wendy
and my dear Daisy

—James Cook

For Irene,
who is my Tiger Lily and my Wendy
and sometimes my Josephine

—John Leonard Pielmeier

PART ONE

---◆◇◆---

THE LITTLE WHITE BIRD

Chapter One

––––•⦗∞⦘•––––

When I was six years old or thereabouts, I had a horrific nightmare that I still remember quite clearly.

Earlier in the day I had gone walking alone in the Kensington Gardens, which was quite close to my home. I was an independent child, and the dangers lurking in wait for independent children of today were unknown back then, so I felt quite safe. I came upon a thick thorny shrub during my walk, in the middle of which rested a tiny nest containing four eggs. Curious to examine them, I reached my little hand through the thorny protection and was startled when, before I could come close to touching the nest, there appeared out of nowhere a small white bird that began attacking me from above. Undoubtedly, this was the mother keeping a lookout for predators, and on spying my intent she swooped down on me with a sharp high cry. I ducked away from her attack, at the same time jerking my hand out of the bush, and in doing so I scratched myself on the thorns rather badly. With blood running down my fingers, I raced home.

That night my dreams took me back to the incident, only

this time, as the bird swooped, the tiny eggs hatched four little monster-birds who began jabbing their needle-long beaks into my hand. One of them caught hold of a vein and began tugging it as if it were a worm. The others took hold of it too, and started fighting for possession. With each yank more and more of the vein emerged until it broke in two, spouting blood. The pain was excruciating. I seized the babies, all four, in my fist and crushed them, while my free hand grabbed hold of the mother. I put her head in my mouth and bit down hard.

I awoke screaming, my tongue bloody from where I had bitten it. My mother arrived at my bedside, and I was soon comforted, but what strikes me to this day is this: this nightmare of the innocent intent, the swooping bird, the bloodied hand, and my murderous revenge was but a foreshortened narrative of the rest of my life.

Everything you think you know about me is a lie.

I was born James Cook on the twenty-third of February in the year of our Lord 1860. I knew little of my father, James, who was a captain in the Royal Navy and who was lost at sea in the year of my birth. My mother and I lived in a small town house in Kensington, supported by an annual stipend bestowed on us by my father's family, not a single member of whom I had ever met and who steadfastly refused contact with us but for the January deposit paid into my mother's banking account. She missed my father terribly. In me, I imagine, she saw a shadow of his likeness.

My mother and I were quite close. An emotionally delicate woman, she depended on me for company and it was I alone who could brighten her life. She suffered from frequent and severe headaches, punctuated by bouts of melancholia, and would often, during those early years, disappear into her room for days at a time, emerging with apologies and much self-recrimination. I never minded being alone in our little house, however, it being filled with memories of my father.

The ground-floor back room of the house was his library and was stocked with books he had acquired on his travels or received as gifts. Though I was a precocious lad, I did not learn to read until, beginning at the age of seven, I was sent to Mr. Wilkinson's private day school in Kensington. From there I returned nightly to dine with my mother and, once my reading skills were up to it, to devour many of these books, hoping to find some clue as to my father's nature and interests. Most of the books were of the sea.

My favorite of these, *A History of the Voyages of Captain James Cook,* was inscribed with my father's name and the date of his graduation from Eton College. It was, according to my mother, a gift from my father's father, who was a direct descendant of the brave captain himself, though I never knew whether that blood came to me legitimately or by more questionable means. I devoured the *History* as if it were my own.

Cook was quite a famous person even in *my* day; indeed he was perhaps the greatest English explorer who ever lived. He circumnavigated the globe two and a half times, discovering most of what we know today as the South Sea Islands, not to mention New Zealand and Australia. Much maligned and misunderstood by people then and now (as am I, dear reader), he was a man of science, of peace, and of unbounded curiosity. He was murdered in the middle of his last voyage by the natives of the Sandwich Islands. They reportedly "cooked" and ate him. My young imagination envisioned them serving him with grilled tomato, in a sandwich.

When my mother first came upon me perusing this book, she burst into tears. I asked her why. "It reminds me of your dear father," she said, "but it is wrong of me to miss him so, for he is here in you, in your face and your hands, your dear sweet hands." And she kissed my fingers and held me tight. I asked her then how she and my father first met, but she avoided a direct answer, simply saying that he was the handsomest man she had ever laid eyes on, and she fell in love with him at once. Had she met any of his family, I queried, and she replied "only at the service." At first I thought she meant the marriage service, but then I realized that it was the final one, after he was lost.

On those occasions when my mother was feeling especially poorly, we were visited by Doctor Uriah Slinque, the only adult who called at our house with any regularity. A tall man, he always gave me a lemon-flavored sweet to suck before sequestering himself in my mother's room. I felt uneasy whenever he arrived, most likely because these arrivals always marked a low point in my mother's constitution, but his visits generally led to my mother emerging from her room at her best and brightest, and for that I was thankful. I would learn more of him, sadly, in the years to come.

When I was thirteen, my mother received instructions from our benefactors' lawyer that I was to be sent to Eton

College, after my father. It was with great sadness that I took leave of her, who through her tears promised that we would be together again soon, come the Christmas holidays. I vowed to write every day. Though the distance to Eton was not great, it might as well have been half a globe away. I remember watching her pale face vanishing in the crowd as my carriage pulled away from the station platform. Little did I know that I was never to set eyes on her again.

My entrance into Eton was difficult, to say the least. Most of the boys hailed from wealthy families, containing two parents and often several siblings. They were loud and boisterous and well connected, while I was shy and poor and semi-orphaned, and it became their great sport to ignore me in the classroom and pummel me on the playing fields. It was not until I announced my family's provenance one day during a class on the history of the Crown that any attention or respect was paid to me at all. As the words left my mouth I could sense the entire room sitting straighter with surprise and fascination.

Before I come to that, however, I must speak of my greatest adversary there—my father, or rather my father's reputation. He had been first of his form in nearly everything that counts: first in bravery, first in cricket, first in leadership. He was a member of Pop as well as Sixth Form Select. His mischief, while officially disapproved of by the instructors, was secretly admired. His bravura during his frequent caning was such that masters broke wands on him in order to get him to cry out; no one succeeded. His voice was angelic, whether as a rich alto in his younger years or as a silky baritone as he matured. His Mercutio was unforgettable; his Mrs. Malaprop bettered Mrs. Siddons's. His sense of style was admired and copied; his winning streak on the playing fields, admired and unquestioned; his devilish soul and sensitive spirit, admired, admired, admired.

Many sons would have grown to hate him. I only loved him all the more.

Of course I couldn't possibly approach his reputation. Viewed initially as a boy with Great Promise, I was within weeks demoted to Unmitigated Disappointment. "It's a good thing your father isn't alive to know of this," one master told me after I misconjugated a Latin verb. I would have preferred caning to his words. I cried myself to sleep that night, and nearly every night thereafter. My father was untouchable, not only because he was legendary but also because he was dead. His heroism had tripled in memory. To compete with him was impossible. Still, I tried.

And I always failed. Boys soon ceased to cover their mouths when they laughed at me; their mockery was open, and the masters seldom stopped it. It wasn't until one day in the aforementioned history class that my fortune, for a short while, changed.

Our instructor, Mr. Stevenson, had asked the boys to speak briefly of their immediate ancestry, expecting nothing more, I am sure, than the occupations or titles of their fathers and grandfathers. When my turn came I stated that I was a direct descendant of Captain James Cook. I admit that my announcement grew more from a desperate reach for approval than from a desire to fulfill Stevenson's instructions, but as soon as I spoke a hush fell over the room. Suddenly all eyes were on me, and since I had perused my father's library, and the *History* in particular, I was quite well versed in the captain's story and, in elaborating on the voyages, trumped even Mr. Stevenson in knowledge of Cook's Discoveries in the South Seas. Being an adolescent, and sensing my schoolmates' approval of my declaration, I naturally embroidered my own story with elements meant to elevate the position I held in their eyes. Not only did I possess my great-great-grandfather's *History*, I told some of them after class, but I owned the brave captain's spyglass, as well as a farewell letter written to his wife (my great-great-grandmother), its parchment stained with the blood spilled by his Sandwich Island murderers. A few of the boys scoffed at this, but the majority were wide-eyed in wonder, and that night I entertained my dinner companions with stories of the captain's astonishing adventures, some of which contained a few elements of truth.

The days that followed were, perhaps, the happiest of my life, and certainly (as of this writing) nearly the last happy days of my existence. (An exception is to follow, dear reader, but I plead for your patience.) Had I but known what was to come, I might have reveled in these days of glory all the more. For too short a time I was the star of the school, or at least of my house, for this new confidence in myself and my abilities soon evinced itself on the playing field—where I scored several goals in football—and in the classroom— where I excelled briefly in maths and Latin, the two subjects in which heretofore I had always stumbled. Sadly, I neglected writing my mother for nearly a week, an act of omission that I know had little to do with what happened but for which I have blamed myself throughout all the years of my unfortunate existence.

On the Tuesday of the second week of my popularity I was called to the headmaster's office. Old Carlyle (as he was called, there being an instructor at the college who was dubbed Young Carlyle) asked me to take a chair and once I was stiffly seated told me bluntly that my mother had died. She had had a seizure, Old Carlyle explained, while she was bathing, and had drowned in the tub. (Indeed, she had been subject on occasion to seizures in the past, which she called her "spells," this being one reason given for her frequent retreats to her room and the saving visits by Doctor Slinque; I was prevented from having to witness any of these episodes in person, and their frequency diminished as I grew older.) Her body had not been discovered for several days, Old Carlyle added, and so was in no fit condition for viewing. The funeral was to be held on Thursday, after which I was to return to school.

Leaving his office I went directly to the Eton Wall, its brick facade comforting in its curves. I climbed atop and sat there for some time. I did not cry; instead I wished myself dead.

I remember little of the following days. The funeral was attended by myself, my great-aunt Emily, and a lawyer from my late father's family estate. He afterward told me that the house in Kensington was to be sold as soon as possible. (It had been owned, I discovered, by my Cook benefactors, who had allowed my mother to occupy it while I grew.) Furthermore, he said, my education at Eton was to continue until "such time as it ended," a cryptic remark if ever there was one. I was allowed to claim my clothing and whatever else I could carry "manually" (the lawyer's term) from my mother's house, and nothing more. Great-Aunt Emily, who was my only surviving relative on my mother's side, tearfully held me close and told me that I was welcome at her little cottage in Yorkshire during the holidays, given sufficient notice. Her breath smelled of mint, and her mustache irritated my cheek.

Doctor Slinque alone offered me distraction, extending an invitation to visit his laboratory. (But more of this later.)

I returned to Eton the following day, bringing with me a trunkful of clothing as well as the *History of the Voyages of Captain James Cook,* my mother's wedding ring, and a golden locket (which I had never before set eyes on) containing a small daguerreotype of my father's face opposite one of my mother's. I opened the locket but two or three times during the weeks it was in my possession; my pater's visage was quite blurred, as though he could not keep still (and I *did* like to think of him as a man of action), and the sight of my poor mother's youthful countenance so broke my heart that I could not bear to look at her. The wedding ring was inscribed with the words *To My Eternal Love.* I wore it on my finger at night; during school hours I hid it in my nightshirt pocket.

I was pitied at first by the other boys at school, but soon the mantle of Orphan became a burden, viewed as it was as a fault that anyone of good breeding could easily have avoided. When several of the boys asked to see the captain's spyglass and the bloodied letter (since they assumed that I had retrieved them from my lost home, and had brought them with me to school), I told them that the items had been destroyed in a fire. They quickly saw through this bald lie, and once again I became the target of their mockery.

The next few weeks were pure wretchedness, each day a further descent into Dante's lower depths, though the Hell of my experience held many more than nine circles; it was bottomless. Its fires burned hottest when my "piratical nature" (as Old Carlyle put it) was uncovered.

Old Carlyle was a pompous sort who prided himself on his knowledge of the ancient Greeks. His most prized possession was a manuscript he had acquired of Plato's *Republic,* a "medieval" tome of spurious provenance that he kept under glass in his office. It was on a Monday morning shortly after the Christmas holidays (which I spent alone at the college) that on entering his office he discovered the glass box shattered and a page unceremoniously ripped from the manuscript. The missing page was nowhere in sight.

To say that the actions that followed were nothing short of loot and pillage would be an understatement. The boys' dormitories were turned inside out, with pupils' trunks gutted, their mattresses stripped and flipped, and their clothing and schoolbooks manhandled as if by the lowest of ruffians. Some boys were "unmasked" when photographs and magazines of the French sort were discovered hidden among their underclothes. But the blade fell full force when the missing page, smeared with excrement, was finally found in the bottom of the trunk of one Jacobus Cook, namely myself. I was, needless to say, completely innocent.

The piracy, I suppose, was committed by any one of a number of boys who wanted some fun at my expense. They got their fun, and then some. I was hauled before the assembled student body, where I was ordered to disrobe and bend over, baring my bum to the sniggering audience, after which Carlyle caned me to within an inch of my life. Blood running down my shins, I was then forced to kneel and apologize to Carlyle and the entire student body—past, present, and future—for my sinful ways.

My expulsion was expected any day, though even Old Carlyle could not bring himself to expel a boy lying bleeding in an infirmary bed, so the dreaded announcement was postponed, I imagine, until my wounds might be deemed closer to some sort of healing. My father's family was notified of my crime, though of course I heard not a word from them, either in sympathy or in recrimination. As I lay on my bloodied sheets recovering, I resolved to leave the school on my own before being drummed out publicly, and to either seek my fortune with my father's family (whose uncertain company was preferable to my great-aunt Emily's) or find it alone. As soon as I was able to walk I rose silently in the night, gathered my possessions into a makeshift knapsack fashioned from my pillow casing, and headed out on the road to Penzance, in the heart of which my father's family resided.

I was determined that they should ignore me no longer. I would prove my worth, and soon be welcomed among them as my father's noble and deserving heir.

I walked for several weeks, occasionally winning a ride on the back of a wagon heading west. My legs were scabbed and raw, and caused me no end of pain, though I bore it as well as I could. The weather turned wet and cold, and it was a miracle that I did not die of exposure along the way. One night, when I was perhaps a dozen miles from Penzance and wondering how my father's family would receive me, I passed an inn (christened the Wretched Traveler, a name I found sadly appropriate to my state) that looked bright and inviting. Roars of laughter and good cheer were echoing from the bar. Here I might rest, I thought, so that I could meet my relatives refreshed and renewed on the morrow. I had no money to pay for a room and bath, but I hoped to find some warmth among the horses stabled in the nearby barn, and if luck were with me I could beg a bite of sustenance from a good-hearted farmhand come for a pint and a pie.

I entered the barn to stow my knapsack before dining. Three of the four horse stalls were occupied, but the smallest one nearest the door was free, and I arranged the straw piled there into a comfortable bed. Suddenly, as I was pillowing the hay, I found myself pushed to the barn floor and the weight of another person pressing down on top of me.

"Are you beggar or thief?" rasped a harsh voice. The owner's breath was foul, and I wrinkled my nose in disgust.

"Neither, sir," I returned. "I'm a weary traveler who has no gold to buy a place to sleep. As a Christian I beg you, sir, allow me this small comfort."

Rough hands turned me over to lie on my back. His face was that of a pimply youth missing his lower front teeth. It hovered horribly but a few inches above mine.

"No gold? What's this then?" he asked, and his grubby fingers clutched at my mother's locket, which I now wore around my neck. He brought it close to his eyes.

"It belonged to my mother, who is dead. Please, sir, 'tis the only image I have of her."

"No it's not," said the pimple-faced footpad. "Cause now *I* have it." He laughed as he yanked hard at the chain. For a moment I thought he would strangle me. Then the chain broke free from my neck.

"Give it back!" I shouted and scrambled to retrieve it.

He kneed me with malicious force. The pain took away my breath.

"You're welcome to sleep here, boy. Consider your room well paid for. Go into the inn and get my ma to feed you whatever slop she has for the pigs. Tell her Scroff sends you." Smiling, he backed off as he pocketed the locket and chain. "And thank me while you're at it. I'm a Christian too." He laughed and stepped out into the night.

Once I regained my breath I entered the inn looking for something or someone on which to beat out my fury. A large blowsy woman stood behind the bar. She too was missing her lower front teeth, and I assumed she was Scroff's ma. But before I could approach her and accuse her son of thievery, I was pounced on by a tall muscular man who handed me a pint and dragged me to a corner table. Undeniably voluble and friendly, he plopped a small plate of sausage and mash before me without my even asking. I needed to gain some strength before confronting Scroff or his ma, and so I devoured the meat and potatoes, thanking him with mouth stuffed, then quaffed the beer. As soon as one pint was empty, another full one was placed before me, and I (who had never allowed strong drink to pass my lips, and very little beer) drank my fill. This will give me courage, I remember thinking, and the next thing I knew I was tumbling face-forward onto the dinner plate and thence into darkness.

Whether I lost consciousness because of my wounds, my starvation, or my inebriation, or because the beer was doctored with an opiate, matters little. I know only that I awoke in a ship's hold, pressed into service by the tall muscular man (whose name was Starkey) and Her Majesty's Royal Navy. A few other hapless young men from the inn were lying beside me, equally confused and groggy. I staggered to the top deck, where I instantly emptied the contents of my stomach overboard. No land was in sight.

One piece of good fortune was that my pillowcase-knapsack had made it on board. Without it the tale that follows would be brief and woefully uneventful.

Starkey soon hauled the rest of my kidnapped companions on deck, where he gently mocked us as a sad passel of "lost lads." He would make men of us, he said, for we were now bound to serve the Queen for several years at sea, and he waved a piece of paper before us containing scrawled signatures that we were too ill to examine closely. I was the youngest of his "lads," and was soon to celebrate my fourteenth birthday in the middle of the Atlantic Ocean without ceremony.

The ship was dubbed *Victoria Gloriosa*, a three-masted noncombat vessel of the clipper variety. She was bound, in this time of peace, to the West Indies with a hold full of sundries and provisions to be exchanged for rum. Her captain was named Styles, a man for whom the word *emotion* was but an unhappy description of the weakness of others. The ship's doctor was a Doctor Flynn, though the sailors referred to him as Doctor Gin, since that was his most oft-prescribed medication as well as his own drug of choice. He was overly fond, I was told, of amputation, and the sailors joked that his solution to the common cold was the removal of the sick man's nose. It was Gin's assistant, however, whom I came to know best, a soft round Irishman of uncertain age whose head was a billiard ball surrounded by soft fuzz and whose heart was equally soft and fuzzy. He resembled, I like to think, one of those rotund men of snow I occasionally built as a child in the Kensington Gardens, whose head was but an orb smaller than his middle, and whose middle was but a globe smaller than his hips. I no longer remember his given name; I only know him by the name I came to call him.

I was tired and I was ill and I was dispirited, and so without a will to protest I bent to my seaman's chores. They were slavey's chores mostly, hauling and cleaning and serving and polishing. It was in my second week aboard, pointlessly scrubbing the deck in the middle of a soft winter's snowfall (Starkey liked to keep us busy, even when there was little work to be done), that I collapsed with a fever. My forehead was beaded with sweat and my Eton wounds had festered, and when Doctor Gin had the pants off me and was examining the half-healed scars on my thighs, now red with infection, he loudly declared that the best way to treat them was to have both my legs off at once. I protested and struggled, but I was weak in limb and half-delirious with fever, and he had the bottle of gin to my lips and as much of its contents as he could manage down my throat before I could escape. I saw him sharpening his flensing knife as I passed into sleep.

When I drifted back to consciousness, I expected to find myself but half a boy. My legs, however, were still attached, and a soft hand pressed itself to my forehead. "Rest, boy, rest" came a gentle voice. My sight was blurred, and when I asked who it was who spoke, I heard only the words "It's me" in a soft Irish brogue.

When I opened my eyes again, hours or days later, he was

still standing over me, his billiard ball of a head atop his round middle and hips. "It's me," he said again, and from that day onward I called him what I thought he called himself: Smee.

Smee had saved my legs, and most likely my life. He had distracted Doctor Gin by plying the thirsty fellow with the very medication with which I had been doused. Soon Gin was snoring away, and Smee spread a disinfectant of his own concoction on my wounds. When the doctor awoke and staggered to his feet, Smee declared that I had taken a miraculous turn for the better, thanks to the good doctor's timely ministrations. Gin shrugged and returned to his bed.

I never learned the composition of Smee's medication. It had something of fish in it, and something of plant oil, and something of his "dear granny's secret solution for sup-purating pustules." I healed at last and took my place once again under Starkey, with this difference: I now had a friend. Indeed, when I told Smee of my naval ancestry, he forever after jokingly called me Cap'n.

One Sunday morning, when we had been over a month at sea, I lay in my cot with a few moments of time to myself. Styles was a religious man (as long as any religious expression had nothing of emotion in it), and we were allowed a few hours of our own to Keep Holy the Lord's Day unless there were something to be done on the Lord's Day that would prove advantageous to Her Majesty's Commerce. Sitting on the edge of my cot, I realized that it was my fourteenth birthday. I blinked back tears as I remembered my mother and her terrible end. I regretted the loss of the locket more than ever. Fortunately I still kept the wedding ring, for I'd had the foresight, before absconding from Eton, to sew it into the cuff of my trousers. I felt for it now and thought of the words *Eternal Love* inscribed within its circle. It was still in its hiding place, and the relief I felt turned my mind to pleasanter things. I reached into my knapsack and pulled out my father's *History*. Perhaps some moisture from the sea air had penetrated the binding, because I noticed for the first time a thickening beneath the front cover's leather. One corner of the frontispiece had loosened, and, peeling it away, I discovered a scrap of sailcloth hidden beneath.

It was a map of the Western Atlantic. The island of Bermuda was marked, and to the southwest of the island stood a crimson *X*, followed by the designation *N 31° 44′ 48″ W 67° 3′ 37″* and a crudely drawn creature that resembled a dragon. An unmarked island? I wondered. A treasure?

Beneath the map was scribbled a phrase in Latin. My Eton schooling helped but little in its translation. The word *star* was there, and I half-recognized a word that I took to mean "lesser." The rest of the phrase remained a mystery.

Whatever else it was, the map and its contents seemed to be some kind of message from my late father, a birthday gift as I entered my early maturity. But being fourteen and still quite young, and not knowing to whom I could turn for advice, I turned to Smee. The man is all kindness, true, but as an intellect he has a long way to travel. When I showed him the map, he suggested I share it with the captain, for if this was indeed a treasure map, the only way to take our ship to the marked latitude and longitude was through his orders. So I gathered my courage, and that evening after dinner I nervously knocked at the captain's cabin door. He bid me enter. I stuttered when he demanded the reason for my visit, until finally I held out the map and explained its source. He looked at it and laughed.

"You're a fool, boy," he said. "The ocean is deep there, with no land in sight. If a treasure is sunk in that spot, it is too far beneath the waves for any man to retrieve it." I asked him kindly for a translation of the Latin phrase. He studied it, looked up a word, and said that it referred to a "lesser star to starboard," which was pure nonsense. He laughed again and sent me away.

I reported this to Smee, who could not stop dreaming of the treasure. "He may be wrong," he said of the captain. "Nay, he must be wrong. I have an idea." He told me nothing more but that he had to "ruminate." I should have known better than to trust Smee's "ideas" and "rumination," but the man had saved my legs and life, and so I let him be.

One night within the week I was shaken awake by Starkey. "Give it here, lad," he ordered, meaning the map. Smee had told him of my discovery. Had I known where this request would lead, I would not have handed it over. I would have told him I had tossed it overboard, or had dreamed it in a fevered sleep. But instead I showed him the document, and as he perused it I saw the greed a-glimmer in his eyes and I knew I had made a grave error.

Sweet as sugared molasses, he begged leave to borrow the map for a short while. I nodded—what else could I do?—and he thanked me. It was two days later that the mutiny took place, and my destiny changed forever.

A handful of seamen, led by Starkey and armed to the teeth (I later learned), burst into the captain's cabin at midnight. Styles was hauled to the top deck in his nightshirt, after which the entire crew (myself among them) was roused. There Starkey declared himself captain, explaining that this change of command was due to a certain treasure he had learned of, a treasure that Captain Styles meant to keep to himself rather than share with any aboard. All who sided with himself, Starkey announced, would share equally in that treasure, which would prove without question to be unsurpassed in the history of treasures. Those who sided with Styles would meet a fishy end. Naturally the majority of seamen agreed to join with Starkey, whether from avarice or from fear I do not know. Because I was young, I agreed too.

Those who were loyal to the captain voiced their protest, and Starkey and his band turned on them with horrid results. Swords were drawn, blood was spilled, and the sharks of the Western Atlantic were well fed that night. Styles himself was forced to walk a narrow plank and, when he refused to leap of his own volition, was shot in the back. He fell to the water below, shouting, "D—n ye for being such a—" His curse remained unfinished when he struck the waves.

We set sail directly for the coordinates marked on the treasure map, and Smee—who was handy with needle and thread—sewed us a new flag to replace the Queen's colors. This flag was black with a human skull stitched in white. Such a flag had not been flown for many decades, but the *Victoria Gloriosa*—now redubbed the *Roger* (after Roger Starkey)—flew it once again.

We reached the map's coordinates within two and a half days, for the wind was with us. Styles was right. There was no island, no treasure, nothing but a fierce storm descending quickly from the west. We too were bound for our graves, I feared, for the gale attacked like a pride of hungry lions. It tore the sails from the masts, being wilder than any storm I have experienced since, and for a time I believed that Styles's curse—whatever it might have been—was coming true. Several men were lost. Nearly all turned to prayer. When night descended we could not determine: the hurricane was so fierce it was as if a black cloud had enveloped us, making "day" and "night" immaterial. Then quite suddenly it stopped. We had entered the hurricane's eye, Smee said, adding, " 'Tis but a false respite, Cap'n, before Death deals its final blow." But the respite continued, and when the sun rose we found ourselves in a calm sea with a palm-covered island off to port. The weather was warm. Nothing seemed familiar.

The Latin phrase on my father's map, I later learned, was more accurately translated as "second star to the right." Those of you familiar with my enemy's tale know its meaning.

Chapter Two

————— ·⟨∞⟩· —————

My enemy. I refuse to write his name, though it is a name well known, oft-illuminated by the gaudy lights of money-raking theatrical houses, where it is exploited for glamour and gain. Wherever his name is lauded mine is hissed. We are forever linked. The same audiences who pretend to save a supercilious fairy's life by applause either laugh at me as a piratical clown or sneer at me as the Devil Incarnate. Children cast the least popular child to play me in the nursery, while their professional counterparts hire histrionic overachievers to portray me. Heavens, what villainy! And all because of a lying tale told by a dour Scotsman that casts *him* as Hero and me as the Dastardly Villain who would stop at nothing to see him dead.

Well, perhaps at one time I would, but it's his own d—mnable fault. I loved him as a brother once. But I race ahead of my tale.

I promise you this, dear reader: I will not lie about him as he (and his biographer) did of me. Allow me to name but a few of these slanders, if only to defuse my wrath before I continue with my story.

I will begin with my name. It is Cook, it has always been

Cook, I was christened Cook, confirmed Cook, and Cook I shall remain. The Scotsman says so himself in his description of me: "Hook was not his true name." But because of the wicked attack that maimed me for life, I will be forever called by that other name, as Doctor Flynn became Gin, as Headmaster Carlyle became Old Carlyle: a joke, a simple rhyme, a reference to an unfortunate physical burden. Potential publishers, I've been warned, may insist on naming this history with the very nickname I despise (possibly using the word *pirate*, which I never was, somewhere in the book's description), because "it will sell better, old man, and you can gripe about it all the way to the bloody bank."

And for some inexplicable reason, possibly having to do with the undeniably pompous actor who first portrayed me professionally, I will always be depicted as bearing an unfortunate likeness to King Charles II. Frilly shirts, long curly hair, high-heeled pumps (ye gods!) are my affected wardrobe in all depictions of the Pirate Moi, though I have never dressed as such in my entire life. True, my hair is black and has grown to some length, but I do not *curl* it. Nor do I sport a beauty mark on my cheek (or anywhere else for that matter, although my eyes are indeed a lovely periwinkle blue). I have (sadly, but for the eyes) nothing beautiful about me; my face is ordinary, and my costume consists of ordinary seaman's garb perfumed with an ordinary seaman's fishy smell. I have (to my inestimable sorrow) exchanged expressions of sincere devotion with only four women in my life thus far (the first one being my mother), a list that doesn't begin to compare with the notorious harem of King Charles. I bear neither undue admiration nor disapproval toward that Good

Sovereign, but *I am not him*! Though I do like a dash of color on certain celebratory occasions.

Nor was I (I've said it before and say it once more) "Blackbeard's bo'sun," as the Scotsman claims. Another lie! That pirate's morals were beneath contempt; besides, he lived a century and a half before me.

And as for that duplicitous fairy, not to mention sweet Tiger Lily—bah! In time, my good readers, all will become clear. Until then, permit me to return to the predicament in which Cabin Boy Cook found himself at the end of the terrible storm.

Those of you familiar with my enemy's account already may have made an educated guess as to the identity of the sunny island burning less than a mile to the *Roger*'s port side, but you would be wrong. It was but one of a dozen islands in this tropical archipelago, the largest of which you know as Neverland (there—I've said it!), a fanciful title that makes absolutely no sense once one has set foot on that *very real* oasis. No, Neverland has mountains and jungles and wild animals, while this isle was flat and sandy and sported but a few palms to shade it from the burning sun. We called it Long Tom, after the sailor among us who first hailed it. It was, I suppose, relatively Long, but had nothing Tom-ish about it.

By midmorning, a boat was launched to explore the island. Volunteers were requested, and I readily raised my hand. Four of us were lowered in the ship's longboat, and we began to row vigorously.

My heart leapt at the possibility that here was the treasure my father's map had promised. As we neared, I, positioned at the rudder and thus facing the island, believed I saw a marker of some sort. Could the spot be so obvious? As soon as we four waded ashore I identified, sticking out of the hot sand near the base of an extremely tall palm tree, the handles of two shovels marking (I hoped) the treasure's grave. I raced toward it, followed eagerly by the other three. Long Tom (being one of them) nearly outdistanced me, for his legs defined his name, but my excited enthusiasm gave me the energy to pull ahead, and it was myself who tripped over the human leg bone lying semiconcealed in the dunes.

The skeletons were two, dressed in rags rotted by the sea air. For a moment I thought that these were the last survivors of some previous ship that had landed on Long Tom. They had starved, or died through lack of potable water, or perished from loneliness and despair. But closer examination made it plain: they were the unfortunate wielders of the shovels whose task was to bury Something beneath the shifting sands before a third party inserted a musket ball into each of their skulls. We learned this when Long Tom picked one up, affecting to play at Hamlet, and a rusty iron orb fell from Yorick's eye socket.

The other two, Sniffles and Bloody Pete, seized the shovels and proceeded to dig with great enthusiasm, hoping to uncover the chest that all four of us imagined buried at our feet. Visions of Spanish gold, Incan chalices, necklaces of precious jewels pirouetted in our heads, and these dreams served only to deepen our horror on finding, instead of a chest, four more corpses, some with flesh still clinging to their browned bones. Two sailors had buried the bodies of the unfortunate others, and these two—when their gruesome task was completed—were in turn dispatched by some third villain: thus was the secret of Long Tom revealed, though its mystery remained unsolved.

After three of us became thoroughly sick (Tom, our ship's fool, clapped his hands with delight at the gruesome discovery), all four returned to the longboat. It was then, stumbling in shock across the beach, that I came upon another treasure, one that would change my life forever.

A flock of gulls was pecking at something buried in a small dune, and as I approached they screamed at me and flew away. I looked closely. A deposit of nearly two dozen eggs lay embedded in the sand; food for the gulls and—better yet—fresh food for us. Whether of turtle or bird I cared not. I called to the others, and soon our shirts were nesting our find. On returning to the boat, we told of the mass grave while handing over our culinary treasure; indeed we were so starved for something other than salt beef and hardtack that the eggs were valued higher than a chestful of doubloons. The cook (whose name was Bill Jukes) snatched them, scrambled them, and the crew ate its fill.

I have mentioned here some names—Sniffles, Bloody Pete, Bill Jukes—without formally introducing their owners, and while we devour our omelets perhaps I should acquaint you with our crew, even though most of them will disappear before too long and play but minor parts in my tragedy.

Our captain, Roger Starkey, was also known as Gentleman Starkey, and with good reason. A man in his middle forties, he too had been publicly schooled, like myself, though he had lasted somewhat longer than I at his particular institution (which, for the sake of its reputation, shall remain anonymous). The circumstances of his dismissal were dark and bloody, and I will say nothing of them save that only one boy died, and I'm certain that even in that instance Starkey was soft-spoken and polite as he drew the murder weapon. He was ever thus. In disposing of Captain Styles, Starkey asked him "pretty please" to turn around. Styles obstinately refused, and so it was not Bad Form that forced Starkey to shoot him in the back; it was our late captain's stubborn pride. One misconception about Starkey, hinted at by the sorry Scotsman, was that he was a "jolly" Roger; Starkey's smiles were frequent but cold. Our ship, named for him *without* the adjective, was never Jolly.

Of the other sailors, the ones who will play some part in my story are quickly enumerated. There was Cecco, very Italian, so Italian that his English was incomprehensible, and whenever he spoke to me I was unable to tell whether he was remarking on the weather, describing his homeland, or detailing one of his many assassinations. Bill Jukes was our sea cook, a pleasant fellow with little affinity for the galley; he had been trained under one John Silver, and his sole innovation was to put apples in every recipe; unfortunately there were no apples to be had on the *Roger*, so every dish to come from his oven tasted as if it lacked something. Black Murphy was very black and not very Irish; his teeth were filed to points and his earlobes hung loose with large holes for bejeweled insertions that had long since been lost in gambling (one of his many bad habits), so that whenever he became agitated or animated—which was often—these lobes swung like tiny nooses dangling from his shaven head. Noodler, it was rumored, had had his hands removed by Doctor Gin and then resewn on backward; this was patently false, for he suffered sadly from a muscular disease that caused his extremities to contract severely. On land he limped as on a rolling ship—it was only at sea that he walked balanced and upright. Sniffles, a darling name if there ever was one, was anything but darling; he was possibly the most bloodthirsty of us all, if the tales he told of himself were true. He once claimed to have tickled a Frenchman to death with his cutlass; he imitated Monsieur's dying screams to our delight whenever we held a Night of Talent and Entertainment (a sort of music hall at sea consisting of rum, bawdy jokes, sad songs, rum, bawdy dance, mimicry, and rum). Bloody Pete was neither cruel nor bloodthirsty; his name was derived from the frequency with which he cut himself shaving or hammering his thumbs or running a nail through his hand. He was our ship's carpenter, and his scars—the one time I saw him naked—were numerous as the freckles on a redheaded seaman. Long Tom, as I have already mentioned, was something of our ship's fool: his father thought him worthless, and the cruel man's frequent beatings had literally dented Tom's head, so that it too bore an elongated shape that may have contributed as much as his legs to his nickname.

There were many others (and a few to be added), but for the moment my cast list of vital supporting characters is complete.

After I had eaten my ration of omelet, I went on night watch, climbing the rope ladder to the crow's nest. The sea was calm and the sky beautifully starlit; Danger was not on the horizon this blessed eve. After the ordeal of the storm, I was certain that most of the crew would sleep soundly, and I spent my nesting hours in dreamy solitude. At one point I reached into my pocket for a smoke (yes, even at fourteen I had begun that delightful habit), and found alongside my tobacco pouch one egg that I had overlooked.

I pulled it out and studied it by starlight.

It appeared to be a pale mottled green. What bird had laid it? I wondered. Perhaps, because it was buried on the shoreline, it was not avian-sourced at all, but held a tiny sea turtle within. Indeed the eggs that Bill Jukes had served had had an occasional crunch to them; tiny bones scrambled in among the yolks gave texture to a meal that Bill complained "wanted of apples."

This egg was all mine. I contemplated eating it, with no one being the wiser. But the softness of the night had made me think of home, and of my mother, and I suddenly felt sorry for the little one inside. Perhaps its mother was dead, like mine. I resolved to keep the egg a while longer, to hide it from the others, to hatch it if possible, and to raise the tiny creature as I would my own child, offering it all the love I had to give (which was then and is now nearly infinite).

And so I placed it in a shirt pocket stitched across my bosom. I wondered if it would hear my beating heart.

The next morning dawned bright and early. My more astute readers might respond that *all* mornings dawn early, but I mean the expression literally: the darkest part of the night seemed to last no more than five or six hours. In fact one of the peculiarities we soon noticed about this stretch of sea was that the twenty-four-hour period we were used to calling "day" lasted here but nineteen or twenty hours. Time was shorter, but the further effects of this curiosity on us we had not begun to realize.

During the night, of course, Captain Starkey had come on deck to measure with sextant the distance between the crescent moon and other celestial bodies; the problem he encountered was that no stars or constellations above us were recognizable. As soon as the sun rose he was on deck once again, using both sextant and quadrant to determine our precise location. His calculations matched the exact latitude and longitude on the treasure map, though we appeared to be nowhere near where we had encountered the gale that swept us here. Furthermore he learned, as we set sail in what appeared to be a southerly direction (our storm-battered sails having been repaired and replaced during our day of rest), that the latitude and longitude *never changed*! Even after the island we called Long Tom had sunk beneath the horizon, his measurements remained fixed. And perhaps what was most remarkable was that, though north and south were clearly indicated by his compass, the sun actually *rose in the west*! Of course we sailors knew nothing of this; we assumed that wherever the sun first appeared was more or less east, and where it set was in the direction of the Americas. Starkey kept the astonishing truth to himself, and it wasn't until some weeks later that we learned of these anomalies.

That second day after the storm we spent traveling at sea, headed (so far as we knew at the time) in a southerly direction. The day passed without event, but on the morning of the third day we all awoke to the cry of "Land ho!" It was an island decidedly larger and taller than Long Tom, and though Black Murphy had spotted it and therefore should have provided its name, Captain Starkey had always wanted something more than a ship named for him and so claimed the island as his own. Starkey's Island it was originally called, but soon this was shortened to Stark's Land, then Starkland, and stark it was. As we sailed closer it seemed nothing but rocks, rocks piled on rocks, culminating in a large round mound in the middle so that the island resembled nothing other than a gigantic bald head (with caves for eyes) rising out of a heap of rubble, with the occasional oasis of palm trees growing askew and clumped like tufts of wild hair about its ears and nostrils.

No sooner had Starkey gathered us on deck to ask for volunteers for the longboat than we heard a booming sound, followed shortly thereafter by a projectile landing heavily in the nearby water, missing our port side by only a few feet and splashing some of us with sea brine. On turning in the direction of the sound, we spotted, rounding one corner of the island, a ship not unlike our own, its sails spread and flying Her Majesty's colors. A puff of smoke drifted above the mouth of its large black cannon: it had fired upon us! Before we could reply in kind, the distant cannon fired again, and we could do nothing but watch as a large black ball arced through the air, heading in our direction. Had not a fortunate wind arisen and carried our floating home a few feet farther into the bay, the ball would have poked a terrible hole midships through which the ocean could have pioneered. As it was it missed us by inches.

Under Captain Styles we had all rehearsed what to do in the unlikely case of attack, and now instinct and habit kicked in. Our one large port-side gun was quickly pulled back from its porthole, then primed with gunpowder and loaded and tamped (by Long Tom) before being pushed back into place. Noodler struck a match and lit the fuse. By this time the enemy ship had had time to fire off a third cannonade, which projectile sailed over our heads, taking out some top rigging and snapping off the tip of one of the masts.

Our gun fired and sent its missile whistling through the air. It landed very near its mark: Cecco (in charge of the gun) had a near-infallible aim and a second shot was sure to succeed. The cannon was retracted, but a giggling Long Tom was in such excited haste that he neglected to sponge it clean. Instead he inserted powder and ball, then rammed the charge home. Before he could remove the rammer from the mouth of the gun, the heat from the last shot ignited the powder, and Tom, whooping with joy, went sailing with ball and rammer over the water toward our enemy. Those of us watching could see him waving back at us as he traveled, and though one would suppose that the added weight would drop the missile far short of its mark, Tom, rammer, and ball landed instead smack in the middle of the enemy's deck. A mysterious explosion followed, near the place where Tom landed, followed by screams of men in panic. This, it seemed, was enough to end the battle. Before our gun crew could recover from the loss of Tom and reload, the enemy ship began to turn. We were not prepared to follow them; a sea battle was the last thing we were expecting, and we needed time to catch our mariners' breath.

We later learned that Tom had landed on top of the enemy's powder keg. His clothes, ignited by the cannon blast, were smoldering with tiny embers, and it was his incendiary self that set off the mysterious explosion. The rammer, in turn, had rammed its way through the man in charge of their gun crew, incapacitating him sorely, just as the cannonball itself had unceremoniously slammed a hole in the enemy's deck before dropping straight through their ship's rotting wood into the crew's quarters below. There a snoozing midshipman stopped its descent (to his widow's regret), else it would have continued down through the hull and sent the ship to the bay's bottom.

Our eventful morning ended with a short service for Long Tom, after which we named our port-side gun after him. Ah, to have both an island and a weapon christened in one's name within the space of forty-eight hours—Tom would have been proud and his father suitably chastised for thinking him worthless!

After we had recovered from our attack, and still scratching our collective heads regarding the presence and identity of our attacker, the crew gathered to elicit volunteers for exploring Starkland. Captain Starkey himself intended to alight, and I asked to tag along. Black Murphy and Bloody Pete joined us, and soon we were skimming across the water toward the rocky beach. As the island was so much larger than Long Tom, we split into four different directions to reconnoiter.

I headed straight upward toward the two socket-like caves. I still harbored hope for a treasure, and thought that, were *I* a pirate, I would secure my loot deep in one of these convenient grottoes. But the climb was steep, and the scree over which

I initially scrambled constantly gave way under my feet, so that it took me nearly an hour to reach the base of the steeper rock. Then it became a matter of cracks and toeholds, and a refusal to look down. I later learned of an easier way to access the sockets, but for now this was the only path that was apparent, and my boyish sense of adventure reveled in the challenge. After another hour of ascent (and descent and re-ascent in between patches of recovery), I reached the lip of the nearest socket.

Of course, in my adolescent enthusiasm and lack of foresight, I had neglected to bring a lantern, or any means of starting a fire. The cave was dark, and its coolness and dampness increased the farther I ventured into its depths. So too did the stench, which was sickening, and I soon learned its source, for a misstep stirred a mini—rock slide and in a trice the air around me was filled with the wings of bats, soaring, diving, brushing my hair, my face, my body, so that I could do nothing but crouch and wait for them to tear out into the light. Their guano crunched under my feet, or stuck like glue where it was fresh, and emitted an odor that would have made a charnel house seem a bouquet of roses by comparison.

Once the bats vacated, I inched forward, holding my breath. Before long I could go no farther; the darkness was so dense as to be impassable. As I waited several minutes for my eyes to become accustomed to the lack of light, I felt with my hand a set of markings carved into the starboard stone wall. They must have been etched into the rock with some sharp instrument, and by tracing them over and over again with my fingertips I was able to make out the letters of two individual messages. The first read "Here a Panther

Became a Man"; the second spelled out the sentence "Gunn visited for a time."

I never learned who or what Gunn was (in *this* part of my history, that is), but I did meet the Panther of the first phrase, to my Joy and eventual Sorrow.

Stumped in my exploration of what I will call the "starboard eye socket," I headed across the bridge of the nose to enter the port-side one. It was here I found a *kind* of Treasure, one that brought me surprising Delight along with incredible Pain.

The stench in this particular eye socket was considerably milder; either the bats preferred the other cave, or already I had become accustomed to the odor. I quickly learned that the first choice was probably the correct one, for no sooner had I taken a few steps into the mouth of the socket than I heard a sound, like that of an animal stirring. I quickly picked up a rock; I had never expected to find a living being on the island, and so I had neglected to bring a knife or a gun. I waited with bated breath. I heard nothing more. As I eased forward, rock at the ready, I squinted my eyes to see better into the blackness before me. After a moment I made out a patch of whiteness lying on the ground. I stood very still. The whiteness seemed to shift. I waited. It pounced.

The attack was unexpected, and even though I had my rock in hand, I was so startled that I dropped it as the thing sprang to my chest, pushing me backward. My head hit the ground behind me; it was a miracle that I retained consciousness. I felt its hot breath, heard its growl. Its face was covered in fur and its teeth were white and flashing. Before it could tear into my throat, I seized its neck and squeezed. Its claws raked my chest, ripping my shirt and drawing blood. It knelt on my groin, and the pressure made me breathless. I knew that if I did not save myself within seconds and break its neck, I soon would be Victim and most likely Meal. My feet found leverage and I heaved my body up and to port side. In a moment our positions were reversed, and I was on top of the beast. I released one hand from its neck and seized hold of the rock that I had dropped, and as I raised the stone to strike, I saw that the beast below me, its eyes wide now with fear, was human.

I sprang backward in shock, and soon was on my feet again, rock at the ready, for the battle seemed far from over. The man—for it was a man—was on his knees, then on his feet in a squat, ready to pounce a second time. For a long moment we faced each other—I the Crusoe in defense of his life, and he the cannibal Friday crouched to attack. Then he fell to his knees again and bent his head to the ground to grovel at my feet. His sobs were heartrending, and I could do nothing but kneel beside him and stroke his head as I would that of a frightened dog.

After several minutes he looked up at me with grateful, tear-filled eyes. "What's your name?" I asked. He looked bewildered. I spoke louder this time: *"Who are you?"* But either he did not understand English or he was still in such shock that words failed him. I touched his face and he nuzzled my palm. Then he kissed it, again and again, and I knew its meaning at once. He was lost and now he was found. He was hungry and I could give him sustenance. He was lonely and I would be his friend.

Gradually I eased him out of the cave. The sunlight blinded him, and he dropped to his haunches and covered his eyes with his hands. But the sunlight gave *me* sight, and I could now discern this unexpected Treasure more readily.

He was quite naked. His hair was long and matted, as was his beard; his skin—where it peeked through the crust of dirt that covered him—was so white it appeared as if he had not left his cave for some months. How he survived I could not imagine. He snuck out of the cave at night, I later learned, to harvest birds and their eggs when he could find nests, to pick berries from the low fruit-bearing bushes that dotted the island, to crunch on the occasional crab that scrambled among the seaside rocks, or to snare the hapless fish that might have washed ashore.

Once he had seized hold of me, he would not let me go. He clung to me as a babe to its mother. Again he sobbed, and his tears dug rivers of white out of the crust of filth on his cheeks. He pressed his face to my chest, and left grimy stains on my white shirt. I knew at once what I had to do. Taking his hand, I raised him to his feet and made signs that we would descend together to the shore. When I headed toward the steep path up which I had climbed, he tugged me in the other direction and showed me an easier way, a longer but gentler descent to the bay.

Halfway down he suddenly turned and raced back to the top. I called for him to stop, then followed after. He was too quick for me, and by the time I breathlessly arrived back at the socket, I was sure I had lost him. But I was wrong: just as I was about to shout for him again, he emerged from his cave, bearing a burlap sack bound with string and containing something oddly shaped and heavy. Happy at last, he readily followed me to the ocean side.

Upon arriving on the beach, I hallooed for my companions. There were no signs of them as yet, but that pleased me well, for it gave me time to make my new friend somewhat presentable. I led him into the water, which he was reluctant to enter, until I ventured a few feet and sat in the tide line, the water coming up only to my hips. He followed suit, and I proceeded to wash some of the dirt off his back. He soon understood my intent, and before long he was washing himself, legs and arms and chest. We never succeeded in this first bath in cleaning him entirely, for what he needed was soap and a good long soaking, but we made sufficient progress to display him as more man than animal. I then removed my own shirt and tied its sleeves around his middle, so as to conceal his nakedness and make him acceptable to our modest Christian society, at least insofar as we on board the *Roger* were modest and Christian. We then waited for the others, and I chatted to him as if we were at tea. He smiled a little and seemed to understand.

He did not appear to be as terrified of our ship—which was visible on the edge of the bay—as I assumed he would be. I was certain that he had glimpsed something of the battle at sea: had I been in his place the first explosion would have drawn me to the window of the cave and from there I could have watched the entire adventure. I later learned that this was indeed what had happened. It was the *other* ship that terrified him, and he viewed us as his defenders.

Soon the others returned and I made my introductions. They were astonished at finding me with company. They called him Friday, after Crusoe's fellow, and Bloody Pete even made to shake his hand. My new friend grasped the proffered hand and took it to his lips. With his other hand Pete quickly drew his knife, expecting to lose a finger or two to Friday's hunger, but my friend merely kissed the hand, then fell to his knees and kissed Black Murphy's hands and Captain Starkey's feet. Starkey drew back suddenly, and when my friend met Starkey's eyes, there seemed to flash a gleam of recognition.

As we five entered the longboat, my companions reported their lack of success. Captain Starkey and Black Murphy had found nothing of interest; Bloody Pete had found sharp rocks, upon which he slipped and fell and drew blood, as well as some crabs, which he tried to catch and which pinched him and bit him and drew blood.

We returned to the ship, where Bill Jukes fed Friday some salt beef and hardtack that my new friend devoured as if they were sweetmeats and cake. He was then given what remained of Long Tom's wardrobe (though it was a bit long in leg and arm), and put to rest in Long Tom's hammock, where he slept for the next twenty-seven hours. When he awoke he was moved to the sick bay for observation. His burlap sack remained ever by his side, and he was wary of anyone who might be curious enough to open it. We let him keep his treasure secret for the moment, certain that in time it would be revealed.

I collapsed into my own sleeping berth, exhausted by my adventures, and before closing my eyes made certain that my dear egg had not been discovered. Before I had departed on the longboat that day, I had tucked my fragile charge into a corner of my knapsack-pillowcase. I had left pillowcase (and egg) lying in the warmth of the afternoon sun, and I now reached inside to ascertain whether my egg was still safe. Instead of finding the egg, I found but bits of shell. My heart sank. Had a shipboard rat located my treasure and made a lunch of my precious souvenir? Exploring further, I felt a sharp sting. I quickly extracted my hand from the pillowcase and found attached to it a tiny creature, its jaws sucking blood from my middle finger as if it were a teat. I gently removed this bloodthirsty infant from its source of nourishment and held it high for examination. Its yellow eyes blinked back at me with surprise and, I like to think, a modicum of affection.

It was a newly hatched crocodile. I named it Daisy, after my mother.

Chapter Three

———⋅⋅❦⋅⋅———

*I*t was some days before I saw my friend from Starkland again. By that time he had found his voice. At first it was weak and weary, and the initial words from his parched lips (yes, he spoke English, and was indeed an Englishman) were to ask after "the boy who rescued him." I was brought before him, abed in the sick bay, and found the poor man much changed from when I last saw him, and all for the better. He remained unshaven, but his beard had been trimmed and his hair cut short (by Bloody Pete, who bloodied himself in the cutting). He had been washed in a hot bath with lye soap and vinegar, since these were the only solvents that would work their way through his grime (removing, I grant you, some skin in the process), and he was now much cleaner and dressed in Long Tom's clothing with the cuffs rolled back to fit his limbs. He appeared to be in his mid-thirties, perhaps even younger. (This surprised me, for I had taken him to be a much older fellow when we met in the cave.) When I arrived at his bedside, he took my hand, again brought it to his lips, and kissed it. He kindly asked my name, and when I spoke it, I saw his eyes widen and felt his grip on me tighten.

"What is it, sir?" I asked. "Later," he replied, "I will explain later, boy. James, may I call you James?" "I wish you would, sir," I answered, happy to hear my Christian name again, for all on board the *Roger* called me Cook, or Cookie, or Cap'n (mockingly, after Smee), or worse. He then turned his face to the wall, and within moments fell fast asleep.

A few days later he found the strength to tell his story to our captain. I heard it secondhand from Jukes (I was gutting fish in the galley), and what I learned nearly brought me to my knees.

His name was Arthur Raleigh. He had been midshipman on the *Princess Alice*, a merchant vessel sailing to India in the winter of 1860. Terrible storms had driven the ship off course, to a spot near the island of Bermuda, where an out-of-season hurricane descended on them late in the month of February. ("The very time we met *our* storm," Jukes remarked, "and in the very place!") The winds were ferocious, and all hands feared themselves lost until quite suddenly the storm ceased its awful blowing, and when the sun rose the next morn they found themselves in these tropical waters. ("Our very story," Jukes marveled again, but already I had begun to suspect that all this was less than coincidence. I will soon tell you why, dear reader, but for now I beg your patience.)

Raleigh's fellow crewmen were confused and restless, and soon forgot the horrors of the storm from which they had been delivered and became anxious to sail either onward to India or homeward to England. But try as they might to find their way out of this archipelago, they met only failure. (More of *this too*, patient reader, I promise.) They turned on their captain, at first in supplication and then in anger.

He did what he could to quell their restlessness, but all for naught. The crew soon became a mob, led by Quartermaster Edward Teynte (the spelling of whose last name I later learned, but which I now heard as "Taint." Indeed he was a "tainted" fellow, tainted with the blood of the assassin). Under Teynte's command, the mob soon seized the captain, stripped him, whipped him, and tossed him overboard. The blood streaming from his shredded back drew sharks, and thus did their captain perish, torn to pieces before Raleigh's horrified eyes.

There remained a handful of sailors loyal to this good man, Raleigh being one of them. As he watched the sharks do their bloody work, he made up his mind to escape the ship as soon as possible, for he feared that those still true to the late captain would, in a short time, be feeding sharks too. But before he could act, all seven of the faithful remainder were clapped in irons, and the next morn five were brought out to be hanged from the yardarm. The other two, who were scarcely more than boys, would be pardoned—or so Teynte swore—if they did the hanging themselves and disposed of the bodies. The five were delivered to their executioners, and nooses were looped around their necks. At gunpoint they were forced onto the yardarm, but before any could be pushed off to tread tropical air, Raleigh managed to free himself from his bonds, slip from the noose, and dive into the water below. He began swimming away from the ship as fast as he could. A few musket balls tore into the water as he swam, but none came close. He supposed that the mutineers believed the sharks would find him, and so they gave up on their quarry and turned their attention back to the remaining loyalists. In time Raleigh found a tree trunk floating in the salty brine, seized hold of it, and eventually kicked his way to Starkland.

As for the other four, he could only assume that they were executed and disposed of. (Alas, I knew where those four lay buried, as well as the two boys who hanged their compatriots and dug their sandy grave. But why their bodies, gruesome as this is to think, were not thrown into the sea after their good captain was a mystery I could not explain. Nor did every detail of the execution, as I ruminated on its description, make perfect sense to me. In time I learned the truth.)

Raleigh lived on the island for many months, but for exactly how many he could not say. When he was told by Captain Starkey that it had been fourteen years since the *Alice* had gone missing, he could scarcely believe it. The remarkable thing was that, though he was a man now nearing fifty, he looked—as I said—no older than thirty-five.

I took all this in as I cleaned and gutted fish for Jukes. We had recently made a lucky catch—a netful of little pinkish denizens of these waters. (Their native name, I later learned, was *pupu-pupu-hunu-hunu-a-pua'a*.) Their skin was spotted in places by small dots of violet and green, and they were unlike any fish I had ever seen before. Their flesh was tender and their taste delightful, though, and they soon became a primary source of food for us. (Having eaten them for oh so long, I am now revolted by them.) At any rate, as soon as I had finished my chores—having heard the end of Raleigh's story—I asked to be excused.

I went to my cot and lay down, not so much to think, but rather to quiet my thumping heart. For you see, dear reader, what no one but I knew was this: the *Princess Alice* had been my father's ship, disappearing in the very month of my birth. Reflecting on this story, I could not stop my tears, and I resolved to visit Raleigh alone as soon as possible. I now understood his widening eyes and tightened grip on hearing my name; it was also the name of my father, his beloved captain.

Daisy had, by this time, been weaned of my finger and was dining on small bits of salt beef moistened by a drop or two of my blood. The odd thing was that, although she seemed quite healthy and possessed a ravenous appetite, she did not appear to grow. I increased her dinner portion, starving myself in order to give her the lion's share of my ration (and a good deal of blood besides), but her size remained constant. I worried, as any parent would, hoping that perhaps she was a kind of pygmy croc, a species that might be common to these isles even though I had never heard of its like in all the reading I did of the South Seas (to which, I believed at the time, the gale had blown us). This was not the case, and I soon learned the reason why.

Meanwhile, since we had taken Raleigh on board and left Starkland, we continued sailing south. We passed between two other islands—little more than rocks with birds—which Captain Starkey named Scylla and Charybdis. (As I said, he was an educated man.) The other sailors took to calling them Silly and the Other One, and so they were named on our maps. We gathered birds' eggs there, and dined on yolky custards for some days.

But on the fourth day of our leaving Starkland, a remarkable sight appeared before us. Noodler, who was in the crow's nest, shouted, "Land ho!" and what should that land be but the island we had named Long Tom! In sailing in one direction (what we believed at the time was southerly), we had circled back to where we had begun. Curious indeed! We wondered at first if we had not somehow got turned around in the night. But since we had departed Long Tom heading south (as we supposed), and now approached Long Tom arriving from the north with the same sun daily moving east to west (as we supposed!), this theory was quickly discarded.

It was at this point that Captain Starkey confessed all that he had been holding back from us: our latitudinal and longitudinal coordinates remained unchanged no matter where we sailed, identical to the ones marked on my father's map; not only were we lost at sea, but that very sea seemed to disobey the rules of astronomy, geography, and nautical science. It was as if, he said as he shook his head in disbelief, we were in another world.

For a day and a night we lay anchored again off Long Tom, and if ever the *Roger* did not deserve the adjective *Jolly*, that time was then. Our sailors were sunk in dark thought, remembering their loved ones, their homes, even dear England (against which they had mutinied, but this inconvenient fact seemed to have slipped their minds). Not a man (or boy) of us was not melancholy; a few wept; some prayed; Smee (who had a superstitious streak in him, being Irish) wondered if perhaps we had indeed perished in the gale, and that this was some form of hellish afterlife, a purgatory for pirates.

The following morning, however, Captain Starkey rallied

us, saying that all hope was far from lost, and this time we set sail westward, or at least in the direction that we called "west." Who knew what wonders we would find?

A few nights after we changed course, I was put on night watch, along with Sniffles (for we had doubled the men on watch now, ever since our encounter with the enemy ship). I was stationed high in the crow's nest, while Sniffles stood at the ship's prow. Daisy lay curled in my trouser pocket, sleeping (if that's what crocodiles do) until her next meal. The night was clear, with not a ship in sight, and so I took this opportunity, knowing I risked severe punishment if I were caught, to descend to the sick bay, where Raleigh was sleeping.

I snuck into his tiny cabin and touched his shoulder. His hand darted out, grabbing me by the collar and slamming me against the wall, as if I were a would-be assassin. This was instinct surely, for as soon as he saw it was I he released his hold and apologized. I spoke to him in a whisper, and his reply was in kind. "You knew my father," I said.

"You're his spitting image," he answered. "I sensed it even before I knew your name."

"Alas, I *never* knew him," I sighed. "He died bravely? I wish to hear it from your own lips."

"I never met a braver man, nor a kinder one. I loved him as a brother, James."

"And was he a good captain?" I asked, blinking back tears.

"Aye. The best."

My heart, for a brief moment, swelled with pride. I took a breath before I asked the next question.

"He knew of a map with a cross in red, didn't he? One with the precise latitude and longitude of your ship's 'disappearance.'"

He too took a breath.

"Aye, that he did. He shared his knowledge with me, for I was his good friend. He deliberately steered us off course. He sailed the *Princess Alice* to the coordinates marked on the map—I believe he thought he'd find treasure there, or *something*—and it was there the gale snatched us up and carried us to these waters." Then he added, struck by a thought: "But how did *you* come here?"

"When my mother died—"

And here his face sank, and he sighed in sympathy. "Oh, James, I'm so sorry. What happened?"

"It's too long a story to tell you now. Suffice it to say I ran away and was taken on board, against my will, by our good Captain Starkey. I had with me a book my father left for me, in the lining of which he had sewn the map. He must have memorized the coordinates before sailing."

"Aye, of course." Raleigh sighed. "Poor Jim. I think he hoped that, if anything went amiss, you might someday discover his whereabouts, or at least an explanation for his disappearance."

"Did he tell you how he found this map?"

"A dying sailor, he said. He didn't elaborate. I hoped to learn more from him one day but . . ." His voice trailed off.

I too thought of my father's demise. "This man Edward Teynte—he led the mutiny against my father?"

He nodded. "His hand held the whip that scourged your father. His voice pronounced sentence, and at his command Captain Jim Cook was tossed into the sea."

My heart swelled again, at the thought of my father's brave death, but there were no tears; instead there was only bold determination.

"I will feed Teynte to the sharks myself, whenever I find him," I answered. "What does he look like?"

"Like a man who fancies himself a magnet to the ladies. He wears bright dandyish colors, and is always careful not to stain his coat with the blood of his victims."

"And the ship that attacked us—that was the *Alice*, yes?"

"Aye, that it was."

"Is Teynte still aboard?"

"I have no idea. I imagine so."

"Is that why it was near your island? Was Teynte still looking for you?"

His brow wrinkled. The very thought of Teynte made him uncomfortable. "I find that hard to fathom. It's been some time since I was marooned, and Teynte must have thought me dead. He couldn't hate me *that* much, could he, to pursue me for—what is it?—fourteen years? Perhaps they came to the island for provisions. There is fresh water if you know where to look, and crabs scuttling everywhere. I can't believe they were looking for *me*."

Another silence, and my heart spoke its need.

"Tell me more of him," I asked. "Tell me more of my father. You called him Jim?"

"When we were alone, yes. He was a fine companion and a highly educated man."

"He went to Eton, I know. He made quite an impression. They speak of him still. What do you know of his family?"

"You never met them?"

I shook my head.

"You were fortunate, then. It was not a pleasant one. He was the second of three sons. His mother died in childbirth, so he barely knew her. His father was a merchant, relatively wealthy, but a strict religious man believing that all but a handful of mankind—himself excluded, of course—were doomed by destiny to the fires of hell. Jim told me this one night when we were both many sheets to the wind." Raleigh smiled at the memory of that night. "He wouldn't speak of them otherwise—never said an unkind word about anyone." Raleigh's wistful smile faded. "His older brother, the only member of his family he was fond of, was a wastrel who spent their father's money, and spent, and spent, until he was disinherited. After which he drank himself into an early grave. His younger brother, Arthur, remained at home, taking after their father in his beliefs and joining the ministry. When Jim met your mother—" He paused here, as if wondering if he should continue.

"Please go on," I begged, emotion rising in my throat.

"Because she was not of his father's faith, his family instantly disapproved. He feared that if he died, or was lost at sea, they would leave her destitute."

"They did not. They gave her a house to live in and me an education."

"Sufficiently Christian of them, I suppose. I met your grandfather once, when your father brought me to his home for a brief visit between voyages. A hard man, and that's the nicest thing I can say of him. And that was before your father chose a woman who did not meet their"—he searched for the phrase—"strict moral standards. She danced, she sang, she even dared in public to hold your father's hand. I daresay the old man grew even *harder* then."

"Did you ever meet my mother?"

A brief sigh. "He showed me her likeness, often. She was beautiful. I teased him that he was lucky *I* didn't find her *first*."

"And did he speak of her?"

"Constantly." His face softened. "He loved her dearly, and once we were lost he agonized that he might never see her again. Or you. Your mother was soon to give birth, I believe, when we were transported here. He wanted a boy, I can say that much."

And now my tears flowed freely. I wiped them away, but others followed quicker than I could dash them from my cheeks. Raleigh too became misty-eyed, and reached out an arm to pull me close. Now it was *I* who wept on *his* chest. And the more he pressed me to his bosom, the more I imagined that it was my father's heart I felt beating there, my father's love that enveloped me.

We remained thus for some time. When I was recovered I had one last question to put to him.

"All this happened," I said, "in the winter of 1860, in the month I was born. Fourteen years have passed since then. How old were you when you took ship?"

He looked more than astonished. "I was thirty-four. It was my third voyage, the second with your father. I can't believe so much time has passed!"

"So you're forty-eight now?"

"Yes, I suppose so. Why?"

"You look thirty-four still."

He was surprised. From a small table near the bed I took a mirror and held it to his face. He touched his cheeks, his eyes. "How remarkable," he remarked.

*   *   *

The sun spinning backward, west to east. The shorter days and nights. The unfamiliar night sky. The rules—the laws of astronomy and geography and physics—even *time*—all broken. It is these, and perhaps other factors, that contribute to the Strange Phenomenon, I imagine, though there is little logic in this reasoning. But the effects cannot be denied: whoever lives in this archipelago, whether boy, man, or crocodile, does not age.

"ALL HANDS ON DECK!"

The cry interrupted Raleigh's self-examination. Ah, God, I thought, paling. Has my absence been discovered? I raced out of the room, clambered up the ladder to the deck. Perhaps I could run to the mast and pretend I had just *descended*. If something had gone amiss, I might confess that I had fallen asleep—a forgivable sin, and one that might escape corporal punishment.

No such luck.

Sniffles himself had dozed off, and his snores and my absence allowed the enemy an opening. She had been following us, the *Princess Alice*, and with all lights on board her extinguished, she had crept closer and closer in the darkness. Peering through their spyglass, Edward Teynte (for it was he at the helm) spied our empty crow's nest and the snoozing lookout, and in a trice they closed ranks. Grappling irons were cast onto our side rails and rigging, and we were under attack.

Reaching the top of the ladder and leaping onto the deck, I skidded in a puddle of blood.

As soon as the three great iron hooks had caught on our ship's rail and drawn our vessels together, Sniffles awoke. He sounded the alarm, drew his sword, and attacked, but he could not move fast enough, and in a moment our ship was flooded with the enemy. There were probably no more than thirty of them, but they seemed three hundred, and the advantage was definitely running in their favor.

Sniffles thrust his saber through the neck of one unlucky raider and severed the arm of a second. Soon it was his own bloodcurdling death scream that rang from his lips, as a giant of a sailor buried a carpenter's ax in Sniffles's broad back. By now several of my crewmates had reached the deck, but many were still groggy with sleep, and so the enemy made quick work of them. Indeed, too many of us died before we could defend our vessel, and for more than a moment the battle seemed a losing one. It was Smee who made the difference.

When he woke from his bunk, the first weapon he seized was his sewing kit, and so it was with fists full of needles and pins that he entered the fray. Being very short and very round, you might imagine, would not be advantageous to a fighter, but it was quite the opposite: the enemy either overlooked him entirely or thought him not worth the effort, and turned their fury on larger, stronger, better-armed men, allowing Smee to take advantage of his insignificance. He leapt on backs and buried long metal straight pins into eyes; he punctured buttocks as though his needles were so many maddened bees on the loose, distracting swordsmen enough so that their opponents could stab them in the heart;

one especially long darning needle he rammed deep into the chest of a Goliath of a man, toppling him instantly to the deck.

Starkey too was among us now, dancing from enemy to enemy as if he were at a public school ball. His talent with the dirk was renowned (bear witness to the unfortunate boy from his public school), and now he wielded two daggers as expertly as if he were carving meat, nimbly slicing here and dicing there, lopping off just enough of a nose, a thumb, an ear to send their owners howling back to their mother ship.

As soon as I recovered my legs, I seized a sword from a fallen enemy and looked for my quarry. The blood of revenge boiled in my heart, and I knew for whom I was searching: one Edward Teynte, my father's murderer. I knew not what he looked like, but I was certain that as soon as I saw him I would recognize him, and indeed spotting him proved far easier than killing him. He was standing in the rear of the brutes like the coward he was, but his pride of fashion betrayed him: he wore a red sash around his middle and a yellow bandanna on his head, making him a man dashing enough to catch a lady's eye, to be sure, but also an easily spotted target for an angry boy. I charged.

He saw me coming and smiled as he raised his cutlass to meet mine. He was a man of thirty-five or so, and his pearly teeth gleamed in the night. But I knew that his apparent age was false; he had been sailing these seas for fourteen years, which made him a man of fifty, and I hoped that, even though his visage was young and handsome, his constitution was ancient and failing. If so, I would be more than his match.

Our swords rang together once, twice, and the sparks flew. On the third clang of steel on steel his strength overpowered me and my weapon flew from my hand. His saber swished through the air and cut me; I felt my chest dripping warm and wet from what I knew was my own blood. Weaponless, I lowered my head and ran at him now, hoping to butt him off balance and perhaps gain the upper hand. He stepped aside and grabbed hold of my shirt collar, like a toreador neatly handling an angry calf. He threw me to the deck and pressed the tip of his blade to my throat. "I've never killed a child before," he said with a grin.

"I'm not a child!" I shouted back. "I'm James Cook, and my father was your captain! He trusted you!" Quite suddenly he froze.

The melee continued starboard and port, fore and aft, but it was as if he and I were on an island alone with nothing but quiet sands and calm water surrounding us. "Your father?" he asked. And for a moment he grew pale. "I loved your father, once," he lied, as he raised his sword above his head in preparation for dealing the fatal blow. "But he betrayed us all," he said, then brought the steel down hard, hard enough to split me in twain. I had not a moment even to pray, but before his weapon cracked open my skull another weapon stopped it. It was a scythe, with a blade that seemed to be made of solid iron. Both Teynte and I looked to the man wielding it. It was Arthur Raleigh.

Teynte turned to face him, and the duel now truly began. Both were exquisite swordsmen, and their weapons were sharp and deadly. A misstep on either side would have been a fatal one. Teynte thrust, Raleigh parried, metal gleamed, sparks flew, and I lay on the deck transfixed by the ballet danced above me. Raleigh wielded the scythe as if he were

Death personified, but he was still weak from his ordeal and he was losing ground. It wasn't long before it dawned on me: I had the advantage; with but a slight interference I could turn the battle in Raleigh's favor. I waited for an opening and dove forward to wrap myself around Teynte's velvet boot; I cared little if a swishing cutlass caught me in the back, I was so determined to avenge my father. Thrust off balance, Teynte toppled to his side, and Raleigh's scythe pressed against his throat. Blood ran. "No!" I shouted up at my defender. "Don't kill him!" Raleigh paused, and in that pause I finished my thought: "Let *me* do it."

But by then the battle had turned; we were winning, and on seeing their commander fallen and about to lose his life, the raiders threw down their weapons and begged for mercy like the yellow cowards they were. A few of them died in that moment of surrender, struck down by my impatient shipmates, but Gentleman Starkey quickly established order and commanded his men to put up arms and treat the enemy as prisoners, not assassins. It was Bad Form to fell an unarmed fellow pirate, or so he believed, even though that fellow pirate may have been bent on decapitating you but moments before. So before I could see his blood staining our decks, Edward Teynte was bound in ropes together with his shipmates, and led below to the hold.

The rest of the night was spent in quiet mourning. Too many of our dear friends had died. Too many ragged wounds needed patching. Too many brave sailors perished of these wounds before dawn. And when the sun rose at last, both dead friends and enemy were cast into the sea together, and the sharks had a filling repast.

The deck was scrubbed; buckets of sea water mixed with oceans of blood. I worked side by side with Raleigh, who mopped and rinsed and polished as hard as anyone. I thanked him for saving my life. "My pleasure, James," was all he said. "I owed it to your father."

"Your weapon—" I continued, my curiosity near-killing me. "The—scythe?"

"Yes?"

"Was that what was in your burlap bag?"

He smiled. "You're a clever lad. I feared if I pulled it out too readily, one of your mates would have my head."

"It looked frightfully heavy. Is it iron?"

"Something like that, yes."

"Where did you find it?"

"Ah, that's a long story." He sighed, then decided to continue. "I took it off a man who subsequently died. We were having a race of sorts. He won."

"You killed him?"

He hesitated. "I cut off his hand. He bled to death."

"Why'd you cut off his hand?"

"To save him. He asked me to. If I hadn't cut it off, he would have died anyway, only more slowly and in a great deal more pain."

"I don't understand. You mean the two of you were racing—"

"—and if *I* had won *I* would have died instead. The prize was a box, you see, and *inside* the box, though neither of us knew it, was Certain Death. So he won, and opened the box, and died, and I got his weapon. It looks very old, so I suspect it is. Possibly snatched from the clutches of Death Itself." He was joking, I was sure. "Do you think it holds a curse? Most old things do."

"I'm terribly confused, sir. What did you *think* was in the box?"

He waved a hand in front of his face, as if the memory was a fly on his nose and he wished to chase it away. "I can't explain it now, James. Someday, perhaps, I will. Now would you be so kind as to refill this bucket?"

While we mopped, the enemy ship, still coupled to us, was boarded and explored. The remainder of its crew, some wounded and all hiding below the decks of the *Alice*, were found and forced to join the rest of our captives. Their storehouse was raided, and anything of value was brought on board the *Roger*. The *Alice* itself, being in poor condition after fourteen years at sea, was no better than a leaky tub and would do no one any good for very much longer, so it was decided that she would burn, a pyre warning any other ships (if there were any) that we were not to be tampered with. The day ended with Starkey announcing that the morrow would commence with a series of trials—of the criminals who attacked us, yes, but also of the traitor on board our own ship who through his negligence had allowed the *Roger*'s near capture.

Since Sniffles was dead, I assumed he meant me.

Starkey nodded in my direction, and Cecco seized hold of me to lead me below. Confused, frightened, I did not struggle. I was clapped into irons in the hold, and forced to spend the long night near my fiercest enemy.

* * *

The hold was overcrowded, and I shared leg irons with a man I later came to know as Charles Turley. "Why did you attack us?" I asked him in all innocence. "We meant you no harm."

He curled his lip at my naïve question, spitting a reply at me as if I should know better. "You're pirates," he said.

"As are you," I answered, and his eyes widened in surprise.

"How dare you?" he gasped. "We are the Queen's men, loyal and true." And then he turned his back on me, and said not a word further. No one else would speak either—they would have strangled me that very night, if they weren't certain that my own captain would perform that worthy service on the morrow.

The following morning I was hauled onto deck, hands bound behind me, to stand before Captain Starkey, who, being a Gentleman, always loved a good trial. (And because he was a Gentleman, he always knew the trial's outcome ahead of time; Gentlemen are quite sure of themselves when it comes to matters of Guilt and Innocence.) I was surrounded by my crewmates, who eyed me with a mixture of pity and scorn. I was a boy soon to die, and thus the pity. I had allowed the enemy their surprise attack, and therefore the scorn.

Raleigh was nowhere in sight.

"You left your post, Cook," Starkey stated in a voice loud enough for all to hear. "As a result, many of our crew were killed or wounded. What have you to say for yourself?"

"I—I fell asleep, sir," I lied. Perhaps, if he believed me, he would be lenient.

"Then what were you doing belowdecks?" came his sharp reply. Someone had seen me there, and tattled.

I did not know what to say.

"Guilty, then," he announced with proper hauteur. "Twenty lashes, and then the rope."

I felt sick. The twenty lashes alone would kill me. Cecco tore open my shirt and pulled it to my hips, baring my back. Then he turned to fetch the nine-clawed cat.

There was a stir among the crew. Some had grown fond of me, and regretted the merciless verdict. It was Smee who spoke up.

"Cap'n," he squeaked, "would not the rope be sufficient? There's no point in hanging a dead man."

I know he meant to spare me unnecessary pain, but his plea for mercy did not go as far as I had hoped it would.

"True, true," mused Starkey, ever fair. "Very well. String him up and be done with it."

A rope, its noose knotted in anticipation of the inevitable, was thrown over the mainmast's lowest arm. My blood ran cold, and though I wished to beg for my life, my tongue dried against the roof of my mouth and my words were blocked. I was led by Cecco toward the dangling strangler, his arm gently slung around my shoulders. He said a few words to me, but whether they were words of kindness or cruelty I could not tell, his accent was so d—mnably thick.

"Not so fast!" a voice called out, and I turned to see Raleigh emerging from below. He was pale; it was clear that the sword fight with Teynte had exhausted him, using up any reserve of energy he might have accumulated since his rescue. He had been resting in the sick bay when he heard of my sentence. "He was with *me*, Captain. He left his post to visit *me*."

"Is that true, Cook?" Starkey asked me sternly.

"Aye, Captain," I answered.

"Why? What was so urgent that you needed to abandon your watch at such a critical hour?"

I did not want to tell my father's sad story; at best it would elicit sympathy, but would it be enough to commute my sentence?

"I *asked* him to come," Raleigh replied before I could speak. "I wanted to thank him once again for saving my life. I wished to give him my blessing."

Starkey took this in, and considered. "Nevertheless, the boy should not have left his post," he concluded. "Proceed." He nodded in Cecco's direction.

Cecco looped the noose around my neck.

"Please, sir, one word more!" Raleigh called out, and once again the proceedings were halted.

I waited for him to find something eloquent to say, a heart-rending plea that would spare my young life.

"Why not burn the boy?" he finally said.

Even the hardened mutineers around me let out a gasp of horror. Cecco muttered an oath (in Italian, of course). (At least I assume it was in Italian.) (And an oath.)

Raleigh continued: "If you are bent on killing the lad, give him the nobility of death by fire. I know you intend to torch the *Princess Alice*. Why not bind the boy to the mast and let him go down with *that* ship? A fitting end, perhaps, and a nobler one. He *did*, after all, fight on our side once he realized his error. Besides, many of the crew, as I can clearly see, are fond of him, and it would spare them the emotional trauma of seeing a child's neck cruelly snapped and his poor emaciated body picked clean by gulls until what remained rotted to bones."

His vivid description disturbed me, of course, but was he truly suggesting a substitute death by fire? I could not fathom why the man would turn so cruel, after I had saved his life.

"A Viking death," Starkey remarked, being an overeducated man, "yes, I like that. Let's do it."

And so it was done. I was hauled by Cecco onto the *Alice* and bound fast to the mast. Pitch was poured over the vessel's deck, torches were fetched, and a few of my crewmates were allowed to say their farewells to me. "I'll miss you, Cap'n," Smee said to me as tears dripped down his ruddy round cheeks. Cecco muttered something in his native tongue, whether a curse or a blessing I could not tell. Starkey told me to die like a Gentleman and make Eton proud. Raleigh was the last, and he kissed me gently on each cheek, and it was while bussing the port-side one that he whispered in my ear, "There's an island to the northwest. Lower the longboat and make your way there." He then embraced me tight, his shoulders heaving with seeming emotion as he slipped a knife into my bound hands.

Bloody Pete lit a torch and tossed it onto the pitchy deck, burning his fingers in the process. Black Murphy lit and tossed a second one. As the pitch on the foredeck caught fire and black smoke rose like a dark prayer to heaven, all returned to the *Roger*. Black Murphy severed the grappling ropes that held the two ships together, and the *Roger* pushed off.

I began sawing through the ties that bound me to the mast.

It was clumsy work, and somewhat bloody, for I sliced my fingers more than once in the process. The fire spread quickly and I had little time. When I finally severed the ropes (and foolishly dropped the knife among them as they fell to my feet), I could see that the *Roger* remained barely a hundred yards off the *Alice*'s starboard rail, and so I held back from stepping away from the mast for fear that someone with a spyglass might see me and report my escape to Starkey. Knowing that he would consider my actions a far cry from Fair Play, I was certain he would then aim Long Tom at me and fire away. But as the flames burned higher and closer, I could hold back no longer. I ran to port, where a longboat was kept. Looking over the rail, I beheld with horror that its bottom was stove full of holes—Starkey (or someone) had anticipated Raleigh's intent, and cut short any possible escape route with a few well-aimed blows. I ran to starboard, concealed as I was now by roiling clouds of black smoke, and found the second longboat in the same condition. I was lost.

To escape the flames I began to climb. As I scampered up ropes toward the crow's nest, I considered my chances as a swimmer. No land was in sight—Raleigh's whispered island may have been days away, for all I knew—and my prowess in the water, though quite remarkable for an Englishman, would never keep me afloat for more than several hours. I would be sharks' food before noon. Still, drowning is a merciful death, or so I'd been told. I decided to cast myself into my salty grave with a last cry of "*Floreat Etona!*" as my epitaph. I said a prayer: "One moment more, dear Lord, of life and breath and air and hope, before I take the plunge." I reached the crow's nest and climbed inside. I prayed to God and to my dear mother, asking both for mercy, for forgiveness. I heard a creak of wood, and looking down I saw that the flames were licking their way through the mast. I prayed to my father, whose spirit was set free in the bloody waters of this ocean's tide, to cradle me in his arms and make my death a pleasant one. Black smoke rose like the hand of the Reaper, wrapping its fingers around my neck and choking the life from me. The noose, perhaps, would have been swifter, kinder; I could no longer breathe, and as I filled my lungs with the noxious poison, I began to hallucinate. I heard a cock crow, signaling Death, the final hour, the dawn of my New Life. And the next thing I knew, I was in the arms of an angel, and we were flying over the water to heaven.

PART TWO

THE GREAT WHITE FATHER

Chapter Four

—◦◦⦿◦◦—

*A*las, it was no angel. It was (and here I must say his name. Why avoid it? Why use a pseudonym that would fool no one, dear reader, for you know it already, sadly, better than you know my own, which is *not and never was* Hook) P. Pan.

I realized I was still alive when we flew no closer to the clouds of heaven (where I hoped my dear parents awaited me) but instead began to descend. Ah no, I thought, what have I done to deserve the fiery pit? Then I noticed that my rescuer was a boy no older than myself, and possibly several years younger. Most astonishing of all—he had no wings! This was no angel, I determined. I panicked, and for a moment I struggled in his arms. But he held me all the tighter, and I realized that giving in to the unknown might be better than plunging hundreds of feet into the ocean.

But how could he hold me, let alone carry me aloft? I was bigger and heavier than he, or so it appeared. Perhaps whatever had given him the gift of flight had also made *me* weightless, at least so long as he had hold of me. As we flew I studied him more closely.

He appeared to be a boy of twelve or thereabouts. His face was smooth and his cheeks pink with excitement. His hair was curly brown, but it could have been dirt that gave it color, for it was tousled and I could see that he seldom if ever washed it. Nor, from the smell of him, did he wash much else. He smelled of earth, not of fish, a smell that I welcomed after long months at sea. He never cast his eyes (brown with flecks of gold, in contrast to my own periwinkle blue) on me but only on the horizon, as if he were looking for some marker to give him direction. His lips were tight in concentration, so that two dimples dented the port and starboard of his mouth. His nose was dusted with freckles. His eyelashes were quite long, adding something girlish to his visage (though I would never tell him that; he would have murdered me). He was—so far as it is possible for any child to be—beautiful.

He dipped even lower. At this point I turned my gaze from his face and looked ahead. There appeared on the horizon a mountainous island, which rapidly grew closer. The ocean around it was of a turquoise color, and prettier water I have never beheld. Apart from the bright yellow sands edging its beaches, the island was deep green, furred (or so it seemed) with an emerald jungle. We circled the island once, and as we did so I spotted a lovely lagoon on the far western side, dotted with rocks upon which sea lions (or so I imagined, for I had never seen those mammals in life but only in drawings) lounged. On the high cliffs to the north was what appeared to be a village of tents. Was this our destination? No, for we sailed over it and continued east in the direction from which we had just arrived, then spiraled lower and dove toward the island's middle, where the wilderness was thickest.

The boy did not decrease his speed as we descended; rather we sped toward earth as if he were bent on crashing us both into the jungle. But a few feet above the treetops he somehow slowed, and we gently descended through leaves and lianas to the ground. He landed on his feet, and as soon as he touched dirt he dropped me, as if quite suddenly he could no longer bear my weight. I landed with an "Oof!" He laughed.

"Thank you, kind sir," I said to him, once I had caught my breath.

"I'm not a sir," he said, in proper English. "I'm a boy. My name's Peter. What's yours?"

"James," I replied, and as I stood I held out my hand for him to shake. He simply stared at it.

"Are you giving me something?" he asked.

"My hand," I replied.

He seemed puzzled. "But there's nothing in it," he said.

"I'm giving you my hand," I said again, uncertain how to make my intention clearer. "Please take it."

"I don't want it, I have two of my own."

I thought he was joking, and I laughed.

"Do you think I'm funny?" he asked sternly.

"I think what you said was funny."

"Was it?" And now *he* laughed, and soon we both were laughing together.

"I saw your house burning and that you were in trouble. I was playing hide-and-seek with Tink, else I would never have found you. It was *her* turn to hide, and sometimes she goes quite far away."

"It wasn't my house, it was a ship," I explained, puzzled at his choice of words. "And who is Tink?"

"Oh, you'll meet her soon enough. She's very irritating at times, but she's all I have to play with. Until now." He grinned, studying me head to toe as if I were his captive. "What is that?" He was pointing at my trousers.

"Trousers," I answered. It was now I noticed that he was clothed in leaves and mud, with a few seashells dangling from a liana belt that barely served up a modicum of modesty. Had he dressed like that in London, he would have been arrested.

"Trousers? But there's only one of them," he observed with grammatical correctness.

"Well," I said, somewhat at a loss, "there are *two legs*."

"Oh" was all he answered.

"Where are we?" I asked, looking around.

"Home," he said and started walking away from me. I instantly followed.

"Do you have a name for it?"

"Home."

"I mean, the island."

"Home."

"I see."

"What would *you* call it?" he asked, stopping and turning to face me.

"I don't know. I've never been any place *like* this."

"Never?"

"No. Never."

"Then it's Never, to *you*. Home to *me*."

Before I could reply a tremendous ROAR stopped me in my tracks. To starboard, at the foot of a large tree, was an enormous bear standing upright between us and two mewling cubs. Its teeth were long, its claws extended, and it waved its paws at us as if it were deciding how to divide our delicate morsels between itself and its offspring. I stood very still, then began quite carefully to back away. But the boy took a step *closer* to the monster.

"Peter," I whispered, "Peter—don't."

He ignored me and stepped even closer. The beast watched him. Everything was still. Then the bear leapt on the boy, knocked him onto his back and proceeded to take his head in its jaws in preparation for the final crunch. I turned away, too frightened to watch, but felt myself a terrible coward and so turned back at the last moment, expecting to see the monster's teeth puncture his skull with a terrible pop. Imagine how surprised I was to see Peter pull from his liana belt a blunt stick, with which he proceeded to stab the bear in its heart. The bear reared back, held one paw to the inflicted wound, then toppled onto its side with a pitiful scream. In a moment all was over, and the two orphaned cubs ran to their late parent (I did not know if it was father or mother) and began to lick its face pathetically, crying so as to break my heart. I felt the tears spring to my eyes—I so identified with these poor young ones—only to turn astonished to a laughing Peter.

"Boy, why are you crying?" he asked.

"I too am an orphan," I declared, and, before I could thank him for his brave actions in once again saving my life, I heard another ROAR and lo! the bear was back on its feet. Not only does Time stand still in this place, I remember thinking, but the Dead Walk Again! The bear waddled toward Peter, and Peter jumped into its arms, and soon both were rolling in the jungle leaves, Peter laughing and the bear snorting (in what I took to be its form of laughter). The cubs joined in, and after a time (while I watched gaping) Peter broke away and introduced us.

"This is James," he said to the bear. "He's my new friend."

The bear waddled toward me, and I backed away.

"Why are you afraid?" Peter asked me.

"It tried to kill you. And *you* killed *it*!"

"Oh, it's just a game we play. Today it was *my* turn to win. Tomorrow it will be Barnaby's. Yesterday he pretended to gnaw off my leg and feed it to the children. Brilliant! Come along." And before I could react he continued farther into the jungle. Barnaby snorted his farewell (or so I took it to mean), and I followed my new friend.

In a few minutes we arrived at a large deciduous tree, which towered above all the others. It was covered in pink and yellow blossoms, and seemed quite out of place in the middle of a jungle. Peter pulled aside a bush nestled against its base to reveal a large hole in its trunk. He stepped into the hole, and I moved to follow. "No, this is *mine*," he said. He pointed to another bush. "*That* can be yours." He disappeared.

I pulled aside this second bush and discovered another large hole. I carefully stepped inside and found my foot on the top rung of what I soon learned was a ladder. Gingerly I descended. Reaching the bottom rung, I turned and beheld an oddly shaped room, tangled in roots and rocks and lit with burning candles. "Welcome," said Peter, for he had already arrived. From a tabletop made of a stump he picked up a clay pipe and instantly lit its contents from a nearby candle. He took a puff and handed it to me. I put it to my mouth and inhaled, then exhaled quite suddenly, coughing.

"You have to hold your breath. Let the smoke do its work," he instructed. I took another puff and held the smoke inside for as long as possible. "This is remarkable," I said, exhaling while looking around at his underground abode. "Did you dig this yourself?" I offered him back the pipe, and he took another puff before speaking.

"No, I had help," he answered, but offered no further explanation.

"But where did you get the candles?"

"A house landed on the beach yesterday," he said, "like the one you were burning in but smaller. It was *filled* with candles."

"Yesterday?" I asked, incredulous.

"I think so" was his evasive answer. I soon learned that all past events happened "yesterday" for him, just as the only future before us—whether it was seconds or years ahead—was "tomorrow."

The tobacco we smoked was quite sharp, but held a lovely herbal aroma, and its effects grew on me quickly. I admit I rather liked it. "What is this tobacco? It's lovely. Where'd you get it?" I asked.

"Panther gave it to me. In exchange for a favor or something. They smoke it all the time."

The name Panther reminded me of the scribbling I'd found on the eye-socket wall on Starkland.

"Who's Panther?" I asked.

"You'll meet him," he replied. "Tomorrow."

It was then that I felt a stirring in my trouser pocket. I

reached in and pulled out Daisy, who was only now waking, having slept through the attack of the *Alice*, my imprisonment and trial, and ultimately my rescue. "Oh. This is Daisy," I said, holding her out toward Peter in the palm of my hand.

He recoiled in terror.

"Put it away, put it away!" he screamed.

"She won't harm you, she's so small she couldn't hurt you even if she wished to. She's safer than Barnaby."

"Put it away!"

I held her to my face, kissed the top of her head (she nipped at my lip), and slipped her back inside my pocket.

"Where'd it come from?" he asked, calming somewhat once she was out of sight.

"I hatched her. I don't know if she's a 'her,' I've only guessed."

"I mean now. Where'd she come from *now*?" he asked again. "Are you a magician? Panther's brother is, but not as good as you."

"What? No. I'm not a magician. She was in my pocket."

"What's 'pocket'?"

I looked again at his skimpy costume. "You don't have them, do you?" I stood to show him mine and buried my hand in my starboard one.

He screamed. "Where'd your hand go?"

"It's right here," I said, pulling it out again.

"How'd you make it disappear?"

"I put it in my pocket. Like the one I keep Daisy in." I "disappeared" my hand again.

"Don't!" He cowered. "Please! Put the Daisy away!"

"Daisy's in the *other* one. Here. Look. I have two pockets. This one's empty." And I turned it inside out.

He marveled, as if I had just turned straw to gold. "Do it again," he said.

I did.

"Oh my," he gasped. "*I'd* like trousers someday. If they come with things like that in them."

"Not all do, but most," I answered, and he was pleased.

"Perhaps Barnaby would like some too. What's an orphan?" he asked, abruptly changing the subject. (He did this, I soon learned, with astonishing frequency.) For a moment I didn't understand. "You said when I killed Barnaby that you were an orphan."

"Oh, yes. An orphan is someone—young, I suppose—who has lost his father and mother."

"I see. Where did you lose them? Did you put them in a pocket?"

"No, no! I mean, they died."

"I see." A moment passed, and he asked, "When are they coming back?"

"At the End of Time," I said, remembering my catechism, "when Christ comes to judge the Living and the Dead."

"Is that a friend of yours?"

"Who?"

"Christ."

"You don't know about Christ?"

"No. Do tell."

"You mean you haven't been saved?"

"Oh, I've been saved many times. Barnaby saved me yesterday when I nearly fell off a cliff. Tink *says* she saved me, but she thinks too much of herself and wants me to like her more."

"I mean—have you not been baptized?"

"I don't believe I have. Is it fun?"

"I don't remember. I was quite small when *I* was baptized. They pour water on you and say special words."

"The mermaids pour water on *me* all the time."

"The mermaids?"

"Yes. You'll meet them tomorrow."

I paused to gather my wits again. "I mean—well—if you were small when *you* were baptized, you wouldn't remember it either."

"Ah. Of course. So I might have been baptized yesterday."

I took a breath. "Yes, I suppose so." Then: "Are *you* an orphan? Have your father and mother . . . died?"

And suddenly a tear sprang to his eye. "I don't know. Have they?"

"Where are they?"

And now his lip quivered. "I don't know. I don't think I ever had any."

"Of course you did. *Everyone* does."

He wiped his cheeks and wrinkled his brow. "I do re-member a—someone—I think I called her Mother. She was very large."

"Yes, they *are*, at first."

"She threw me out the window."

"Really?" I gasped.

He grinned. "No, I just made that up. I'm hungry. Let's eat." He stood and walked to a ladder that I took to be the one on which he'd descended. He clambered up it without looking back.

We spent the rest of the day picking mushrooms and

consuming them raw and wandering about the jungle and getting lost (or so Peter said) and then finding the large tree again. Ever curious (I had regained my strength and hence my sense of wonder), I plied him with questions as we walked.

"How long have you been here?"

"I only got here yesterday."

"How old are you?"

"I think I'm your age. How old are *you*?"

"Fourteen. Just."

"Yes. That seems about right."

"When's your birthday?"

This stopped him in his tracks. He thought for a moment. "Yesterday," he told me, then continued on. We stopped at some fruited bushes, and he began picking the berries. I followed suit. They were a deep purple.

"You're certain these aren't poison?" I asked.

"Oh, but they are," he said as he popped some into his mouth.

"Won't you be sick?" I asked, alarmed.

"They're not *all* poison, only every *other* one." He tossed a random few of them onto the ground.

I tasted one. It was delicious. "How do I know which is which?"

"Oh, that's easy. If you eat one, it's not poison. You can't eat poison, it's vile."

He moved toward a stream after he had eaten his fill. Sunshine glinted off it, and a miniature rainbow sparkled at the foot of a tiny waterfall.

"It's beautiful. Does it have a name?"

"The Serpentine."

"Really? Just like the one in London."

"I don't know. Are there serpents in London?"

"Not in the Serpentine. I don't *think* there are. I've never *seen* one."

"Then why's it called the Serpentine?"

"Well, why call *this* the— Oh." I now saw that what I had taken for a rainbow was really a long snake, with all the colors of the rainbow gleaming on its back. It looked quite dangerous. Peter saluted it and moved on.

"Did you come here from England?" I asked, watching to see if any serpents were following us.

"Well of course I did. I'm not a barbarian. What's England?"

"That's *my* home."

"Oh. Then that means it's *my* Never."

I couldn't follow his logic.

"Who was Queen when you left?" I asked.

"Queen?"

"Was it Victoria?"

"Yes. That sounds right. Victoria Blackburn. I remember that name very well."

"No. Victoria Regina. Who's Victoria Blackburn?"

"I think I remember my—what's the word?—mother?— telling Victoria Blackburn to watch me while Mother went shopping. She threw me out the window."

"Peter," I admonished, and he laughed.

"I do think I remember a queen. Her name was Maud. Yes, *she* was Queen when I left."

"Queen Maud?" I tried to remember—*was* there a Queen Maud? "That must have been hundreds of years ago."

"No, it was only yesterday." Then he laughed again, and I stopped asking historical questions. Instead I changed the subject.

"How do you fly?"

"I think lovely thoughts." We had returned to the tree, but instead of descending he flung himself to the ground and lay back with one arm resting on his forehead.

"Really?"

"Of course not. Don't be silly. There's a kind of sand. Tink gives it to me. She has a large supply of it."

"Who's Tink?" I asked again, my frustration growing. I lay beside him.

"You'll meet her—"

"I know, I know—tomorrow."

"No. Now. I expect she's given up on me trying to find her. We always meet up here—and here she is!"

I could see no one.

"Tink, this is James," he said, sitting up.

"I don't see her."

"She's right here. She thinks you're very handsome."

"Is she invisible?"

"No. But she can be quite small at times. Say hello to her."

"Hello, Tink," I said, rising to greet her. She was nowhere to be seen.

"It's called 'trousers,'" he said illogically. "It has pockets which are magic and you can hide things in them." Then he explained: "She doesn't know what you have on your legs. She's never seen anything so funny." He paused, as if listening. "She wants you to take them off, so she can see you properly."

"No!" I blushed.

"Don't mind her. She can be very rude. But she's only a fairy. She's never even been to England." He listened again. "She says she has," he continued after a moment. "Describe it then." Another pause followed, and he turned to me with a grin. "She says there are hundreds and thousands of people. She's such a liar."

"But there *are*."

This made him laugh. "Do you like to lie too? I *love* it. It's such fun, especially if others believe you. Like telling them you've sprinkled them with Flying Sand and then they walk off a cliff and fall." He giggled. This was the first inkling I had of his Darker Nature.

"Oh, look what *you* have." He pointed to something on the ground beside me.

"What?" I could see nothing.

"Panther has one of those too. *I* don't, but I'd like one."

"One what?"

"One of those!" He pointed to the ground beside me once again.

"I don't see anything," I insisted.

"Are you blind? It's right beside you. That dark thing."

"What dark thing?"

"There! It's hooked to your feet!"

"My shadow?"

It was then I first noticed—he had none.

"Is that what it's called? I want it. Could you lend it to me, just till tomorrow?"

"I don't think I can detach it. It's not physical, Peter. It happens when the sun . . ."

At that I looked up and realized—the sun had set and darkness was quickly descending. Still, my shadow was quite distinct.

"Tiger Lily says it makes one solid and real," he announced with confidence.

"Who's Tiger Lily? Is she a friend of Tink's?"

"Oh my, no! At any rate, she has a . . . what is it?"

"Shadow."

"She has one too. So does Barnaby. If I had one I must have lost it yesterday."

I didn't know what to say.

My night was restless.

Peter slept on the ground. I lay down nearby, and Tink told him she would spend the night with *us*. He had made a small house for her sometime in the past, and now retrieved it from belowground and perched it among the roots. Then he opened the little door for her and ushered her inside. I still could not see her, but as I drifted off to sleep I thought I saw a faint light twinkling inside her "home," which resembled a tiny Cotswold cottage. Peter, though he denied it, must have remembered *something* of England.

Once Peter was asleep and snoring—his snores were soft and gentle, like a baby's—I took Daisy from my pocket and allowed her to feed on my thumb, not having any other food to give her. Her needle-sharp teeth punctured the skin, and as blood ran down she lapped it up like a cat drinking milk. Meanwhile I felt for my mother's wedding ring, making certain it was still hidden in my trouser cuff, which it was. When

Daisy was finished, I put her once again in my trouser pocket, and followed Peter into Dreamland.

I had the pleasantest of dreams. I dreamed I was alone in the jungle, and that an invisible hand was exploring my empty pocket, only this hand was very very small. It tickled my thigh and I felt myself smiling, and the more it tickled the more I smiled. And then I felt like I had to make water, and I tried not to but trying not to made me smile even more, and soon the mysterious hand in my pocket was so wet it moved to my other pocket to dry itself off. It buried deep, exploring, until suddenly I felt a sudden jerking movement and I thought I heard a tiny scream. I awoke to find that *both* my pockets were wet. My starboard pocket was sticky and cold, with what substance I knew not, but my port-side pocket was warm with something else, something familiar. I touched it and then put my hand to my nose—it smelled of blood. Had Daisy bitten me? I shuddered at the thought. I reached in to pull her out, and she was chomping on something. A tiny mouse, perhaps, had snuck into my pocket for warmth, and Daisy at last had her dinner. I tried to think nothing more of this, and drifted once again into sleep.

I awoke with a cry, not mine, but Peter's. "Tink! Tink! Where are you, Tink?" he wailed, and when I stood up, wiping the sleep from my eyes, he stared wide-eyed at my Daisy pocket and pointed at my thigh. "Look! Blood!" And peering down I saw the dried blood on my trouser leg. "It's mouse blood, or something," I tried to explain. "Daisy dined on mouse last night."

"Villain!" he cried and drew his blunt stick. "It's Tink! Your Daisy ate Tink!"

"Really, Peter, I don't think so. Get hold of yourself. Tink's around here somewhere. Crocodiles don't eat fairies."

"They do if they're hungry!" he wailed. Then he collapsed to the floor, and such unconsolable sobs were never heard from any boy before. Gingerly I approached and knelt beside him, then placed a hand on his back. He turned and held me tight, sobbing into my chest as if I were his only friend, not the accused assassin of his resident fairy. We remained that way for a long time. After a while he became quiet, and very still. I could hear his baby snores. He had fallen asleep. When finally he awoke again all was forgiven, and he was as bright and cheery as he had been the day before.

"I'm sorry about Tink," I apologized. "If it *was* Tink. She probably arose quite early and went off somewhere. But if she *did* creep into the Daisy pocket, well—is there anything I can do to make you feel better?"

"As a matter of fact there is," he said with a beaming smile. "You can give me your shadow."

"I don't know how to do that," I told him.

"But if you find a way to remove it, may I have it? For a day at least?"

"Yes, of course. If it will make you happy."

And so I gave him the loan of my shadow, on the condition that it could be removed, little thinking anything would come of this gifting. His spirits rose even higher.

For the remainder of the day, Tink was never mentioned. It was as if she had disappeared *years before*, and was now but a distant memory.

* * *

"Mermaids," I said when he asked what I wanted to do. "You said we'd meet them tomorrow, and now it *is* tomorrow."

"No it's not, James. It's *today*."

I didn't argue.

We set off through the jungle. Peter led. The morning grew quite hot, and I took Daisy out of my pocket and let her ride on my shoulder. Peter plowed happily onward, never turning back and so never seeing my reptilian charge. It took several hours to arrive at our destination, and during our march Peter seemed content to hum merrily to himself rather than carry on with yesterday's conversation. I was happy with the silence.

We arrived at the lagoon on the western side of the island when the sun was directly overhead. As you may have already guessed, the creatures that I took for sea lions were actually women with fish tails, lounging on rocks (the largest of which Peter named Marooner's Rock) and combing the plankton from their whiskers. Yes, dear reader, I said whiskers. Of the walrus variety. I am certain that you, like myself, have always imagined mermaids to be irresistibly attractive, and indeed their bosoms are comely and unencumbered by corsets, but they also smell of rotting fish, and their teeth are sharp and pointed. Their breath is raspy when they are out of the water, for they breathe through gills growing on either side of their short necks. Their mermen spend much of the time in the deep ocean and shun humans, but the ladies adore playing water games with sailors and such, always with the nefarious purpose of making the sailors fall in love with them, so that they can drag them underwater to their deaths. But because these ladies are, for the most part, quite hideous, that seldom happens.

Besides, we were boys, and boys cannot love.

Still, hideous as they are on land (or rather rock), once in the water mermaids are sleek and swift and quite beautiful to watch. That is why, I believe, Peter adored playing with them; though he could never swim as well as they, he liked to try, and with each game of Find the Cockle or Pin the Tail on the Merman, he grew more adept in their wet playground. As soon as he arrived at the lagoon, he shed liana and leaves and whatever else was covering his nakedness, and dove into the tropical bath.

I sat down on the pebbled shore to watch him at play. There were half a dozen mermaids, all of whom were delighted at his arrival, and those sunning themselves on the midwater rocks immediately slipped off them and flew underwater to his side. After that it was a matter of leaping and diving, then disappearing for what seemed long minutes under the aquamarine surface until they shot into the air with a scream or a laugh triumphant. I took as much delight in watching them, I'm sure, as Peter did in swimming with them. He cavorted like he was a fish himself among these semi-nudes. Their exposed bosoms I found quite fascinating, but, in the spirit of my famous ancestor whenever he visited bare-breasted Tahiti (Cook was every inch of him a faithful Christian husband), I tried to keep my study of said bosoms purely scientific: how do the mermaids dive to the lagoon's bottom when their mammaries appear to be so buoyant? and so forth. Nevertheless, I freely admit that, when on occasion one of the ladies seized hold of Peter's hair and pulled his face into her chest and wiggled, I grew quite envious.

In the meantime I gently set Daisy on the water's edge,

thinking she might enjoy its newness, for though she had seen water from a distance, she had never touched its surface. Crocodiles, after all, make their homes in such places as this, and I planned to allow her gradual immersion until the day came when she might grow comfortable with it, and perhaps take to it for long healthy swims. As soon as I transferred her to the pebbly beach, however, she skittered into the lagoon, and before I could call her back she disappeared into its depths.

I was uncertain how to react. Would she return? Was she lost forever? It was then that I heard Peter calling. "Come join us, James!" he shouted. I stood and politely shook my head with a smile. I was shy of these ladies, truth be told; my excuse was lame and laughable: "I don't wish to get my trousers wet!"

"Then take them off!" was his reply.

Oh dear.

As you may recall, my shirt had been torn open by Cecco in preparation for my lashing, and ever since that moment I had been bare-chested and soaking up the sun. My feet were bare, as befits a sailor's life, and toughened to a life at sea (as well as to the thorny pathways of the Never-Isle), but my trousers, pockets and all, were the last hold I had on civilization and I was too modest to part with them. I shook my head firmly, looking toward Peter to tell him no, but he was gone.

In a moment he resurfaced at the water's edge, accompanied by two of his fishy friends. He leapt onto the shore and with a smile seized my waistband and pulled. My diet, of late, had been quite skimpy, and I was astonished to discover that my trousers slipped down to my ankles with barely a bump. The mermaids giggled and pointed, and I covered myself as best I could. I do not, dear reader, wish to go into any details that might offend you, but suffice it to say that I was at least a year older than Peter, and that year made an enormous difference.

Peter took no notice. He grabbed me by the hand and yanked me into the water. It was surprisingly warm, I felt my muscles relax in an instant, and I dove into the depths and looked around.

Perhaps, I hoped, I would spot Daisy.

The underworld of the lagoon was quite bright and easily visible. The sunlight frolicked as much as Peter, bouncing off shiny fish scales and mica-streaked rocks. Colorful marine life and coral abounded. All around me there were dozens of mermaids. It seemed they had been hiding (or living) underwater, enjoying the coolness of the lagoon's depths rather than face the wrath of the sun. Looking at them underwater, I found them infinitely more beautiful: their whiskers disappeared, their tails were lithe and lovely, and their bosoms were worthy of, well, closer examination. In shedding my trousers, it was as if I had shed my inhibitions too. In the next few hours I had the time of my life, cavorting with them, wrestling with them, discovering rather astonishing things about them (on which discoveries my Christian upbringing forbids me to elaborate). But the specifics of my playtime have nothing to do with the story I wish to tell, and so I shall leave them in the past, frolicking in the lagoon. Suffice it to say that I did not drown.

Eventually, exhausted, Peter and I emerged from the

water and lay on the beach to dry in the sun. Peter picked up my trousers and tried them on, but he didn't like their feel against his skin and wondered aloud how I could wear them. I bethought me of Daisy then, and looked around for her. At last I spotted her, resting on a stone some twenty feet offshore. I looked to see if Peter had seen her, but he was playing with my pockets. I stood and began to wade in her direction. She saw me coming, turned tail, and disappeared under the surface again. She far preferred Lagoon to Pocket, and I can't say I blamed her.

I slung my trousers over my shoulder as Peter and I walked home together, as naked as we had been with the merladies, and I didn't mind this one bit. The jungle air felt good on my skin; there were no mosquitoes; my independence from clothes seemed a metaphor for other freedoms as well. I was happier than I had been since I told my Eton classmates about my nautical ancestor. Best of all, I felt that for the first time in my life I had made a true friend.

I slept that night, beside Peter in the under-tree room, better and deeper than I had slept in a long time. Gradually, however, my dreams were touched with a sting that I found vaguely unpleasant; that sting grew to a sharp searing pain, and suddenly I was back on the *Victoria Gloriosa* with a laughing Doctor Gin sawing off my legs. I awoke with a howl.

"Oh, sorry," said Peter. "It's almost off. Just give me another moment. You can bite on this stick if it hurts."

He handed me the stick with which he had "stabbed" Barnaby, then went back to work. Only a single candle was burning, so it took me a while to see what he was doing. "Ow!" I cried again, and spied in his hand a knife, a true knife, the keen edge of the blade glinting in the candlelight. *"What are you doing?"*

"Sorry," he said. "Almost there."

He held my ankle tight and began a sawing motion at my heel. The pain was intense. I screamed again. "Bloody hell! LET GO!"

He sat back. "Done. You're not bleeding. I didn't think it would hurt *that* much."

"What . . . what were you doing? Were you cutting off my foot?"

"No. Don't be silly. I was borrowing this." He held it up for me to see, a dark piece of something gathered in his fist, a something that seemed to have less substance than cloth while being smoky and viscous at the same time. Quite suddenly I realized what it was. It was my shadow.

Only now was I truly naked.

He grinned. The gold in his eyes flickered in the candlelight. The boy was mad.

Chapter Five

—·—·—◁∞▷—·—·—

*E*ver since I heard the name Panther from Peter, I had wanted to know more about him. Thus began my greatest adventure on the Never-Isle, one that brought me the greatest joy, taught me the greatest fear, and punished me with the greatest sorrow.

"You said I'd meet Panther," I said to Peter in the morning. "Is he a real panther?" The soles of my feet were tender, and I moved gingerly about the underground room.

"Of course he's real." Peter was walking around, trying out my shadow. He would take a few steps, then stop, look at the ground behind him, and grin. He tried to run away from it, but since it was firmly attached to him (by some sort of tree sap, I believe), it followed. He found this delightful. No matter what he did it copied him; wherever he went it came with him. It was, of course, larger than he, as was I. Its size tripped him up on occasion, and more than once he fell over it to land flat on his face. At these times he would grow irritated and try to kick it away, but it always held fast. Then he would laugh. "What fun!" he said, as if he had found a new playmate. "Let's see if it will fly."

He reached into Tink's Cotswold Cottage and came out with a handful of something. "Tink won't mind, she's got plenty," he said to me, forgetting for the moment that Tink was dead. Then he raced up his ladder, and I followed on mine, and we met together on the surface. I had been meaning to inquire further about his ability to fly, and now I hoped to see how he did it.

He shook his closed fist over himself, as if he were peppering his limbs in preparation for eating them.

"What's that?" I asked.

"Oh, it's the Flying Sand. Would you like some?"

"Yes, please."

He proceeded to pepper *me*.

"How does it work?" I queried.

"I don't know."

"Do I jump off something?"

"You can. There's a cliff nearby."

I remembered his mentioning a cliff yesterday, in the context of describing how he liked to lie to people. "Is that necessary?"

"I don't know."

I peered at my arms. The hairs on my forearm stood erect, as they do sometimes in the London winter when my clothes crackle. "How long does it last?" I asked.

He didn't reply. I turned to look at him and he wasn't there.

"Peter?" I called.

"Up here!"

I looked up and there he was, standing *beside* the tree trunk, perhaps twenty feet off the ground.

I was speechless. Feeling a tingling, I looked down at myself again. The hairs on my legs were upright too.

"What did you say?" he called.

"I asked you 'How long does it last?'" I sensed his presence, turned, and there he was. "Oh, there you are. Thanks for coming down again."

He laughed.

"What are you laughing at?"

"I didn't come down."

And now I looked at my legs one more time. My feet were floating in the air, beside his.

I was speechless yet again.

I was flying.

I never understood how it worked, nor do I know now. It begins with the Flying Sand, of course, which was stored in Tink's Cottage. I don't know if this was Peter's *only* supply, nor did I ask if it was mined somewhere on Never-Isle, or possibly on Long Tom or an isle I hadn't visited. I assumed at the time that fairies had sole access to it—I certainly never saw Barnaby fly, or Panther or Tiger Lily. Tink had gifted it to Peter, and now Peter gifted it to me. A fair exchange, I assumed at the time, for a shadow.

At any rate, peppering oneself with Flying Sand seemed no guarantee of flight. It was some moments before Peter flew, and another several seconds before I joined him. Perhaps it took time for it to "soak in," or required some element of belief. One thing I *did* know, shortly after I found myself afloat: once one was airborne, it required a good deal of practice to master one's limbs, direction, and speed, not to mention one's ability to land on one's feet and not on one's head or behind. Rather like learning to walk, I imagined, and I comforted myself with the knowledge that it had taken me almost two years to master the art of walking, and so I should not think less of myself for being unable to fly very well at the beginning.

The rest of the day was spent in practice. I struck my head on tree limbs, and once knocked the breath out of me when I flew directly into the trunk of a coconut palm. On my first descent I came down upside down, and remained unconscious (according to Peter) for several minutes. I bled, I bruised, I used language that the Very Reverend Undershaft, chaplain at Wilkinson's school, would never sanction. Sometime in the middle of the afternoon I burst into tears of frustration. Surprisingly, Peter as my personal instructor was never anything but Kindness Personified. He counseled patience. He demonstrated technique. He took my hand after my breakdown, and we flew together to the lagoon, where we made a gentle water landing. We frolicked a bit with the mermaids, which put me in a much better mood, and then we took off, still hand in hand, and returned to our Underground Home. I fell asleep that night in joy, in pain, in disbelief, in excitement, in pride, in a mixture of all of these emotions. I vaguely remember hearing Peter arguing with someone (himself?) as I drifted off, but I was too tired to open my eyes.

* * *

The next morning I asked if we had had a visitor.

"Oh," he said. "I didn't mean to wake you. I was arguing with Tink."

"She's back?"

"Of course she is. She always comes back. She was furious at me for taking some Flying Sand without her permission, but I told her that since she kept it in *my home,* I was entitled to use it whenever I wished. She's sulking now. She'll recover."

"So Daisy *didn't* eat her," I declared.

"Oh yes, I think she *did*. At least Tink *says* she did. But then again, Tink is such a liar."

"She *must* be lying. Because—*if* Daisy ate her—how can Tink be alive?"

"I told you. She *always comes back*."

"Oh. I see." Which of course I *didn't*.

For several days I worked on improving my flying, and Peter guided me over many parts of the island. We soared above lions and tigers lolling on the southern savanna, but Peter said that they weren't near as fun as Barnaby and paid attention to him only when they thought he had food or when they wanted their backs scratched. We flew to a midisland mountain crest, where Peter said it occasionally snowed, but the temperature there was almost as hot as it was in the jungle, and I had trouble believing him. We glided over what he said was the fairy village, but I could see nothing but mounds of dirt that resembled anthills, and Peter said he never liked to visit because it was mostly deserted, since nearly all of the fairies were dead. Were these their graves? I wondered.

All the while I asked him questions about his past and how he got here, and he usually said that he didn't know, or made up an answer that was so absurd I could only laugh. I wondered if he were deliberately concealing something from me. Upon reflection at the end of each day, I found that what was most remarkable about my questions and his answers was that he never asked any questions in return. He seemed to have absolutely no curiosity about me, about who *I* was and how I got here.

At the end of the fourth day I confronted him. "Peter," I said, "aren't you curious about *me*?"

"Why should I be?" he answered in all innocence. Then his eyes widened. "Do you have a secret?"

"Well, not really. I mean, I have a *past*. Doesn't that interest you?"

"You mean, what you did yesterday? But I know all that. I was *with* you."

"Yes but—wasn't there a yesterday before yesterday? What I'm trying to say is—how can you—how can you *like* me if you don't know who I am?"

"But I *do* know who you are. You're James," he said bluntly. "Aren't you?"

"But I . . . I could be a criminal . . . or a king. Or . . . or a *nobody*."

"*Are* you a criminal?" I could tell that he hoped that I was.

"No, and I'm not a king either."

"And you're certainly not a nobody. Because you're a James."

By the tone of his voice I knew he thought me daft.

"But you—you like me? In spite of knowing nothing about me?"

"You're my friend," he replied, as if he were stating the day's weather, or what he'd had for breakfast. "Why should I want to know anything more?"

My throat swelled and I found it difficult to swallow. For a moment I thought that *my* questions of *him* were so—so *unnecessary*. What did it matter who or what he was, so long as he remained gay and innocent and carefree? I rather liked this incuriosity; it implied a trust and openheartedness that I had never met with in England.

After a week or so (I found that I was becoming very vague about the passage of time; it was so much easier to think only in terms of "yesterday" and "tomorrow") I asked Peter again about Panther.

"Would you like to meet him?" he asked, as if I had never inquired about Panther before.

"Very much so, yes."

"I'll take you there tomorrow then."

I made certain, on the following day, to remind him of his promise.

When I awoke (was this really "the following day"?) I felt, well, an *Evil* dwelling in my heart. I used to feel this on occasion during catechism at Wilkinson's school, when the Very Reverend Undershaft reminded us of the unspeakable sin of Adam and Eve, which forever stained our immortal souls. "Try as you might," he said, "you can never scrub it away. Only if you lead an exemplary life, by shunning all impure thoughts, respecting the clergy, and contributing generously to the Church, will God allow you to pass through the Heavenly Gates, and even then only if He's feeling magnanimous. Many good people burn in the Everlasting Fire in spite of their leading saintly lives."

Such thoughts used to burden my soul, but since I'd been falsely accused at Eton and then pressed into service at sea, my troubles on earth had become so enormous that they rubbed out all worries I had about the afterlife. (Assuming that I would live a long life, as most children do, I put off any Concerns of the Soul until much later.) Now, in the long leisurely days I spent with Peter, I began to feel these worries creeping back into my consciousness. It was almost as if, in losing my shadow, I needed to find *something else* to take its place, and that something was the Dark Side of my Soul, my true shadow-self.

But I said nothing of this to Peter, who would not understand.

"We're going to visit Panther today," I told him instead.

"Of course we are. Why are you dawdling?"

I smiled at his accusation, for I was more than ready to depart. "Shall we fly?" I asked, heading for Tink's Cottage.

"No, they don't like us to arrive that way. They may shoot us down and tie us to a spit and roast and eat us," he said matter-of-factly.

"They? Who's they?"

"Panther's tribe."

"So he *is* human."

"Of course he is."

"And a cannibal?"

"What's a cannibal?"

"Someone who eats other people."

"Of course he isn't. That's disgusting."

"But you just said . . ."

"What?"

I sighed. "Never mind."

We donned clothing again—Peter his liana and shells and I my trousers, which were now so sadly torn that they provided scarcely more modesty than Peter's liana. Still, we needed the pockets. We filled them with food (for we would be walking much of the day), climbed our separate ladders, and headed off into the jungle.

That overimaginative Scotsman who wrote Peter's story calls Panther and his tribe the Piccaninnies, a poor gibberish version of their true name, which is Pa-Ku-U-Na-Ini, meaning "Persons of Honor and Trust." They were depicted in his tale as members of the "red" race, a description that couldn't have been further from their true appearance. Their skin was a light chocolate brown, and they resembled the natives of our Pacific's Southern Seas, or at least appeared so to me, who had seen illustrations of the Sandwich, Tahitian, and Samoan islanders in the books of my father's library. They are a kind, generous people—or were when I first met them—just as Barnaby was once playful and the lions and tigers were once (and to tell the truth still are) indifferent. The Pa-Ku-U-Na-Ini, as their name implies, always kept their word.

It took us the entire day to reach their village.

It was perched on the north side of the island, the village of tents over which Peter had carried me on the day of my rescue from the burning *Alice*. It rested on a rocky promontory, longer than it was wide and raked on a gradual incline, sticking out like a four-fingered hand high over the ocean. The natives had built a wall of logs across the wrist of the hand, thus providing them with some sort of protection against predators, though I must confess I had yet to meet any human, bird, or animal that might do them harm. Perhaps the wall was symbolic more than anything, for they were a people who prized their traditions, and the barrier may have served to remind them that they were a group set apart.

As we approached the wall, which appeared quite suddenly on the edge of the jungle, Peter let out a crow, similar to the one I'd heard as I prepared for my fiery death in the crow's nest. (What a homonymic coincidence, first hearing his "crow" from a "nest.") A birdcall answered him, of the jungle variety, and we pushed out of the foliage toward a tall gate, its doors just now opening for our admission. As we neared this entrance, I noticed a single black feather (crow?) hanging above the open doors.

"Ah," Peter said, hesitating. "I see this is not a good time."

"Why?" I queried. "How can you tell?"

"There's a funeral feast tonight" was all he said.

"Shall we come back tomorrow?" I asked.

He was quiet, as if he had not heard me. Then he proceeded, but he hung his head low and dragged his feet a bit. "Copy me," he whispered, and I followed suit. We walked through the open gate, slumped and studying the ground.

"Peter, old man," a deep voice greeted us. It belonged to a tall, muscular, handsome fellow clad in a waistcloth and speaking in a very proper British accent. (He sounded, indeed, as if his education had been Etonian.) "Who is your guest?"

"Lone Wolf, this is James," Peter said, still hanging his head low, as if observing some rule of etiquette.

Foolishly, I looked up. "How do you do? Peter only just told me of your loss. I'm so sorry. I hope it wasn't anyone in your family."

Lone Wolf stood a little straighter, as if I had said something slightly offensive.

"We are all family here," he replied.

"Oh" was all I could think to say. Peter elbowed me, and I lowered my head, copying his posture as before.

"Tiger Lily was to be my wife. Our engagement, though not official, was understood. Now that union will never take place."

I remembered Peter mentioning this name. I glanced over at him and saw a tear drop from his eye to land with a plop on the top of his foot.

"Welcome," Lone Wolf said at last, and it was only then that Peter raised his head. I followed suit.

"Tiger Lily?" Peter exclaimed softly. His voice caught in his throat.

"It's good that you came, Peter."

"I wouldn't have missed it. But I *will* miss *her*," Peter said with a glint of excited anticipation. He now acted as if the sole purpose of our visit was to pay our respects at the funeral feast, yet I could swear that he knew nothing of this affair until he first saw the black feather.

"When did she die?" I asked in all innocence.

"She hasn't yet," snapped Lone Wolf. "She won't die until tomorrow."

I was utterly confused. "Has she been ill very long?" I asked with as much sympathy as I could muster.

"Not at all," Lone Wolf scoffed. "She's in excellent health. We would have postponed the death if she hadn't been up to it."

I could tell that he took great offense at my question, and thought me rather impolite and stupid. Perhaps he *had* been Eton-educated.

He turned and led us toward the largest tent of the village, where the funeral feast was in progress.

The tent was packed with between forty and fifty natives—every member of the tribe, I later learned. We were politely welcomed, and invited to sit cross-legged on the tent floor in the middle of the congregated company. I was placed beside a large round woman with an enormous bosom and very bad teeth who introduced herself as Blue Bonnet. Her English gave no hint of any native lilt but rather smacked of Shoreditch. (I here make no attempt to reproduce her poor grammar or odd dialect; suffice it to say that had I met her on the streets of London I would have been wary of her company.) She was indeed as gentle a woman as I have ever known, and she soon cleared up any confusion about the sad circumstances we had stumbled upon.

The chief of the tribe, Great Panther, had been blessed with many daughters, the youngest of whom was the loveliest. He named her Tiger Lily, after his favorite flower. (There was an abundance of these on the island.) His wife, Sunflower, had borne him no sons, or at least none that lived. But when she was carrying their latest child and her birth pains began, Panther made a promise to the Great-God-Below-Who-Is-Death that if the child were a boy, and if that boy lived, Panther would sacrifice his most precious possession in gratitude for sparing the boy's life. Panther owned many rare and beautiful seashells from his travels (which presumably encompassed the dozen or so islands of this Never-Archipelago), and he would have been happy to part with any or all of them in exchange for his son's life. But when the boy (for it *was* a boy) was born healthy, and still thrived after a month, Panther asked the Great-God-Below-Who-Is-Death which of these precious shells he desired, and in answer Panther was given a dream. In that dream the Great-God-Below-Who-Is-Death told Panther that the God would be satisfied only with what was promised, and what was promised was Panther's most precious possession, which was not a seashell or an entire collection of seashells. It was Princess Tiger Lily. And so, being a man of his word (which was true of all members of the Pa-Ku-U-Na-Ini tribe), Panther was to take Tiger Lily on the morrow to the lip of the Deep Well, where she was to descend to the Great-God-Below-Who-Is-Death, who would take her as his bride and keep her until her bones had turned to dust.

After hearing this sad tale, I found it difficult to eat any of the delicious fish stew Peter and I were served. I thought instead of my mother and of my father, both of whom had been summoned by the Great-God-Below-Who-Is-Death. But my mother had drowned in her bath and my father had been devoured by sharks, and these circumstances, while horrible, were quite different from those of a lovely young maiden in the pink of health who was to voluntarily offer herself to the God in less than twelve hours. She sat not twenty feet away from me, flanked on one side by Great Panther and on the other by Lone Wolf. All three were served by Sunflower, her mother, who could not cease weeping and who carried Little Panther, the infant who had caused all this sorrow, in a sling at her bosom. I could not take my eyes off the princess, she was so beautiful in her stately resignation.

She was—I blush even now as I think of her—the most striking creature I had ever laid eyes on. Her skin was a shade of toasted almond, touched with a rouge of coral on cheek and lips. Her eyes were almost too large—just the right size, really, in which to drown oneself. Her teeth— Oh, it pains me to go on. And so, gentle reader, please picture the first love of *your* life. She was as beautiful as that.

After the meal (eventually I managed to eat more than my share) those who knew Tiger Lily approached to say their farewells. Peter, who couldn't bear saying goodbyes, refused to face the girl and instead led me outside the great tent to a smaller one reserved for guests; there we bedded down for the night. Usually loquacious at bedtime, he said not a word.

I could not sleep at all. After an hour or so of tossing and turning, as Peter snored softly beside me, I arose and crept outside. The village was quite still. Skirting the few campfires yet burning, I walked to the cliff edge of the village and onto one of the four rocky "fingers" that extended out over the ocean. I took a few steps along the ridge of this finger, then sat down to contemplate the night sky.

I pondered Death, and how he could be a presence even here, on this Never-Isle where Time seemed to have stopped. In theory, I supposed, Peter and Panther and Tiger Lily and all the island residents might be thousands of years old, or older. Yet, even frozen, Time *did advance* here, in the passing of hours and days. There was birth (witness Daisy, witness Little Panther) just as there was some kind of Final Exit (witness Tiger Lily on the morrow, not to mention my father and all the men who had died in our recent sea battle). Was death here always sudden? How could that be? For if birth, which is a gradual process, was possible, then in its own way Death— the slow sickbed sort of death that touches most residents of London—must also be an expected event. I wondered then if Time had not so much *stopped* here as it had *slowed*. In some ways I *was* older today than I had been yesterday, if only in experience, and so in time, in a very very long time, I too would grow old, as would Peter, as would Daisy, and we all would—eventually—die.

"It's a gorgeous night, isn't it?" asked a voice behind me.

I turned round and saw a slim figure silhouetted against the campfires of the village. It was Princess Tiger Lily.

"May I join you?" she asked.

"Please, yes, I would be honored," I said and shifted to make room. She allowed her legs to dangle over the high cliff.

"You're Peter's new friend," she declared.

"Yes. I'm James, Your Highness. He saved my life." I instantly worried that my mention of "life" would stir unhappy thoughts in her.

"He's a brave boy with a good heart," she said. "He's at times too *much* of a boy. He's always entertaining, but he doesn't know how to handle—well—*other* emotions very well. He was afraid to say goodbye to me."

She sounded like a woman of wisdom, of careful observation learned from the experience of a long life. This, of course, was probably true; she may have been even older than Peter, in Never-Isle terms. But it was the "womanness" of her wisdom that struck a chord within me. My mother, at her best, might say things like this; still, there was a heat in Tiger Lily's words that made me aware of things about her that went beyond mothering. She wasn't as delightfully womanly as the mermaids, of course, but still she stirred something within me, something that superseded mere affection.

"I'm glad you came with him," she added.

"Why? I'm a stranger."

"But you're *new* to this world, aren't you?"

I nodded.

"I like that. There's something about you that still *sees* things. Too many people here—mostly the men and boys— forget that there is more to life than just the Now. For that I'm glad of my leaving. My father and Lone Wolf and most of the males in the tribe are suddenly thinking about things they don't usually pay the least bit of attention to. Even with all that, they're sleeping soundly tonight, dreaming of food or the hunt or some new adventure. No one is taking the moment to look at the stars and think about what it all might mean. Like you."

"But I *don't* know what it all might mean. Nor do I understand why your father doesn't simply say no. Toss a few shells to the Great-God or whatever it is and be done with it."

"He's given his word. That is more precious to him even than *I* am. And I must say I'm proud of him for that."

"But you could run away, couldn't you? And there's nothing your father could do about it. If you weren't available and the God still demanded something precious, he might still hand over a very nice shell."

She smiled. "Thank you, James. That's a very clever solution. But I'm a little too duty bound for my own good, I admit. I don't think I could live with myself if I ran away from the village. I could certainly never face Father again, not to mention Lone Wolf."

"But if they love you, don't they want you alive, Princess?"

"Life is no condition for Loving, James. More often than not it makes Loving more complicated. And vice versa."

I thought about this for a moment. It made me sad. The person I loved the most, until now, was my mother, and it wasn't easy keeping her in mind nearly every moment of every day. I worried that if loving a *living* someone was more of a challenge, how could I *ever* manage it? I didn't like to think about this, and so I changed the subject.

"Are you afraid, Princess? Of dying?"

"A little. I try to think of it as Curiosity more than Fear. I like adventure too, and Death will be an awfully big one."

In the silence that followed I studied her face. Desperate, I plumbed for Hope.

"You're going to descend into something called the Deep Well, yes?"

She nodded.

"Are you sure there's a god down there? 'Who-Is-Death'? I mean, maybe there's nothing. Maybe you'll spend a damp morning in the well and then you'll simply come back up."

"No one who's descended in the past has ever returned.

We-Who-Are-Above listen, and we hear screams, and sometimes a great roar, and then there's silence again. Granted, most of the Voluntary Descents tend to be old people or the occasional Disappointed Lover, so there's little expectation for a triumphant return. We *did* send the Great White Father down, but we don't like to speak of that."

"The Great White Father? Who's that?"

"We don't like to speak of it, James," she sternly reminded me. "Besides, he didn't return either, which was all for the best."

"Still, whatever is down there may not be immortal."

"It's always been there, at least according to the songs. They used to toss people down, on occasion, to make the God happy, but even when they did he never laughed, so I don't think happiness was an achievable outcome. Anyway, they stopped doing that long ago. They just pray now, and on occasion throw him a few rutabagas."

"But if he—or it—is mortal, it could be conquered. Why doesn't someone go down *with* you? Lone Wolf—he looks like a proper warrior. He could fight the God, and perhaps even kill him. And then you and he could live happily ever after. Or something like that."

"Yes, I've wondered about that too but you see—" She stopped, as if she knew a secret she was afraid to spill. "I shouldn't say."

"What? I won't tell."

She took a deep breath, then sighed. "Lone Wolf is afraid," she whispered. "As is my father. As are all the men. Even Peter. They're *all* afraid of the Great-God-Below-Who-Is-Death."

"But being afraid shouldn't stop anyone. I mean we're *all* afraid of Death. *I* certainly am."

"Yes, but they're also afraid to admit it. Anyway, they won't go down. I'll have a bow and a quiver of arrows with me, and I'm a very good shot, so there's *some* hope."

I looked away for a time, studying the lowest star. Then I took her hand.

"*I'll* go with you."

Tears sprang to her eyes, and I knew right away that, even if it ended badly, this was the best and bravest decision I had ever made in my short life.

I returned to the tent before dawn, and waited beside Peter until he awoke. I told him of my plan.

"Are you *mad*?" he exclaimed.

"Probably," I told him with a smile.

He thought about this for a moment, his brow furrowed in worry, as if he were searching for a jolly ending to *Hamlet*. Then he reached down to his liana belt and pulled out the blunt stick that was his "everyday" knife.

"Here," he said, holding it out to me.

I almost laughed. Instead I took it and put it into a pocket. "Thank you, Peter," I told him.

And then he smiled, as if all problems—his and mine and the world's—were solved with that one generous gesture.

I stood beside Tiger Lily at the lip of the Deep Well, which was in the middle of the village and which looked exactly as any well should look—a circular pit lined with stones disappearing into darkness—with this one exception: a stone spiral staircase rimmed its interior, leading downward. There was little ceremony before the descent, all goodbyes having been said the previous night. Great Panther and his wife were present, and a few of the women. Most of the men and boys, including Lone Wolf and Peter, were nowhere to be seen.

Panther took the news of my offer to accompany his daughter with indifference. He shook my hand in proper English fashion, embraced Tiger Lily, shed a few tears, and turned away. Even he could not bear to watch our departure.

The steps were quite narrow and precipitous, and without a railing. Tiger Lily insisted on preceding me, since it was herself who was promised. She carried a full quiver of arrows and a long bow. I followed behind her, Peter's stick-knife lying uselessly in my pocket. I carried a torch, which shed light on our descent. Our progress was immeasurably slow, becoming all the more difficult the lower we spiraled, for the stone steps were in poor repair farther down and eventually transformed into a sort of narrow mudslide. Handholds carved into the wall were all that prevented our falling the rest of the way. Tiger Lily was nimbler than I, and was forced to pause more than once in order to allow me to catch up.

The air, as we descended, grew quite chilly and the stones themselves slimy and damp. Approximately fifty feet down we became aware of an odor—a smell redolent, I imagined, of an open and occupied grave—which grew stronger the lower we went and soon became overpowering. Death was no stranger to this pit. At one point, forty minutes or so after we left the surface, I knocked loose a rock which tumbled into darkness and eventually hit water with a loud splash. As soon as the sound of that splash met our ears, an even louder sound followed: a ROAR, deeper and darker than any I had ever heard before. This was not like Barnaby's roar, or those of the Big Cats in the savanna; no, this was the roar of a veritable monster, and I could feel my very bowels weaken.

"Allow me, please," I said to the princess once we reached well-bottom. A low underground tunnel lay before us. "Let me go first. I have the light, which might blind him, if he's not used to it."

Out of the tunnel flowed a stream of water that looked to be several feet deep. Ducking our heads, we followed a path upstream into the tunnel. The walkway edging the stream was lined with the bones of the long dead. Fresher corpses, mostly of fish but, shockingly, a few of merfolk (whether of men or maids I could not tell), floated on the surface of the waterway. We were approaching the monster, and I, somewhat foolishly, reached into my pocket to clutch Peter's stick-knife.

Quite suddenly we were in a cavern, in the center of which lay a small lake. Stalactites dripped water. Other than that there was no sound.

The shore of the lake held more bones, more rotting bodies, and in the middle of the lake there appeared to be an islet, a mound of dirt and sand humped above the waterline. The light of the torch was not strong enough for me to guess its distance or its size, let alone see if any Great-God lay waiting there for us. A large log sat in the water just offshore, and I wondered if this were the boat on which some Never-Isle Charon ferried his customers. But where was this god? I turned in a circle, looking everywhere for the enemy.

We seemed to be quite alone. The water of the lake was

crystal clear, and I could see no sign of life either on its surface or in its depths. I searched high and low, ever alert for the presence of the owner of the great ROAR.

"Hello!" Tiger Lily called. "I've come to fulfill my father's promise!" Her voice echoed. There was no reply.

Of course! Panther's dream was but a dream, a vestige of the superstition that ruled this ancient tribe! There was no Great-God! We had answered the summons, and, finding nothing, we could return to the surface with lightened hearts! We were saved!

As my eyes made one final sweep of the cavern, curiosity took charge. I wondered what was on the islet. Could this possibly be the location of the treasure marked on my father's map? I would return some other day and explore, I decided. Perhaps I could indeed use the log as a boat to straddle and paddle across the lake. I wondered for a moment how the trunk of such a large tree could have found its way this far underground. Was there another ingress? It was then that I noticed a ball of whiteness situated on the log's starboard side and, thinking it some sort of cave fungus, I inserted the torch into a crevasse in the cavern wall and approached.

It appeared to be a large maggot, plump and soft.

As I bent to study it, I noticed its twin, lying equidistant from the center on the port side of the log.

I suddenly grew quite cold.

They were eyes, white with blindness.

And in the moment of epiphany the log leapt, catching hold of me in its toothy jaws. No log it was, but the largest crocodile I had ever seen. It seized my trousers, thinking them part of me, and began dragging me into the water. I tried to tear myself away, but my trousers though ragged were extremely well made (the Eton uniform employing but the sturdiest Highland wool). To make matters worse, the enormous meal of the night before had for the time being expanded my belly, so the trousers did not slip off as readily as they had at the lagoon. I was doomed.

Just then something flew past my ear and embedded itself in the monster's hide. It was one of Tiger Lily's arrows, and was swiftly followed by another, and yet another. The croc's skin was tough, and though the arrows penetrated enough to stick, they were anything but mortal. They *were*, however, distracting and angering, and the cave-blind reptile turned away from me to bite at the sharp annoyances.

"James, move back!" Tiger Lily shouted. Unfortunately the croc's hearing was as sharp as its eyesight was dim. With another ROAR it turned and raced toward the source of the sound.

Tiger Lily was taken by surprise, and in backing away in alarm she tripped and fell. The leviathan was upon her.

But *I* was soon upon *it*. I straddled its back, and, having nothing else with which to attack it, I pulled Peter's blunt wooden stick from my pocket and stabbed. Being both frightened and angry, I plunged the dagger downward with such force that it penetrated a soft area at the base of the dragon's skull. The monster opened its pink mouth wide in pain and emitted a gigantic HISS. Tiger Lily, frantically backing away, stopped to fire several more arrows at the target. They pierced its open maw, traveling down its blood-red throat so that the monster began to choke. Seeing that for a moment we had the advantage, I pressed the dagger even deeper, then pulled it out to strike again. A well of blood spurted from the back of the giant's skull, coating me in gore. Tiger Lily now grabbed her one remaining arrow, and, using its tip like a dart, she stabbed the monster's tongue again and again. The croc bucked like a wild horse. I flew off and landed on my back, losing my breath. The beast's muscular tail whipped around, just missing me. Before it could pendulum back, Tiger Lily pulled me out of its reach. The dragon twisted, writhed, bled buckets, and then after giving a terrible shudder it rolled onto its back and became quite still.

Had we killed it?

We both crept closer.

Indeed we had.

Tiger Lily held me tight, and I in turn held her. We were cold, we were frightened, we were elated, we were champions.

The Great-God-Below-Who-Is-Death was no more.

By the time we climbed back to the surface, it was night. Hand in hand we walked to Great Panther's tent. The noble chief screamed at what he thought were a pair of ghosts, but Tiger Lily quickly calmed him and he clasped her to his bosom. Then he reached out a great muscled arm and pulled me close beside her. He wept, we wept, the adventure ended in joy for all but the poor crocodile.

The following day Lone Wolf and several other young men descended with me to the bottom of the pit. We inserted torches in various niches in the cavern, along with a supply of flint and a piece of steel to allow us, should the torch flames extinguish, to reillumine our work. We then tied a liana rope to the dead giant's tail and, with great effort, hauled the carcass to the surface. That night we had a second feast, of crocodile stewed and crocodile roasted, of crocodile fried and crocodile steamed in banana leaves, of crocodile sweetened with coconut milk and crocodile spiced with island pepper, of crocodile raw and crocodile baked in a pie, of crocodile stuffed with crocodile gizzard topped with crocodile liver and served on platters made from tough crocodile hide.

When we had had our fill, pipes were produced, and we all partook of that marvelous tobacco Peter had acquired from the natives and shared with me in his Underground Home.

After that we slept for two solid days.

Chapter Six

O nce we had recovered from the feast, Peter boasted that had he not overslept on the morning of Tiger Lily's descent into the Deep Well he would have slain the monster himself. Lone Wolf said nothing. I had shamed him, and he was now my enemy. But for the moment at least I was safe, since I was a prince in Great Panther's eyes.

I was more than that in Tiger Lily's.

I did not see her for three days. Peter was growing restless and missing his Underground Home, and so it was decided that we should take our leave, promising to return soon. Great Panther wished to throw us one more celebratory meal before we left. Happily, we all had had our fill of crocodile, and the dinner consisted of various island flowers, stuffed with fruit mixed with honey and prepared in many ingenious ways. Tiger Lily cooked my own meal herself. Aside from being adept with bow and arrow, she made a delicious hibiscus pie.

Afterward, Great Panther stood and sang—literally *sang*—my praises. This made me exceedingly uncomfortable, for I could see that these laudatory verses enraged Lone Wolf. Peter shifted irritably; he was unaccustomed to anyone garnering such praise, except himself. I had always dreamed that a heroic ballad such as this might be composed about me one day, but now that that dream had become reality, I could see that every firework of glory draws to its honoree a cannonade of envy.

As the tribal drums beat in my honor, I looked around—Tiger Lily was nowhere to be seen. And then lo! the flaps of the tent opened wide and in she came, bearing a plate in the center of which lay one enormously stunning blossom—a tiger lily agleam with gold. The gold was actually pollen, a prized harvest from some rare jungle orchid that she had gathered herself for this remarkable dessert. She placed the plate in front of me and watched while I picked the flower up and gently nipped at its petals. I had never tasted anything so astonishing, a mixture of sweetness and sharp pepper that seemed to dance in my mouth. Following the rules of etiquette that I had been carefully taught, I offered a petal to the princess. She blushed and took the petal between her teeth as an exclamation of delight erupted from the crowd. Great Panther looked pleased, Sunflower began to weep with joy, and Lone Wolf stormed out of the gathering. The exchange of dessert petals that had just taken place, I later learned, was an offer and acceptance of marriage.

Once the meaning had been explained to me, I stuttered with astonishment, but did not attempt to withdraw the offer. To tell the truth, dear reader, I was thrilled. Once the supper was over, Tiger Lily and I wandered hand in hand out of the tent, returning to the spot of our first conversation. No one followed. The affianced were to be left to themselves.

We sat on the promontory cliff and looked at the night sky. It was agleam with stars sparkling in mysterious constellations, none of which I recognized. I asked their names, and she said that each person who studies the sky finds their own names for these configurations. "I might look at that one," she explained as she pointed to a celestial grouping, "and see in it a flower and call it Tiger Lily's Blossom, but no one else would call it that, and so it would have a very special meaning for me. You might look at it and name it something else, and so it would have another special and completely unique meaning for you."

"But isn't it easier if everyone calls it Tiger Lily's Blossom?"

"Yes, it may be easier, but that's not the point, James. The point is to take the time and study the heavens, and find your own meaning there. Why should my meaning apply to you?"

"Everything of yours applies to me."

She squeezed my hand. I did not look at her at first, but at the horizon, where a string of five bright stars lay stretched out, like a serpent, or a belt. "Peter's Liana," I named it as I pointed. She laughed with delight. Its reflection was equally bright, floating on the surface of the sea.

"James," she said after a long while. I turned to look at her.

"Yes?" I answered.

She said nothing.

Then she leaned forward very slowly until her lips touched mine. I felt the hairs on my arms and legs lift high, just as they had when I first took flight. Without moving my lips away from hers, I cupped her head in my starboard hand and pressed her closer. Our mouths opened slightly, and the soft tip of her tongue brushed mine.

* * *

The wedding was set for one full moon hence—the first time I heard the future spoken of in any words other than *tomorrow*. Not knowing the length of the lunar cycles in this astonishing place, I had no idea how many "tomorrows" this involved. I knew only that my future happiness awaited its arrival.

Peter and I left the following morning. He was uncharacteristically silent for the first half of our journey. When we stopped for some lunch, I asked him bluntly why he was not speaking to me. He simply shrugged his shoulders.

"Are you angry?"

He said nothing at first, and then he began to cry.

"Peter, what is it?"

"You're leaving me. I've waited forever to have someone to play with, and now you're going away."

I took his hand.

"I'll never leave you, Peter. I'll always be by your side. After all, you have my shadow." He smiled at this. I continued: "I'll visit as often as I can. *Without* Tiger Lily. I promise." This made him even happier. "We'll frolic as we have in the past. You can teach me things I don't know, because you're ever so smarter than I am. We'll swim with the mermaids, and tumble with Barnaby, and try to make friends with the lions and tigers." He was very pleased.

For the rest of our journey he jabbered as if little had changed within the last twenty-four hours. He talked of "yesterday" and "tomorrow" and of nothing at all, and because I was happy at last, I forgave him his childish behavior. He was, after all, my first and closest friend, the very best part of myself.

* * *

Panther had given us a parting gift of tobacco, and so we shared a pipe when we arrived home. We were soon laughing tremendously at nothing at all, we were in such good spirits. Suddenly Peter looked up, cocking his ear to one side. "Well of course you could have come, but I didn't ask you because I know you don't care for them."

He was speaking, I assumed, to Tink.

"Because we had a marvelous time," he said in answer to some fairy question. "James rescued Tiger Lily from an enormous crocodile. He's quite the hero." He listened to a further question and smiled. "I don't know, I'll ask him," he said and turned to me. "She wants to know why you didn't rescue *her*. From your . . . what's her name? Daisy."

"I was asleep," I answered, a bit annoyed. "I didn't even know she was *in* my pocket. Tink, I mean. I knew Daisy was. Besides, she didn't need rescuing. She obviously *wasn't* eaten, in spite of what she tells you."

Peter listened again. He was getting a great kick out of acting as translator. "She says that of course she was eaten. You saw the blood."

"She was wounded, perhaps. But it could have been a mouse's blood. Or my own. Daisy sometimes feeds on *me*, you know."

Peter seemed surprised. "No, I didn't. Where is she, by the way?"

"I left her at the lagoon. She was happier there." And Peter, I admit, seemed relieved. "At any rate, please tell Tink that I apologize for not warning her about Daisy, or pulling her

from the jaws of death. I couldn't even *see* her—please remind her of that. I *still* can't. But I'm glad she survived, and I hope I can someday be her friend."

That, I prayed, was the end of the matter.

But there is no end of the matter with Tink, once she has a notion in her little skull. At least that's what Peter told me.

He now shook his head in exasperation as she apparently rattled on and on. "That's not possible," he finally said to her. She continued, obviously making some childish demand— Peter was rolling his eyes as if he were a music hall comedian playing to the back of the house. "No, Tink, absolutely not, we *have* to go back," he stated emphatically, barely concealing his annoyance. "Because James is engaged." Another beat. "To be married, yes. To Tiger Lily." Another silence, longer this time. "Oh, Tink," he said, cajoling her. Then he sighed. "Hopeless," he muttered.

"What is?"

"She's upset. She's crying now. *Sulking* and crying."

"Whatever for?"

He didn't answer.

"Is she jealous?"

He looked at the Cotswold Cottage, to which, I presumed, Tink had retired. "To be perfectly frank," he whispered, "I think she's in love."

"With whom?" I exclaimed in astonishment.

"With *you,* of course."

That night I dreamed the most marvelous dream. Tiger Lily had become quite small, and was dancing on my lips. She

tiptoed to the precipice of my chin and slid down my neck to the hollow of my throat, which had become a tiny lagoon filled with water. She drank, then climbed the hillock of my breastbone and rolled down the other side to my stomach. I laughed in my sleep, it was such fun. Then she went exploring in my pockets. In the starboard one she found a firecracker, and here for a moment the dream became a bit frightening, for the firecracker's fuse was burning and I tried to warn her to leave before an explosion happened, but when I opened my mouth to speak no words would come. She examined the cracker quite closely, for she had never seen anything like it. The fuse sparked as it burned shorter and shorter until, with a fizzle, it suddenly died. She's safe, I thought, and I relaxed. Ever curious, she drew an arrow from her quiver and pricked the tip of the cracker to see what lay inside. Quite suddenly it blew its top like Mount Vesuvius. Tiny plumes of flame scorched my pocket lining; lava flowed, burning holes wherever it touched. I searched for Tiger Lily everywhere, expecting to find her a heap of charred ash and bones. But there she stood, laughing, only it wasn't Tiger Lily, it was Tink, Tink clad only in cinders and soot. She bent forward and blew me a kiss, then turned and did a naughty little dance with her behind before tunneling into my blanket. I awoke, I must confess, with a smile on my face. I was admired by the ladies! And not just by one, but by two! Never in my most romantic fantasies did I imagine this could happen! Peter, sound asleep beside me, seemed to be smiling too.

* * *

Having been gone from their company for some time, I asked Peter the next morning if we could revisit the mermaids. He readily agreed. To be polite I inquired if Tink might wish to join us, but he said that she was nowhere in sight at the moment, which was just as well (he said) as she didn't care for either water or fish, especially fish who thought of themselves as half-human. (If she liked neither mermaids nor tribal folk, I wondered, was there anyone at all—other than Peter and myself—whose company she *did* enjoy?) He got a fistful of Sand, peppered both of us, and we were off.

The mermaids were delighted to see us. They waved skyward as we approached. No sooner had our feet touched pebbles than we shed our clothing and dove into the delicious warmth.

I had by this time become special friends with one of them, whom Peter called Josephine. Her hair was red as the sunset, and her breasts were quite enormous. I loved to press myself against her, and now she clasped me to her bosom and called me her "handsome little man." Here was a third lady I had charmed! Still, like all successful lotharios, I worried how she would react when I told her that I was soon to be married. Certainly nothing like love had passed between us, but it's difficult (or so my Eton housemates often said) to know the mind of a woman. I decided the best way was to be truthful, and so when we lay on Marooner's Rock, basking in the sun, I told her everything.

"I'm going to be married to Tiger Lily the native princess whom I met recently and then saved from certain death at the jaws of an enormous crocodile which she shot full of arrows while I stabbed it to death and which we both ate."

This statement, made in one breath without pause, was followed by her silence. Oh dear, I thought. She's going to drown me.

Then a smile broke through, and her sharp little teeth gleamed in the sun and she laughed with delight. "How wonderful for you!" Josephine said (her accent was decidedly French) and pressed me close to her bosom once again. "I will give you a wedding gift! What would you like?"

Taken aback by her generous response, I was speechless at first. "Your blessing," I finally answered.

"But of course, of course, I bless you, all over," and she began kissing me and I laughed whenever her whiskers brushed against a place that was especially ticklish.

After that we swam again, and soon found Peter chasing half a dozen of Josephine's sisters. We played Slippery Otter together, and Where's the Shrimp, which Peter always won. Then the ladies retired for their underwater nap and Peter and I lay on the pebbled beach, where we ate mangoes and dozed.

Throughout the frolicsome morning I thought more than once of Daisy, wondering what had happened to her. Had she left the lagoon to swim back to Long Tom? I worried that something might have eaten her, and then fretted that the beating sun had baked her into a crocodile mummy. I stood on the edge of the lagoon and called out her name. Peter stirred, but sank back into Dreamland. Daisy did not respond.

It was then that I decided to look for her underwater. Thanks to Josephine and her friends, my swimming skills had improved considerably, and the warmth of the sun made the lagoon as comfortable as a bath. My ability to dive and remain under the surface while holding my breath was markedly improved too: for some inexplicable reason I could stay below for several minutes at a time without strain. I breaststroked to the middle of the lagoon, and dove.

The sunlight penetrated the water to a remarkable depth; I could see for hundreds of feet in every direction. There were rainbow-hued fish and colorful coral; long strands of seaweed waved up at me from the bottom, where Josephine and her sisters lay curled around one another, dreaming watery dreams. But there was no sign of Daisy.

I surfaced and formed a reconnaissance plan.

The lagoon was bordered on one side by a tall limestone cliff, and now I swam to its base before diving again. I planned on making a complete underwater circuit around the edge of the lagoon, hoping that this might be the best way to seek Daisy out, if indeed she was still here. But before I had advanced more than a dozen feet I spied, perhaps ten feet below the surface, what appeared to be a hollow in the cliff face. Curious, I swam toward it, only to be met on the way by a very excited Daisy.

She was delighted to see me. How can a crocodile show delight? you might ask. She swam around my head, nipping at my ears, my nose, then snapping at my lower lip and drawing blood. A Daisy kiss? I laughed to myself: my fourth female conquest! She turned and headed in the direction of the hollow. Was she asking me to follow?

I trailed behind her. She kept turning and looking back, as if to make sure that I was taking her lead. I began to worry about my breath, but I figured that I had perhaps another forty-five seconds, possibly a minute, of comfort remaining, and so I trusted my instincts while giving in to curiosity. On arriving at the hollow I discovered that it was an entrance to a narrow tunnel in the rock. What boy could resist?

My lungs were about to explode.

I raced to the surface, where I gasped for air. I should return to Peter, I thought, if only to tell him where I was headed. Perhaps he would join me. But curiosity and Daisy's urgency got the better of me. I sucked in several deep breaths and kicked under the surface once again.

Daisy was waiting for me by the tunnel entrance. On seeing my approach, she turned and entered. It was then that I made a courageous—and possibly very foolish—decision. My hips could barely fit through the opening. Once inside, would I be able to turn around in order to return? Daisy disappeared into the darkness ahead of me. I followed.

The tunnel was lined with rocks and coral. Their sharp edges cut me as I advanced. I wanted to cry out in pain, but I could not open my mouth for fear of losing air. I began to panic.

I could not go on. My lungs would not hold. I tried to turn around, but it was impossible. I could only move forward. Daisy paddled ahead of me. Then it occurred to me: how could I see her? If this was an underwater cave, what was the source of its light? Furthermore, how could she breathe? I knew nothing about a crocodile's ability to hold its breath, if that is in fact what it did, but she had been underwater much, much longer than I. Did she know of something that I didn't, of some ray of hope that lay ahead? I could do nothing but follow her.

Gradually the light seemed to grow brighter. It must be my dying brain playing tricks, I thought. I could no longer see my reptilian friend. What had become of her? I gave one or two final kicks, pushing onward, then turned onto my back in order to see the heaven to which I was about to ascend. My lungs were screaming, and the time had come for me to end the agony. Swimming with my face pressed to the rock ceiling, I had no choice but to suck in my watery Death. An awfully big adventure indeed! Peter, alas, would never know what had happened to me. Peter, alas, would forget me by tomorrow.

I opened my mouth to take in water, and filled it instead with the sweetest air I had ever breathed.

My face had found a pocket of atmosphere trapped under the rock, a treasure chest of oxygen acting as a buffer between limestone and lagoon. Was it luck or instinct that made me flip onto my back? No matter. This pocket, but several inches in height, was enough to renew my hope. Ah, but what now? I inched forward a bit, still sucking in air as though I could never get enough of it. And miraculously the pocket continued onward, expanding, increasing in height. My goodness, there was now nearly a foot of open space above me! I pushed forward with my hands, dragging my body along the sharp rock ceiling, razoring my chest and thighs with a dozen tiny cuts. The air pocket continued to climb and grow until—God be praised! A miracle!

It was a small cave, perhaps twenty feet high, lit from above by a hole in the rock ceiling. I looked around. A shoreline! If my strength allowed, I might be able to pull myself out of the water and onto damp earth. I lowered my feet in preparation for an enormous effort of will, and they met bottom. Lo! I could stand with ease.

Once I was out of the water, I lay on this underground beach for several minutes, gasping for breath. I heard a soft peep, and turning my head I discovered Daisy sitting on a rock, either cheering me on or laughing at me.

It seemed that since we had last met she had learned to talk. She peeped again. "I'm coming," I said, "just give me a moment. You're as impatient as Peter."

She waited a few moments more. Carefully I stood. Rivulets of blood ran down my chest and legs. Daisy lapped the blood as it puddled at my feet. This seemed to me only fair and rather eased my guilt: after all, had I not dined quite recently on every bit of edible crocodile imaginable?

Once she had quenched her thirst, she turned and scampered deeper into the cave. Again I followed. Cracks in the ceiling let in sunlight, so that I was never in danger of losing my way. We walked on and on, seemingly for miles. At one point, thinking she must be tired, I picked up Daisy. I had no pocket in which to carry her (my trousers being back on the shore with Peter), so I placed her on top of my head. She rode there for a while, and after a time—seeing, I suppose, that I was headed in the right direction—she curled up and fell asleep.

I couldn't help but wonder: was this path indeed leading to some satisfying end? Why would any sane human trust a crocodile to lead him anywhere? What if I eventually became lost, to die in a maze of underground tunnels? But then again, what choice did I have, other than to turn around? Finally, exhausted, I entered what appeared to be an enormous grotto but dimly lit by the vanishing sun. I'll lie down, I thought, just for a moment and close my eyes. I gently removed Daisy from my hair and stretched out on the rock, nestling her in a small cavity in the floor beside me. The next thing I knew I was awakened by a thin shaft of daylight. I sat up and looked around. Darkness was everywhere, but for this blinding shaft.

Daisy peeped a good morning. She seemed content to remain where I had placed her. Was this room our final destination?

I decided to explore. The air was quite damp; I sensed that there was water here, perhaps the source of the underground stream. As I moved along the wall, farther and farther from the opening through which I had entered, a thought—a fear, actually—began to gnaw at me. I pushed it away, refusing to believe until I had proof. And soon enough I did: my hand came upon something protruding from a crevasse in the wall—a torch! One of several left by Lone Wolf and the other young men when I returned with them down the Deep Well! Daisy had led me along a back-door pathway to the very cavern in which Tiger Lily and I had met our nemesis.

The monster was dead, I knew, but were there others like her? (And it *was* female—a discovery proudly announced by Sunflower when she and the native matrons butchered the carcass.) We had sighted no mate when we came back for the carcass. But now, alone in the dark, I felt a presence. The monster's husband, larger than the she-dragon, lay licking its jaws at the edge of the water—I was sure of it. Naked as I was, I had not even Peter's blunt stick to wield as weapon! I was a dead man.

Daisy had led me here, to the crocodile's underground home.

Daisy had led me, quite possibly, to my death.

As I calmed my breath, I tried to think of what to do. I could run, of course, out of the cavern and up the tunnel to the bottom of the well, but if there were a giant lizard here he would be on me as soon as he heard me scrambling across the rocky shore. I assumed he was sightless like his wife, and had been for many years, making his blindness an asset; whereas my blindness was new, and made me all the more vulnerable. I then recalled that the native men on our descent had left some flint and steel on a ledge nearby, to be used if one of the torches were accidentally extinguished. Fire was a weapon and my only recourse. I stretched out a hand and found the ledge. And yes, there they were! Happily, in my days at the camp, Tiger Lily had instructed me in the intricacies of using flint and iron pyrite to start a flame. (I had watched Peter do it many times, though he had no patience as an instructor.) The steel, I knew, was even more effective, but would it be enough? How damp was the torch? Would the pitch in which it had been dipped still be effective?

I struck flint against steel, holding both near the torch's head. I feared that the sound would draw the creature to me, but I had to risk it. I struck a spark. It had no effect. I struck again. Another spark. And lo! the pitch took the bait, as it were, and in a moment the torch was ablaze.

I wrenched it from the crevasse and held it high, hoping to spot the enemy before he attacked. There was the lake. There was the islet in its center. There were the she-monster's bloodstains on the rocks, her scratch marks in the sand where she had writhed in her final death throes. But there was nothing else—no dragon, no enemy, not even so much as a bat to be feared, save for my overwrought imagination.

Why had Daisy come here? Was she in search of her birth mother? Was the monster that I had slain—oh horrors!—my little Daisy's ma? Daisy's sandy incubator had been located far, far away—could the leviathan have left the cavern by the very path I had followed in arriving? Were there *other* paths? Once outside, she might have swum to Long Tom, quite a long journey but perhaps one dictated by Nature or Habit, and deposited her load of eggs. Something, of course, had *fertilized* those eggs, and perhaps someday I *would* meet Daisy's father, but he certainly didn't seem to be *here*. (Perhaps he was off in the depths of the ocean, eating mermen.) At any rate, Daisy had returned to her mother's lair, and now she had brought me here, possibly to introduce me to the fierce dame. (I had heard of similar tales involving cats and kittens, and remembered reading of astonishing bird and mammal migrations. Why should I doubt that a reptile could do this too?) Following this logic, did Daisy know, in some inner core of her primitive brain, that I had murdered her parent? Had *eaten* her *mother*? Yet she seemed happy in my company. She peeped her joy again and again and again.

And then I wondered: what had brought the mother *here*? I remember reading as a child the myths of Rome and Greece, of Arthur and the Norse gods. Wherever a treasure lay buried, a monster inevitably guarded it. Was this the location indicated on my father's treasure map? I recalled the crudely drawn creature that resembled a dragon. Was it meant to be a crocodile? Of course! Here lay the treasure my father, and so many others, had sought!

I was hungry, but I knew a way out: the Deep Well would easily bring me back to sunlight and Tiger Lily. On my first venture here, I had vowed to return one day and explore. Well, here I was, returned! Why not take this opportunity to uncover a treasure, quite possibly the Never-Isle's "deepest" secret?

The water was frigid. I waded in quickly, then swam the thirty feet or so to the islet. I was shivering terribly when I emerged, and so went to work at once. The islet, as I had guessed, was more or less a mound of sandy soil. The mass of it was no wider than fifteen feet across, and now I walked to the center of the mound, fell onto my knees, and with my bare hands began to dig. The soil was wet and easy to move, and within minutes I was in it to my elbows. The light was not good here. I couldn't bring the torch across the water with me and had returned it to its crevasse. Consequently I was dependent on its distant ambient light, and trusted more to the *feel* of things as I dug and sifted. The soft soil wedged itself under my fingernails and in between my toes. But that's all I found—wet sandy soil. No treasure chest, no ingots of gold or pouches of diamonds—until my thumb bumped against something round and thick and solid, which I pried out of the dirt. Another something came along with it, a chain of sorts, and I quickly discovered—by feel, mind you, not by sight—that I had uncovered a pocket watch. I held it to my ear—it was still ticking! I dug further. Nothing more. Nothing but sand, wet and useless.

I was shivering from cold, and so decided to return to shore and thence to the lovely warm sun of the Never-Isle. I could come back another day, with a pick and shovel and a better source of light. Holding the watch above the water,

I paddled one-armed back to where I had entered the lake. The going was slow, and I thought that my blood might very well turn to ice before my feet touched ground again. Yet I gritted my teeth and paddled on. Dripping wet, I knew I had to get to the surface before I collapsed from the chill. I said my farewell to Daisy, who peeped in return—she clearly had no desire to leave this wretched place—then headed back up the Deep Well's winding stair to the native village above.

It occurred to me only as my head was about to appear above the lip of the well that I had left my trousers back with Peter and the mermaids. I was completely naked.

What to do? I was always somewhat shy about things like this (unlike Peter). I suppose the natives would not have cared a whit; nevertheless, I made sure that no one was in sight before I scampered to some nearby bushes. I soon heard a woman singing to herself, and peering out of the fronds that covered me, I spied Blue Bonnet gathering banana leaves.

"Pssst. Blue Bonnet," I whispered.

She looked around, and when she saw my face her eyes lit up. "James! You've come back!"

"Yes, I—I need a favor. I—I've lost my—my trousers. Could you do me a kindness and please—bring me—something?"

She laughed at this. The old women of the village were known for cracking ribald jokes that made even the bravest of the braves blush with shame. She said something to me which I will not repeat, dear reader, except to say that it had to do with the large banana leaves she was gathering, and then she handed me one. I asked for several more, and a rope, please. Still laughing, she undid her own belt and passed it to me along with a few more leaves, and thus I fashioned a sort of skirt that for the moment served its purpose. I emerged from hiding, thanked Blue Bonnet, and then quick as I could I hastened to pay my respects to Great Panther before seeking out my fiancée. Several of the natives stared, astonished at my dress.

To my surprise he was not pleased to see me. Nor was Tiger Lily, who sat at his feet.

"James, what are you doing here?" she exclaimed.

"I—I found a secret way. I'll tell you about it over dinner. In the meantime— What?"

I could see the alarm on her face. Great Panther jumped in to explain.

"You shouldn't be here, lad. Lone Wolf is angry, jealous, and insulted that he has lost the hand of the princess to an outsider. A boy without a shadow, he complains, but I think that's beside the point. At any rate, he demands a meeting."

"Well, of course I'll meet with him," I replied. "But he won't change my mind."

"You don't understand, James," Tiger Lily explained. "By 'meeting' he means 'battle.' In this case a battle between rival suitors. To the death."

"Oh."

"It's his right, because I threw him over for you."

"Oh." All I could think of was how much older and bigger and stronger Lone Wolf was, compared to my fourteen-year-old musculature.

Panther continued: "We were hoping to hold him off until you returned for the wedding. It would be Bad Form to kill a bridegroom on his wedding day. But of course, any time before then . . ." He left the sentence unfinished.

"I could hide, and then sneak away tonight. He doesn't need to know I'm here."

"Too late for that," said a voice behind me. Turning, I saw Lone Wolf standing in the entrance to the tent, his bronzed muscular arms folded resolutely across his broad muscular chest. He smiled.

It was decided that we would meet two days hence on the savanna at noon. We each were allowed up to two weapons of our own choosing, although the two must "act as one." A bow and arrows, for example, would fit the description. I could, of course, choose to ignore the challenge and hide in Peter's Underground Home, but that would mean not only that I would lose Tiger Lily forever but that she would then have to marry Lone Wolf against her will. (That, at least, was the tradition, and Pa-Ku-U-Na-Ini took pride in their traditions.) If, however, Lone Wolf and I met in battle and I was killed defending her honor, she could choose another suitor, or even decide to keep her maidenhood. Her free will and happiness depended on my showing up for the "meeting," and either beating Lone Wolf to a bloody pulp (which was absurdly unlikely) or being horribly murdered while whispering my undying love for her with my dying lips.

I returned home to Peter the following day. He seemed remarkably unconcerned about my absence, and absolutely thrilled (once I told him) about the forthcoming combat to the death.

"But, Peter, I might die!"

"To die will be an awfully big adventure," he answered. This phrase was becoming something of an annoying cliché.

Tink was the only being who evinced sympathy. "She's very worried," Peter remarked that evening over a pipe. "You know she loves you, and she'd rather see you married to that terrible girl than have you lying dead in a puddle of your own gore. She'll deal with the girl later."

"Thank her for me," I said rather glumly, "I guess."

"Thank her yourself," he said. "She's right here."

"Thank you, Tink," I repeated, even more glumly.

I couldn't sleep, of course. I tossed and turned, and it was only then that I remembered the watch I had found on the islet. Tiger Lily had given me a pouch in which to carry it home, as there was no buttonhole in my banana-leaf skirt through which to thread the fob. All I could think of, at any rate, was my impending death—watches be d—mned—but now that it was only hours away, I could do nothing but sigh deeply and turn my thoughts to anything at hand that might be distracting.

I lit a candle, then pulled the watch from the pouch. Peter slept soundly.

It was solid gold, or so it appeared. The chain and fob were gold too. I held it to my ear once again to hear its tiny heartbeat. I supposed that, if people didn't age, or aged very slowly, on the Never-Isle, then the same principle might apply to inanimate objects. The watch could have been wound centuries before.

I checked the fastening—a simple clasp—and flipped it open.

The watch face was unadorned, but its simplicity was a thing of beauty. On the verso of the cover I found an engraving.

To J.C. with love from A.D. it read. J.C.? A date followed: *January 1860.* The month before my birth. Was this my father's watch? If so, who was A.D.? Not my mother, for those were not her initials. Nor could she have afforded such an extravagance. Beneath the date was a phrase: *Tempus Regit Omnes.* Time Rules All.

Indeed.

I met Lone Wolf on the savanna at noon the following day. Peter was my second, and a native known as Sly Fox was Lone Wolf's. Great Panther was there, as were many members of the tribe, but Tiger Lily could not bear to come. My heart broke a little on learning this, though I understood her reasons.

His weapon was a six-foot spear accompanied by a fishing net. (Did I mention that Lone Wolf was the fishing champion of the tribe?) The spear was headed by an iron spike that looked to be nearly a foot long. I pictured him entangling me in the fishing net, then easily sliding the spear through my body until it poked out of my back. The blade bore several smaller blades sticking out at right angles, so that once the spike was securely inside me Lone Wolf might twist it around in either direction and thus shred whatever organs had come in contact with the aforesaid spike. I hoped that this "meeting of Lone Wolf with the boy James to resolve a preconjugal dispute" (which was how it was described in the official proclamation) would be over so quickly that I would feel very little pain, but I had my doubts.

I was wearing my trousers again (Peter had worn them on his return from the lagoon); my weapons lay concealed, one in each of my pockets, so it appeared at first that I was weaponless. This puzzled all but Lone Wolf, who smiled mockingly.

"Do you hope to beg for your life?" he asked with an Etonian sneer. "Is that your weapon of choice, coward—a plea for my mercy?"

"Well," I answered, "I'm not counting that as a weapon, but yes, I will beg. Not only for my life but for common sense. Your pride has been hurt and I'm sorry for that, Lone Wolf, but it was Tiger Lily's choice, not mine."

"You offered her the flower," he declared. "Which is the custom."

"I didn't know that, I swear. I do love her, and I'm glad she answered the way she did, but I didn't mean it as an offense to *you*. I assumed at the time that she was already yours—there was no choice to be *made*. I was simply being polite, like my mother taught me."

"You truly love Tiger Lily?" he scoffed. "You—a boy without a shadow, let alone any noble blood or family titles—think you're in love?" Clearly he was stuck on this point of "love."

"I'm descended from the Great and Historically Important Captain James Cook, though I doubt you would know who *he* was," I said in as imperious a manner as I could muster. I thought I heard a faint gasp from some in the crowd, but I ignored it and plowed on: "But I *am* in love, and she is too. She *admires* you, Lone Wolf—I mean, who wouldn't? You're very brave and strong. You could have killed the crocodile easily, if you had so chosen. But you didn't, and do you know why? Because you're a coward."

An even louder gasp emerged from the crowd.

"It is *you* who are the coward, dear boy, as I will demonstrate shortly. You will beg for mercy as your blood spurts forth. You will scream like a woman as I decimate your guts. You will whimper like a little girl as I pull out your spleen—and eat it." His imagination was somewhat overcharged, but it had the desired effect.

And with that he raised the spear.

We circled each other at first. He seemed in no hurry. He knew his triumph was inevitable, and the showman in him wished to draw the moment out for the crowd's (and his own) enjoyment. After all, those who came to see the massacre had traveled far, and it simply would not do for me to be skewered in a matter of seconds.

Once we were in a good position, I reached into my starboard pocket and pulled out the pocket watch. I had polished it that morning to a brilliant sheen, and now I aimed it so that it caught the rays of the sun and bounced them back into Lone Wolf's eyes. He blinked, briefly blinded, and I knew I had but a moment to effectively deploy Weapon Number 2. I raced toward him as fast as I could, simultaneously reaching into my port-side pocket and withdrawing a handful of sand. I flung it into his face, then made a very hasty retreat.

He screamed in frustration and brought the hand holding the net to his eyes, which were now gritty with grains. He rubbed, he blinked, and—doubly angry—he turned to face me again.

"I will kill you even more slowly for that," he hissed.

Slowly he approached.

Slowly I circled.

Slowly he countered and moved closer.

Slowly I prayed.

Slowly he whirled the net above his head, preparing to cast it.

Slowly I prepared to die.

Slowly he rose from the earth and ascended to the tree-tops.

For, as I'm sure you've guessed, dear reader, it was Flying Sand I flung at him.

Helpless, he began to scream.

I had hoped to catch him off guard. To my great good luck, and unbeknownst to me at the time (I swear it!), he had a terrible fear of heights.

He dropped the net.

He dropped the spear.

He screamed for his brothers to help him down.

He was actually only thirty feet or so above the savanna. Sly Fox seized hold of the net and flung it back up to him. Lone Wolf reached for it, but the reaching threw him off balance.

He plummeted to earth, his head bounced off the grassy plain, and he soared even higher.

"Lone Wolf, breathe deeply, calm yourself!" I shouted up to him.

He was now hovering upside down. A few curious lions appeared on the edge of the plain and studied him.

"Get me down, boy!" he screamed again. "Get me down, get me down, GET ME DOWN!" And then he began to cry.

"I don't want to die," he squeaked in a very high falsetto.

I spoke quietly to him.

"Lone Wolf, take a breath—relax—tuck your knees to your chest and bring your feet below your hips." I repeated this three more times before he heard me. After several tries he managed to turn himself upright. "Now *will* yourself to earth." He looked down, tensed once again, closed his eyes, and very slowly, *very very* slowly, descended until he was but a foot or so above Sly Fox, who reached up, grabbed an ankle, and gave a sharp tug. Lone Wolf fell on top of his second, and both men toppled to the earth in a tangle of arms and legs and fishing net.

Sadly, Lone Wolf suffered an accident of the bowels.

And so Peter and I returned to the Underground Home that night, triumphant.

"You should have seen it, Tink!" Peter cried. "You would have loved it!"

He listened for a moment.

"She says you owe her your undying gratitude."

"Whatever for?"

"It was *her* Flying Sand you used."

"Yes, well, I thank her for the use of her Sand, but it was *my idea.*"

"No it wasn't." Peter spoke as if *he* were Tink, without the regular pause needed for translation.

I looked at him.

"But it *was,* Peter. *You* didn't tell me what to do, nor did Tink. I thought of it myself."

He looked hurt, and a little bit astonished.

"So you're still going through with it?"

"With what?"

"The wedding. Tink wants to know."

"Of course I am. I love her. Tiger Lily, I love Tiger Lily."

"But you *owe Tink.*"

"I don't owe her a d—mned thing."

There was a decidedly long silence.

"So you'll be leaving us then?" His lower lip trembled.

"Peter, I told you, did you forget? I will come back to visit. As often as possible. We'll play together. We'll visit the mermaids. We'll wrestle with Barnaby."

"What about Tink?"

"What *about* Tink?"

"She *loves* you. She wants you for herself."

I sighed.

"Peter, to be perfectly honest, I've never even *seen* Tink."

He said nothing for a moment.

"Do you not believe in fairies?" he finally asked.

"I don't know. I mean, if Tink *is* real, then—" I stopped midsentence. "Peter, this is beside the point. This is not about Tink being real or not. I'm sure she is. I'm sure that, in time, my eyes will grow accustomed to things here, and she'll be as plain as day. But what this is about is my love for Tiger Lily.

I never thought it possible that I would ever love *anyone*, or anyone would ever love *me*."

"*I* love you."

"Not in *this* way. It's all I've ever hoped for."

He searched for another angle of attack. "But—Tiger Lily could be lying. Tink lies all the time. It's common for women to lie and betray you. My mother betrayed *me*. You and I will *always* be true to each other."

"What do you mean your mother betrayed you? I thought you didn't remember your mother, except that she was bigger than you."

Silence.

"I do remember *some* things."

"Yes, well—" I didn't know what else to say. Finally: "Peter, you're my friend. I care for you in one way and I care for Tiger Lily in another way. I'm not betraying you by marrying her. I'll *always* be your friend."

"Promise?"

"Promise."

"Hope to die?"

"I *never* hope to die. Living here, I hope to *never* die."

He looked at me, then at Tink's Cottage. Then he lay down and closed his eyes. I lay down beside him. Exciting as the day had been, I was exhausted.

As we both were drifting off to sleep, he said to no one in particular: "Things change. I hate that." He sounded very sad.

Over the next week, our relationship returned to normal. Peter forgot everything, or so it seemed. He was cheerful, playful, filling every waking moment with fun. We Barn-abyed, we mermaided, we even rode on the back of a tiger (very briefly). Finally the moon reached its fullness, and it was time for the wedding.

I wanted to walk to the village, but Peter said he would wait and fly that evening. I was to warn the natives that he would be coming by air, so that they should not shoot him. I set off at dawn.

It was a glorious hike, that walk alone. I thought of where I'd come from and what I was to become. I thought of my mother and my father on *their* wedding day. Had they been excited? Nervous? Did they love each other as much as Tiger Lily and I did?

As I crossed the Serpentine I spotted the rainbow ser-pent and nodded hello. It hissed a friendly hello in return. I passed Barnaby and his two cubs. I waved and they waved back. I wondered then where Barnaby's mate was, and why *he* was raising the children. There seemed to be a tremendous number of motherless children on these islands. I thought of Daisy, and wondered if perhaps I might retrieve her before the ceremony and bring her as my honored guest, but I was certain she wouldn't understand. Besides, her presence might cause confusion among those (and there were many) who distrusted crocodiles.

I arrived in the village late in the afternoon. A great pit had been dug for the wedding feast fire. An enormous spit was in place, waiting for whatever fish were to be roasted. The women were busy chopping, baking, preparing. The men were practicing the wedding dance, a complicated ritual involving high kicks, head butts, and a peculiar wiggling motion of the buttocks. Lone Wolf was off netting the Catch of the Night. The wedding was to take place at midnight, under the full moon. I retired to Blue Bonnet's thatched hut to prepare.

I was given a native-dyed cloth of indigo to wrap around my waist. My trousers by now were pretty well worn out, and when I handed them to Blue Bonnet (I was modestly concealed behind a partition), I realized that in saying goodbye to them I was bidding farewell to the last remnant of my English life. I was an island child now—no, an island *man*. I kept the pocket watch, of course, tucked in the pouch Tiger Lily had given me. The bag was dangling like a locket over the center of my chest. I called the watch "my father's watch"—which it very well may have been—and I imagined that its constant ticking was a reminder to my heart that my father, in spirit, was always with me.

Once I had finished dressing, Blue Bonnet—as my surrogate mother—presented me with the ceremonial Wedding Knife, a short sharp blade I would use to cut the Wedding Liana that symbolically bound Tiger Lily to her parents. She then gave me back my trousers and told me to cast them into the small fire burning in the center of her tent. I suddenly remembered my mother's wedding ring and used the Wedding Knife to slice open the stitching of my starboard trouser cuff. I took out the ring and tucked the knife into the waist of my indigo wrap. I promised to burn my trousers *after* the ceremony. I was anxious to meet my bride.

Great Panther was in mourning, a ritual seclusion enacted by every bride's father for three days before the service. As the sun set and cast a beautiful hibiscus shade of pink over the sea, I was to spend the final hours of bachelorhood with my future mate—we were called the "individuals-not-yet-as-one"—so that we could share any secrets from our past that needed to be told and carefully consider one last time whether the choice to join together was the right one. There was no shame in calling off the wedding, even at this late stage. Once the vows were said, however, we were not permitted to hold anything back from each other.

I met her on the promontory. She was even lovelier than the hibiscus-pink sunset.

"You're the first person I ever kissed," I confessed. "Apart from my mother, of course. But I *thought* about kissing others. Before I met you."

"I kissed Lone Wolf. Many times," she confessed. "I think I liked it. A little bit. I know *he* did."

"There's a mermaid I frolicked with. We didn't do anything naughty, but I *thought* about it."

"Was it Josephine?"

"How did you know?"

"She frolics with everyone. Every man, I mean. She's very fond of Lone Wolf. He's told me all about her bosom."

"I'm glad yours isn't as—enormous. She frightens me sometimes."

Tiger Lily lowered her face to hide her blush.

"I thought for a moment of running away," she confessed. "When the crocodile attacked you. I knew I could escape, but I also knew that if you had died, I would never be able to live with myself. I had to risk staying with you, perhaps dying with you, if I hoped to stay true to *me*. Can you forgive me for wavering?"

"We all waver. What's important is making the right choice

in the end. I love you, Tiger Lily. For me, *that* is the right choice. I would have died happy, knowing I saved you."

She said nothing further. She took my hand and we gazed out to sea. The moon had risen, and the path of its reflection led across the water like a trail to heaven.

"Here," I said to her and held out my mother's wedding ring.

"James, it's beautiful. Where did you get it?"

"It belonged to my mother. My father gave it to her on their wedding day. I want *you* to have it."

She studied it in the moonlight.

"It says something. It's difficult to read—"

"To My Eternal Love."

"Is that me?" she asked with a teasing smile.

"Oh yes."

She was quiet for a moment. "What's 'eternal'?" she asked.

"It means 'forever.' It means that something will never change. Like here. Like *this* place. Everyone who lives here, it seems, will live forever."

She caught the hesitation in my voice.

"But that's good, isn't it?"

"It is for *us*. It is for our love. I know with all my heart and being that, wherever we are, my love for you will never change."

She smiled. She leaned in close and kissed me softly on the lips.

It was then that Peter struck.

He swooped down from the heavens, planting the flats of his palms on our shoulders, and pushing us out into the air. Tiger Lily screamed. We plummeted toward the rocks below.

I reached for my pockets, hoping to find some Flying Sand that might save us, but of course there were no pockets, there was no sand. Just before we struck, he swooped under me to lift me up, as he had lifted me from the crow's nest, and in his arms I flew heavenward. Tiger Lily did not.

"Peter! No! What are you *doing*?" I pushed against him.

"They were going to eat you! They were going to roast you on a spit and eat you! Tink heard them planning it! She flew ahead and raced back to tell me! Tiger Lily was going to betray you!"

I hit him. I clenched my hands into fists and struck him in the face again and again. He looked astonished, and finally released me. I dropped ten feet to the promontory, knocking the wind from my chest. Peter landed beside me. There were tears on his cheeks. His nose was bleeding from my furious fists, and his tears mixed with the blood.

I scrambled on hands and knees to the promontory edge and looked down. I saw only jagged rocks in the moonlight, and the waves lashing against them. "Tiger Lily!" I cried. Then I turned to Peter and drew forth the Wedding Knife.

"Liar! You're not my friend! You killed her! You're my enemy!"

I raised the knife to stab him.

He was shocked. "I saved you, James," he said ever so softly.

I did not strike. I should have, but I did not.

* * *

I raced back to Blue Bonnet's tent, to search my trouser pockets for any grains of Flying Sand that remained. I rubbed what I found over my chest, into my hair. Then I took off, flying out of the tent into the air across to the promontory and down to the rocks below.

Tiger Lily lay among them, broken, not yet dead. I held her and sobbed. She reached up and touched my cheek, catching a tear on the tip of her finger and then bringing it to her lips, as if to taste me one final time. Then she opened her hand and held out the wedding ring.

"To My Eternal Love," she whispered.

Carrying her in my arms, I returned to the camp, and placed her broken body at her father's feet. Now he had an honest reason to mourn.

It was Sunflower who spoke.

"You've come back," she said with bitterness. "You who are One with the Great White Father. He came among us, bringing Death. He descended in the Well and now has risen again. Bringing Death. Always bringing Death."

I could not meet her eyes. My eyes instead met Lone Wolf's, and I knew he hated me forever now. They all did. I never told them what had happened or who had done this to their beloved—I was still in too great a shock. Instead I looked one last look at Tiger Lily, then turned and marched to the lip of the Deep Well.

On the third finger of my starboard hand I placed the wedding ring.

Then I descended once again, never to return.

*   *   *

I know that the Scotsman's book claims that I tried to drown her in the lagoon, and that Peter saved her life. Can you imagine what I felt on reading such a lie? It was *he* who betrayed *me*, not *I her*. I will never trust a man or boy again, I thought, or love another woman.

Never. Never again.

By the underground lake I met Daisy. She came to me at once, as if she understood. I could tell she had been nesting on the little island, for she was covered with sand. She floated in the air before me now and nestled in the hollow of my clavicle.

It was then I realized—you, dear reader, may have guessed long ago, but only now did *I* guess—that the treasure of the island, the treasure marked on my father's map and guarded by the dragon, was not buried in the sand; it was the Sand itself.

I swam to the islet and scooped some up, filling the pouch that held the watch (which I now fastened by its chain around my neck), then peppering myself with as many grains as I thought would last the night. Daisy followed as I flew from the islet to the ceiling of the cavern, then squeezed through the narrow crack. Its passage led to a rocky ledge below the promontory, several hundred feet above the sea. Inviting Daisy to join me, I turned toward the stars of Peter's Liana and willed myself up. It was the second star I was aiming for, not the starboard one (on the right) but the one that was port side, to the left, the sinister guiding light. I would fly until dawn, if that were possible, and perhaps I would die on the way. But if I did not die I might succeed in leaving this wretched archipelago forever.

When the sun rose, God willing, I would be in England.

HOOK AT ETON

Chapter Seven

—◦◦∞◦◦—

*A*s the sun rose I spotted the Plymouth coastline. I flew high above the sea, hoping that any fisherman, looking up, might mistake me for a great bird. Heading west, I circled Saint Michael's Mount, then flew north. I plummeted landward as swiftly as possible, and touched ground just as the morning's sun was first gracing rooftops. Daisy, nestled in my hair (to which she had retreated halfway through the flight), awoke and stretched. I adjusted my indigo wrap, drew my Wedding Knife, and walked as boldly as possible into the front room of the Wretched Traveler.

A man of forty-plus years stood behind the bar, washing glasses from the night before. The inn was much shabbier than I remembered it. The man turned to greet me and stood dumbfounded. I could hardly blame him. Before him stood a near-naked fourteen-year-old boy wielding a knife and bearing a miniature crocodile atop his head. I leapt across the room to the top of the bar, aided by a combination of Flying Sand and Never-Isle litheness. Daisy hissed at him as I pointed the knife at his throat.

"I'm looking for Scroff. He took something from me and I want it back."

The barman's mouth dropped open in fear and astonishment. Like Scroff and his ma, he was missing his lower front teeth. Poor dental hygiene clearly ran in the family.

I explained myself: "You're the father, I presume. Your son attacked me in the barn several months ago and stole from me a locket that belonged to my late mother. I've come to retrieve it."

The man managed to choke out a word: "Locket."

"Yes. A locket. He ripped it from my neck."

"No. No."

"Yes. He did. If he's sold it, his life is worthless. Where is he?"

The man swallowed, then began to gasp for breath, as if he were having a fit.

"ONE LAST CHANCE!" I shouted. "WHERE IS YOUR SON?"

"Not possible," he rasped.

I whipped the knife across his throat, not deep enough to cause serious injury, but enough to draw blood. He clutched his neck and staggered back, knocking over several glasses and a bottle of gin. The fumes of the alcohol made my eyes water.

He thought he was dying. He held a hand, wet with blood, in front of his face to ward off another blow. "Please, sir, please," he begged, "have mercy."

"Do you know of this locket?" I demanded.

He nodded.

"And?"

"Course it's sold. It were *gold*!"

"To a pawnshop? A local merchant?"

He nodded.

"Retrieve it. I'll give you an hour."

"Not possible."

This was absurd. He was stalling, wavering, lying to protect his son.

"Why? Why is it not possible? WHERE IS YOUR SON?" I roared as Daisy let out a peep that I'm sure she meant as a threat.

He caught his breath, stood a little straighter. He wiped tears from his eyes. He seemed on the verge of hysteria. He was preparing for death.

"It were me," he mumbled.

"What? What was you?"

"It were me what took it. *I'm* Scroff."

The world stood very still. I couldn't believe my ears *or* eyes.

"You're the *father*. Your son was fifteen, sixteen years old. *Is. Is* sixteen years old."

"No more. I'm thirty now."

Another silence. I felt a sickness fill my stomach. "What's today's date?" I asked.

"November fifteenth. Year of our Lord 1888."

In shock I slowly lowered the knife.

My God.

Fourteen and a half years had passed.

I tried not to think of my predicament. True, in my visit to the Never-Archipelago I had lost track of the time, and could not tell you, dear reader, exactly how many days and weeks had come and gone. Still, I was absolutely certain that nothing like a year had elapsed, let alone fourteen of them. Yet as I looked around the inn and took in its shabbiness, as Scroff showed me a mug commemorating the Queen's Golden Jubilee, as I perused a pile of newspapers that he had stacked for kindling, I could not deny that much had changed in the world in my absence.

Time had brought change to the Wretched Traveler too. Scroff may have been thirty, but he looked forty-five. His mother lay abed in a back room, lost in a world of dementia. He had indeed pawned my mother's locket, but that was too long ago for any hope of reclamation, and the coin he sold it for had been long spent. He had lost his youthful bravura and was clearly terrified of this crocodile-capped madman in his front room.

The moment I let down my guard he would, I was certain, summon the police. So I continued to threaten him until I had obtained some loose clothing lying around the inn. The shirt, shoes, trousers, and jacket were a bit oversize for a fourteen-year-old, but I did what I could to make adjustments. Once I had bound Scroff to the brass footrail by the bar, I stuffed balls of newspaper into the toes of the borrowed shoes and rolled up the trouser cuffs and shirtsleeves, hoping to obtain snugger clothing in good time. I then took what little coin I found in the cash drawer, stuffed my new pockets full of day-old bread, and set off.

I was determined to pick up my journey where fourteen and a half years before it had left off, and I now headed toward Penzance in the hope of finding my father's family. I had no idea, of course, who in that family might still be alive, but I had obtained in my shipboard conversation with Raleigh a bit of information about them, and so prepared myself for the worst.

During my halcyon days at Eton, I had succeeded in securing the address at which my father's family resided, they being regular contributors to the college whose letters were kept in the Donors' File of the Records Office. When I first set off on my pilgrimage fourteen years past, I held that address in mind and—it being only *months* that had slipped by in *my* experience—I remembered it still. And so it was that on a lovely day in November of the fifty-first year of Her Majesty's reign an ill-dressed lad with a crocodile on his head arrived at Number 25 Chapel Street, Penzance, and knocked on the door.

To be honest, I had quite forgotten about Daisy's presence, nested as she was in my thick tresses, and it was with unfortunate haste that I now plucked her from my crown to stick her in a pocket before the door could be opened. Startled, she bit me in the process of transfer, and so the woman who answered my knock beheld a dirty boy sucking a bloody thumb.

"What do you want?" she queried as she gazed down at me imperiously. She was wearing black, head to toe, a widow's garb. "We've no food. Go away." She shut the door in my face.

I noticed a brass nameplate to the port side of the door. JAMES COOK, MERCHANT, it read. (So my grandfather was named James also! Was he still living? Why was the woman dressed in mourning?) I knocked again. "Excuse me but—I'm your nephew!" I shouted, guessing that the woman could be the wife of my father's youngest brother. "I'm James Cook the third!"

After a moment she opened the door again. "We have no nephew," she declared and slammed the door once more.

"My father was James Cook, *Captain* James Cook of Her Majesty's ship the *Princess Alice*! The ship disappeared southwest of Bermuda in the Year of our Lord 1860!"

There was silence. I had not heard any retreating footsteps, so I knew that she remained on the other side of the door. After a few moments more she opened it again.

"Then you could not be his son," she announced with a smile of triumph, as if she had caught me miscounting cards and was playing her trump on my ace. "If he died in 1860, which is true, he could not father a boy of sixteen."

"Fourteen," I corrected her, "and I never said that he died, simply that he disappeared." (Of course he *had* died, but affirming this fact would not help my case.) "Are you my aunt? I'm sorry—I don't know your name. My father never spoke of you, he only talked of his younger brother, Arthur. *Reverend* Arthur—a minister, yes?" (That, at least, is what Raleigh had told me.) "Perhaps Uncle had not yet married by the time my father . . . vanished." (This was all guesswork on my part. Nearly twenty-nine years had passed since his disappearance; therefore this woman—who was clearly fifty if she was a day—could certainly be my aunt by marriage, assuming that my uncle Arthur—who remained at home— had wed.)

She studied me from head to foot before exclaiming, "This is absurd. *You* are absurd. You're dressed like a beggar. You're filthy. Why should I believe you?"

"I have his watch," I said spontaneously, then reached into a non-Daisy pocket and pulled out the instrument.

She took it, studied it, opened it, then read the inscription.

She was right. This *was* absurd. True, the watch bore his initials, but "J.C." is not an uncommon monogram and could belong to many a man (including our Lord!). Why would she believe that this watch came from my father?

She clapped her hand to her mouth and began to sob.

She shut the door again, not as soundly as she had before, and I heard her footsteps retreating. I waited, uncertain what to do next. She had the watch, and it appeared to have meant something to her, but what now? I knocked again. When the door remained firmly closed, I retreated across the street and studied the house from that vantage point.

It was stone, narrow, neat, and probably in line with the modest dwelling of a successful merchant who had religious scruples against ostentation. Was this the house in which my father had been raised, and where he had spent his last night on English soil before boarding the *Princess Alice*?

I recrossed the street and tried to open the door on my own. It was locked.

I pulled out a piece of Scroff's stale bread and ate. I placed some in my Daisy-pocket, which sustenance she devoured hungrily. My legs and arms began to ache, a pain that was bone-deep, and I feared I was coming down with some illness connected to flying. The street, meanwhile, was becoming busy with daily commerce. A few passersby studied me with concern for their safety, and I worried that a policeman might arrive shortly and place me under arrest for loitering. Sure enough, after I had been on the stoop or in its vicinity for an hour or more, a bobby turned a corner and began striding in my direction. At this point the door to Number 25 reopened, and the woman motioned me inside.

A dark narrow hall led to the back of the house. The hall became even darker once the door was shut.

"I'm your aunt Margaret. That is, if you *are* my nephew. If you are not, if you are nothing but a lying thief and beggar, which I suspect is true, then may you burn in the Eternal Flames of Hell, and soon." With these words she turned and headed down the hall toward the back room. I followed.

We entered a tiny bedroom, lit by a fire and as hot, I suspected, as the Eternal Flames to which she had condemned me. In a corner stood a night table with a washbasin and ewer. A bedpan, uncovered and redolent, sat on top of a quilted throw rug, one of several such rugs surrounding a large bed situated in the middle of the room. Propped up against the bedstead was a very old man.

"Grandfather," I said to him. "You're alive!"

"What's that to you, boy?" the old man replied.

Aunt Margaret tossed another log on the fire.

"Come close," the old man commanded.

I did.

He wore a nightcap, but a wisp of white hair hung like a tassel from underneath, covering one pale gray eye. His skin was mottled, his face splotched with large brown marks that appeared in the firelight to resemble scabrous wounds. His breath smelled of onions, and of dead things.

"You say James is your father?" he asked.

"Yessir. He only *disappeared* in 1860." A little lie, nothing more.

He said nothing at first, but his eyes never left mine.

"Do you doubt it?" I asked, fearing he did.

"No," he finally answered. "You're much like him, in face and figure, when he was your age. How old are you?"

"Fourteen, sir."

"Ha! You look old for your years." This surprised me—I had never been told this before.

I was feeling bold and replied, "So do you."

He grinned at this. A few of his teeth were black.

"You have your father's spirit, I'll say that. What's your name?"

"James. The Third."

"Your father had a prior son named James," he said, "so you may be the *fourth*." He was referring, I assumed, to myself, but of course he wouldn't know that. "Why are you here?"

"I wanted to meet you, sir. I wanted to learn some more about my family. My *father's* family."

"Such as what?"

I thought for a moment. How should I begin? "Is it true we're descended from Captain James Cook?" I blurted.

"Who in heaven's name told you that?"

"My father left me a book. A history of the captain's voyages. It was your gift to him, I was given to believe, when he graduated from Eton."

I saw a spark of memory flash in his eyes. "And why would that make you think your ancestor was *that* Captain Cook?"

"My mother said so."

"Ah. And you believe your mother?"

"Why would she lie?"

There followed a beat of silence before he answered. "All

mothers lie. Or their sons wouldn't wish to grow up, knowing what *truly* lay ahead."

I didn't know how to respond.

"And who *was* your mother?" he asked.

What should I say? I felt I couldn't tell him the truth, not just yet, for that would only convince him and my aunt that I *was* a madman and a liar.

"Even if you are who you say you are," my aunt interrupted before I could respond, "why should we trust you? You had a brother, *half* brother, who was a thief and a scoundrel. We paid for his education at Eton, but he was caught red-handed in a scandalous crime and ran away before he could be properly punished. I daresay he's dead now, God be praised—we never heard of him again and I can only assume that he is burning in the Eternal Flames. How do we know that you, James the Fourth, do not take after him?"

I swallowed and answered with sincere humility. "You cannot know that, Aunt Margaret, until you come to know my character. I am not here for money, or personal gain. I simply want to know more—about my father."

"He didn't go down with his ship?" The old man drew my attention back to him.

"No." This much, at least, was true.

"Does he live still?"

"No, sir."

The old man was silent for a moment, absorbing his son's second death. His expression was unreadable. "Why did he not return?" he finally asked. "Or at least send some message home? Was he shipwrecked, like Selkirk, on some undiscovered island?" This last question was colored by sarcasm, and he showed surprise when I answered in the affirmative.

"He was." This was *nearly* true.

"Your mother was a native woman then?" Aunt Margaret remarked in a disapproving tone. "You seem to have her coloring."

I realized then that the weeks (or months or years) that I had spent on the Never-Isle had tanned my skin a soft brown. I said nothing, which she took as an assent.

"And the island was discovered recently by some wandering ship?" Grandfather asked. "I saw nothing of that in the papers."

"It's a very small island," I answered.

"And the watch," my aunt queried. "He still kept the watch after all these years?" This was not so much a question as it was a kind of wondering.

"So it *is* his watch?" I queried.

"Why would you doubt it?" Aunt Margaret asked, skepticism edging her voice.

I had nearly given myself away. I steered the topic in a slightly different direction.

"What I meant to ask is—who is A.D.? The other initials. He never told me."

She blinked back a tear, and in that instant seemed to become even harder, like a seaman battening the hatches against a storm. Was she A.D. herself?

"Margaret," the old man commanded, "see that he's better clothed. Get someone from Harvey and Son to measure him for a suit and some shirts. I don't want my grandson dressed like a filthy highwayman."

And with those words I was dismissed.

Within the hour Mr. Harvey the Son came and measured me in the parlor for a suit of clothes. He also saw that I needed socks, undergarments, handkerchiefs, and a better pair of shoes. Within two more hours I had all but the suit, and before evening fell even that was delivered. My grandfather, I could see, was a powerful man.

I was shown to the top floor of the house, where a low-ceilinged room was to serve as my sleeping quarters. There I changed into the new suit, once it arrived, and was surprised to find that, for all the careful measurements taken by Harvey Junior, the suit was rather tight and a bit short in the legs and arms. I carefully removed Daisy from my old pocket, then stowed the clothes acquired from Scroff, along with the Wedding Knife and the pouch of Flying Sand, in an old travel valise I found in a corner of the room. It bore my father's initials and so, I thought, might have been his equipage during his years at Eton. Why, this very room must be my father's old bedroom! I had found him, in some sense, at last.

Daisy was famished, and I let her suck on the meat of my palm. Something was different about her, but I wasn't sure what that something was at first. And then I realized—she was several inches longer. At last she was beginning to grow! The sea air of England was proving to be bracingly beneficial for crocodile maturation.

It was then that I glanced at my pant legs and jacket sleeves, and another thought came at once. I was growing too: longer, taller, and—my God—older.

Fourteen and a half years had passed and I, returning to Greenwich Mean Time, was catching up. I felt my face. The beginnings of a whiskery stubble were sprouting on my jawline. I rolled up my shirtsleeve. The hair on my forearm was decidedly darker and thicker.

How old *was* I? No longer fourteen. (I now understood why Aunt Margaret and Grandfather had both thought me older.) If this was 1888, then I was twenty-eight years old! Gradually, as the day advanced, I was advancing too.

Quite suddenly all that had taken place in these weeks and years overwhelmed me. For some time I sat in the attic room contemplating everything I had missed. Had I remained in England, I would be well into my career by now, perhaps a vice president of a firm or, if I stayed a sailor, a first mate or master. I would most likely be married, and a father. My oldest son might be as old as eight, thinking himself near-grown and hoping to follow in the old man's footsteps! Had I been blessed with a daughter, she would be breaking little boys' hearts! The Beauty of Penzance! Not as beautiful as her mother, of course, but still—

And then I thought of Tiger Lily. Had she been dead for twenty-four hours, or for fourteen years? My sorrow nearly drowned me at this point. It filled my chest, tightened my throat, watered my eyes until, like a heartsick maiden, I flung myself on my father's boyhood bed and wept.

* * *

A storm was beginning to rage as I descended to the basement kitchen for my evening repast. Aunt Margaret, it seemed, did all the housekeeping herself. Her cleanliness was *above* godliness, as far as I could tell, but her cooking skills were barely rudimentary. The meal she served me was little more than a thin fishy broth punctuated by a few overcooked carrots.

I sat across from her, sipping the "stew" (as she called it). There was something on her mind, yet she hesitated to begin conversation. So I took it upon myself to do so.

"Is Uncle Arthur—" I left the sentence unfinished.

"He traveled to New Guinea, to bring the Lord to the native population. I was to follow in a year." A brief silence ensued. Then: "They ate him."

I couldn't help but think that Uncle Arthur would have made a better stew than what I had been served.

"I'm sorry, Aunt. I see you're still in mourning. Was it recent?"

"Twenty-six years this past August."

"I see."

"His father was kind enough to take me in. The servant and kitchen help had both recently left and Father Cook needed someone to take their place. I was able to help him economize. Your grandfather is a very frugal man."

I took a few more sips of broth. I was hesitant to explore further family history, but do or be d—mned, as they say.

"And the—other brother?"

"I beg your pardon?"

"Not Arthur, the older one."

"James?"

"No, no. My father spoke of his older brother, one he was very fond of, but he never said his name."

"I don't know to whom you're referring. There were only two sons. Their mother died giving birth to Arthur."

I distinctly remembered Raleigh mentioning an older son. "He was—well, from what I remember hearing—he was—disinherited. He overspent, and eventually drank himself into an early grave."

"It must be your father you're speaking of. Only he didn't drink himself to *death*, he just drank."

I didn't understand. "My father was a wastrel?"

"And disinherited for it, yes. Not only did he gamble and drink, he . . ." She stopped, looking away as if remembering something. She did not complete her thought.

"You knew him?"

She stiffened slightly, fighting against some violent emotion.

I decided to dig deeper, in a more roundabout way. "When did you marry Uncle Arthur?"

She seemed relieved at the apparent change of subject. "Shortly before he sailed to New Guinea. I was widowed in less than a year."

I did some quick calculating. If Arthur was twenty-six years dead, he was eaten in '62. Consequently he and Margaret were married in '61. My father vanished in '60.

"So you *couldn't* have known my father. He disappeared at least a year *before* your marriage."

"I knew him," she said, her voice wavering. "*Before* I knew Arthur. Through my sister."

I could tell there was more she wanted to say. She reached into her pocket, I assumed to withdraw a handkerchief, and produced my father's watch instead. Its ticking had stopped;

at last it had run down. She opened it and gazed for a long moment at the inscription.

"'To James Cook with love from Angela Darling,'" she translated. Then she closed the watch and absentmindedly rewound it. Her mind was leagues away.

"This Angela was your sister?" I prompted.

She glared at me as if I had stabbed her with a knife. "She was trapped in an unhappy marriage when she met James. Of course it was a sin, but her husband was a horrible man and James adored her. I connived in concealing her adultery." She looked away again. "She loved him so. James was handsome, and dashing. And the worst thing to ever happen to her."

"Her husband found out?"

"No. No, he believed the child was his. George they named him, after the husband. James had just been given a captaincy. She had this watch inscribed to him as her congratulations. He promised, on his return, to marry her if she could obtain a divorce and to live with her in sin if she could not. He left, he disappeared—drowned, we thought—and shortly after the child was born she—she took her own life."

Aunt Margaret closed the watch as if this were her final statement. In many ways it was. She reached across the table and handed me the watch. Then she rose and without another word climbed the stairs like a departing ghost. Her task was done, her soul unburdened. Now she would sleep, or not, and dream, or not. I never saw her again.

I returned to the attic room to think. I sat on the edge of the bed, Daisy (even larger) snoring beside me. The wind and rain beat against the bedroom window. I studied the ticking watch and its terrible inscription, thinking of my father, of the lies Aunt Margaret had told me, fearful of course that they were not lies. Had my father loved *two* women? His wife my mother and this Angela Darling? And had he fathered two sons, myself and a bastard named George? Indeed he *was* a wastrel, if this were so. I had to learn the truth.

I placed the watch on the bed, secretly wishing I had never discovered it, then descended to the ground floor, where I walked to my grandfather's room. The door was partially open. The fire burned low, its light reflected in the pale gray eyes of the old man.

Outside thunder rumbled.

"Put a log on, James, would you?"

I entered. The heat was stifling. I lifted a small log from the pile beside the hearth and placed it gently on top of the glowing ashes. I stirred the embers with the fireplace poker as sparks chased each other up the chimney.

"Thank you."

I turned and went to his bedside. He seemed a bit afraid of me; I must have resembled, silhouetted in the firelight, the suntanned ghost of his son. His eyes quite suddenly widened with surprise.

"Where is it?" he asked.

"Where's what?"

"Your shadow. You have no shadow."

A perceptive old fellow.

"I gave it away. To a boy I know. I don't really miss it."

He looked away, trembling, staring at the fire. His brow wrinkled, as if he were trying to solve a particularly nasty puzzle. "You're the very Devil, aren't you? Come to bring me home."

Was he joking? He looked back at me, a smile curling his thin lips. Thunder crashed. Lightning outlined the room's heavily curtained window. "What do you want to know?" he finally asked.

I took a deep breath and began.

"My mother. Did you know her?"

"Your mother?" His eyes studied me, as if for a moment he was not sure who I was.

I had continued to grow in the hours since he had last laid eyes on me. The sleeves of my new suit barely reached the middle of my forearms. My trouser legs exposed my socks and muscled calves. I no longer resembled a boy, that's for certain; I looked to be a man of twenty or more. Perhaps now he would believe my story.

"I was born in 1860, Grandfather. *I* was the boy you sent to Eton. I was falsely accused and expelled for thievery. I was on my way to *you* when—something happened."

"Ah" was all he said. Then his face convulsed in pain.

He began to cough, and I sat beside him on the bed and helped him sit up straighter. He motioned for a small dish resting on a bedside table. I handed it to him and he spat a large globule of bloody mucus into it. Then he sat back, as if his troubles were over.

"Your mother." A statement now, not a question. "Was a common whore."

My hands were around his neck, pressing him against the bedstead, squeezing the life from him. "Liar," I rasped. My voice too had changed by now, become deep and gravelly.

He was choking. He made no effort to pull my hands away. I did so of my own volition.

"My mother was Daisy Cook. She and my father were happily married. I lived with her in a house in Kensington, a house that you donated for our use. Until she died and then you cruelly took it away. I had my mother, and then I had nothing."

He took a deep breath. And another. "Your mother—and your father—were never married."

"That's a lie."

Another breath. "Did you ever see"—another breath—"a marriage license?"

"She had a wedding ring. *This* ring." I held out my fist, displaying the thin gold band. "'To My Eternal Love,' it says inside. He loved her."

"Cheaply bought. Any jeweler has them. She wore it for show."

"He *loved* her," I repeated.

Another breath. "He loved"—another breath, shallower this time—"many women."

I wanted to deny this, but remembering Aunt Margaret's tale I said nothing.

"Why did you support us then? If they weren't married, if I was a . . . bastard, why would you house us, and educate me?"

He shrugged as if the answer were obvious. "You were my grandson. Your aunt thought I was foolish, but I hoped to produce the kind of boy that your father most definitely was *not*." A slower breath. "Obviously my experiment failed." He looked at me directly now. Tiny flames flared high in his irises, as if he were stoking a fire inside. "I did not take into account that *both* of your parents were corrupted by vice. Else I would not have wasted my money."

"My mother was a saint."

"Your mother was a drug fiend." He flung his words at me like darts. "Your father met her in the lowest of gambling dens, where she was selling herself for a cheap pipe and instant oblivion." He took pleasure from the pain he was giving. "She was lovely, I imagine, and obviously desperate—James was an easy mark for beautiful, needy women. He fell upon her with the kind of missionary zeal your uncle Arthur professed toward the natives who ate him." The storm outside seemed to energize his cruelty. "He hoped to save her and succeeded to a point, I'll grant him that. He took her out of the pit and weaned her of her habit. He told me this in a final letter, asking me to care for her and his child if he failed to return from his voyage. How prescient of him."

"Do you still have that letter?" I challenged. He was lying once again—I knew it.

"Of course not. I have my vices, but sentiment is not one of them." He waved his hand as if he were dismissing my doubts. "At any rate, by the time you were born his ship was reported missing, and the pain of your birth and his disappearance drove your mother back to her old habits. I heard of this from Doctor Slinque, who was a friend of your father's, and I hired him to treat her." He chuckled, and the odor of decay spilled from his mouth. "It wasn't enough. It never is, with women like her."

In that moment I hated him more than I have ever hated anyone.

Without a second thought I went to the fire and picked up

the poker I had left lying in the embers; turning back to face him, I raised it high to strike. He looked up at me, astonished. I saw him for the bitter, wizened, pathetic worm he truly was; killing him would be a mercy, but I hadn't the courage. Instead I turned and, flinging the poker into a corner, left the room. I cursed him as I slammed the door behind me.

I had barely set foot on the stairs' bottom tread when I heard him scream.

His cries were weak at first, and interrupted by another coughing spell. Soon they continued—louder, more desperate—and my conscience told me to return to the room.

Was this some sort of trickery to bring me back? The door that I had slammed was now stuck fast, and it was the sight of smoke curling from beneath the doorsill, not his escalating cries, that galvanized me. I pulled with all my might against the door, and finally succeeded—after kicking it—in wrenching it open. My grandfather was engulfed in flames.

In seizing the poker earlier, I had inadvertently sent some burning coals tumbling across the floor. His bedding, worn and dry with age (much like himself), caught fire, and now the flames enrobed him in a burning shroud. There was little I could do. I flung the contents of the washbasin and ewer, and then of the bedpan, onto the pyre and lifting the heavy quilted throw rugs did my best to smother the flames. By the time the conflagration was extinguished the old man was nothing but a crisp.

Aunt Margaret, inured to his nighttime retching, slept through it all. I had no desire to wake her; I was through here. I had given her a reason to remain in mourning for *another* twenty-six years. I quickly climbed to the attic, peppered myself with Flying Sand, grabbed my father's valise in one hand and the two-foot-long Daisy in the other, and opened the top-floor window.

The storm had passed. Rain dripped from the eaves, but the night was warm.

Just as I was about to step out into the darkness, I remembered the watch. I returned to the bed, where I had left it, and looked for it but could not find it. It was somewhere near, that I knew, for I could hear its incessant ticking. I deposited Daisy on the dresser, then pulled off the bedclothes, deceased the pillow, turned the mattress onto the floor, but was unable to locate my father's timepiece. It was maddening. Where could it be? I stopped and stood very still, listening. Tick. Tick. Tick. Where was the noise coming from? I cocked my ear and followed the sound. I was led to the one place I would never have thought to look. The ticking of the watch, like the beating of a heart muffled in cotton, was coming from inside Daisy.

As we flew I pondered the science of my sudden growth spurt. Neither Daisy nor myself appeared to have increased in size and age since nightfall, so it was daylight, inexplicably, that seemed to affect our aging. We now were heading east, and soon to meet the rising sun. How much more would we grow? When I attained my 1888 age of twenty-eight, would I stop or grow even older? How much would Daisy's size and weight increase? The Flying Sand made her light as a feather to carry, but as soon as we touched down I would be unable to hold her. How big, in fact, did crocodiles become? The leviathan in the cavern was enormous. How could I possibly explain a crocodile's presence on the streets of London?

For London, indeed, was our destination. My goal was to reach the metropolis before daylight, but I was uncertain how quickly the Sand would allow me to travel. True, I had flown from a distant location in a matter of hours, but would the humid atmosphere of England slow me down? I needn't have worried. Before long the clock face of Big Ben guided me like a beacon toward the Thames.

As a boy, whenever my mother was felled with a headache, I had raced more than once to Doctor Uriah Slinque's home and office in Bayswater. He had taken a liking to me, for reasons I cannot explain, and I remember him extending an invitation to me to visit his laboratory after my mother's funeral. And so it was that, on the afternoon of the saddest day of my young life, I had arrived on his doorstep. He ushered me up three flights of stairs to his surgery, where I marveled at his display of jarred specimens as he explained to me the invaluable contribution of the vivisectionist to science.

He then led me to a table situated under an enormous skylight and near a staircase leading to the roof. There he showed me a frog lying on its back and pinned to a surface of thick black wax. The creature was anesthetized and would feel no pain, he told me as he carefully sliced open the poor thing throat to belly and splayed wide its skin, revealing among brightly colored organs a tiny beating heart. I was sickened and fascinated at the same time. Slinque rested his hand on the back of my neck, and gently massaged as he pointed out stomach, lungs, liver. I couldn't help but imagine *myself* pinned and splayed as he happily poked and prodded the amphibian's insides. He afterward gave me one of his lemony sweets to suck as I wandered home.

I had never seen Slinque's office from above, of course, but I quickly spotted the enormous skylight and swooped down, Daisy in arm, to land on the gently sloping roof beside it. Peering through the skylight in the early dawn, I could see the surgery much as I remembered it, so I knew at once that Slinque was still in residence. I found the trapdoor on the roof leading to the surgery staircase below. Daisy was too large now for me to pocket, so I laid her carefully on the angled surface, where she scrambled with her sharp claws to keep from falling. I tugged and kicked with all my might at the wooden door. The lock soon gave way, and I descended, awkwardly carrying an extremely heavy reptile under one arm and my father's valise under the other, to the abattoir.

I lit the gas lamps around the room and paused to catch my breath. The jarred specimens remained, but no longer fascinated me. The organs and fetal anomalies that they held (all, I supposed wrongly, belonging to the lower forms of animal life) now only disgusted me.

I made no attempt at stealth. Sure enough, I soon heard footsteps arriving from the floor below. As he climbed the stairs and came into view, wearing nightshirt and cap, he raised a pistol and aimed it at my breast.

Slinque remained remarkably unchanged despite the passage of Time; in fact the anesthesia and formaldehyde that he used in his practice had given a sheen of preservation to his face, so that he resembled, in the gaslit dawn, something that might be found suspended in one of his specimen jars. I remembered him as being a tall man, but my height now matched his. He cocked the gun and said to me, "You're a dead man."

"Doctor Slinque," I said as I raised my arms, "you remember me. My mother was Daisy Cook. I'm her son, James. We vivisected a frog together many years ago."

This, of course, gave him pause. He peered at me for a moment, then with his free hand reached into a breast pocket and removed a pair of glasses, which he proceeded to don. He peered at me again. "James Cook?" he said, reaching back into the past.

"Yes. My grandfather hired you to minister to my mother. He sends you his regards. Forgive my unusual entrance, but I did not wish to be seen on the streets of London with my friend." I nodded to the bottom of the trapdoor stairs, and Slinque's gaze followed. He started and nearly dropped the gun.

"My God," he whispered. Daisy opened her mouth and hissed at him. He backed up a step and almost tumbled down the stairs behind him.

She continued, rather loudly, to tick.

"I mean you no harm," I continued, "I simply have a few questions I'd like answered."

"James Cook?" he repeated, as if he had thought me long dead and yet here I was, returned from the grave.

"Please, if you wouldn't mind," I said, nodding to the pistol. He looked at it as if he had forgotten that he carried it. He now lowered it so that it pointed at the floor.

"Do you have any tea or coffee?" I asked. "I'd love something to take off the morning chill."

* * *

We sat in two armchairs in the consulting area of his surgery. I sipped a delectable cup of Black Dragon while Daisy lay curled at my feet like a contented puppy. He too held a cup of tea in his lap, but whenever he raised the cup to his lips, his hand shook so that more tea was spilled than was drunk. His nightshirt was quite wet with Oolong, but he took no notice of it. The Bunsen burner on which he had heated the water still burned behind him, its blue flame adding an eerie shade to the proceedings.

"My mother," I said, initiating the discussion.

"Daisy, yes. Lovely woman. I remember her fondly."

"Grandfather said you were a friend of my father's."

"We were at Eton together, and later shared brotherhood in a Masonic lodge. Jim told me he had written to your grandfather, asking him to care for you and your mother if for any reason he didn't return." He smiled wistfully. "It's almost as if he *knew* he wouldn't."

I thought of the treasure map, and of my father's intention to sail to its coordinates. "I think he knew there was a greater than normal *possibility* that he wouldn't."

Slinque said nothing for a moment, absorbing this bit of intrigue. I could tell he wanted to ask questions of *me*, but restrained himself.

"When things started going . . . wrong," he continued, "I contacted the old fellow to remind him of his obligation."

"My mother—"

"—was a beautiful woman."

"Was she a drug fiend? That's what Grandfather called her."

"*Fiend* is a very harsh word. She was"—here he hesitated, searching for a better word—"drug *dependent*."

"Was she a prostitute?"

He smiled sadly. "She was forced to make certain compromises to support her dependency. You mustn't judge these women harshly. I myself have always been fascinated by them. I'm curious to find what it is *inside* them that makes them tick."

His words reminded me of Daisy, whose ticking was—to me, at least—quite audible. I couldn't believe he didn't hear it too, though he said nothing.

"Your birth was not an easy one," he continued. "Your father's ship had vanished at sea. She was alone in this world. She needed comfort. I provided it."

"You gave her drugs?"

"I gave her *better* drugs. She was fond of opium when your father first met her. He wanted my advice, I advised, and together we ransomed her from the devil-drug. After he was gone, and I saw she was drifting back, I supplied her with cocaine instead. Your grandfather footed the bill."

I took several deep breaths, readying myself for the Whole Truth.

"How did she die?" I asked.

He said nothing.

"I was told she had a fit and drowned in her bathtub," I said.

"She slit her throat with your father's razor."

I felt myself becoming ill. I took another sip of tea. I changed the subject.

"My father—I was told my father—was a gambler—and a drunkard—and a philanderer."

"All true. But he was a very poor gambler, and a cheerful drunkard, and nearly all the women he made love to he fell in love *with*. Your mother especially."

I hoped this wasn't a lie, but if it was, it was a very kind one.

"Did he ever mention a woman named Angela Darling?"

The doctor blinked. "Yes. I believe so."

"He had a child with her?"

"Yes."

"She too killed herself."

"Yes."

I swallowed. "He had quite an effect on women," I lamely joked.

"He had quite an effect on everyone who knew him," Slinque answered. Slinque, I realized, must have loved my father too.

I was becoming quite tired, and needed to rest. Leaving Daisy in the surgery, after feeding her several rabbits he had vivisected the day before, Slinque led me down one floor, where he offered me his own bed, into which I collapsed. By the time I awoke the clock on his bedroom mantel was striking two. Midday! I had slept much longer than I intended. He must have heard me stirring, for in a short time he entered, carrying my valise, and asked me if I was hungry. Indeed I was, I told him, but more than anything I wanted a bath. He showed me to his private bathroom, where he proceeded to fill a tub with hot water from his own tap. (Indoor plumbing, in these last fourteen and a half years, had found its way to Bayswater! Oh wonder!) Once I was alone, I carefully transferred the pouch filled with Flying Sand from the inside pocket of Mr. Harvey's suit to a secure compartment of the valise, then peeled off my new clothes (which now scarcely fit at all), gazed for a moment into a full-length mirror at my strange new self, and stepped into Slinque's white-porcelained tub.

Lying in the steaming bath, I examined my new self more closely. My feet were quite large, long, and unattractively bony. The aches I had felt in my arms and legs but a day before had been, I realized, growing pains. These limbs were now (begging your pardon, dear reader, for any discomfort you may feel regarding anatomical matters) furred with soft black hair, as were certain other unmentionable areas of my person. In short, everything was longer and stronger and leaner and a bit rougher than I was used to and, apart from my feet, curiously interesting. I had become, almost literally, a new man.

On a low table beside the tub rested a stack of newspapers. Slinque, I imagine, perused them when having his morning bath, and I picked one up in order to familiarize myself with the current news. The front page was entirely devoted to a sordid murder that had taken place a few days before in Whitechapel—a prostitute had been slaughtered, the fifth of several in the last few months—and the outcry against the killer and the incompetent constabulary was tremendous. Of course this put me in mind of my mother and her sad death, so I cast the paper aside and could not bring myself to look at it again.

After I had been soaking in the tub for about twenty minutes, Slinque entered without knocking and presented for my inspection a complete set of clothes, which he said he hoped would fit me. They were his own, he added, and since we appeared to be of approximately the same size now, I was certain that they would at least fit me *better* than Mr. Harvey's suit. I thanked him, and sat back in the water, waiting for him to leave. He pulled up a wooden stool instead, and sat down on it. It seemed it was time for him to ask questions of *me*.

"Where have you been?" he began.

Since I now looked closer to twenty-four than to fourteen, I didn't need to explain any aging anomalies. I told him much of the truth—that I had been pressed into a life at sea and that after living for some time on a distant archipelago I had finally found my way back home.

"And how did you get onto my roof?"

This was a bit trickier to answer. "I did a lot of climbing on the islands—coconut trees and volcanoes and such. The facade of your building is easier to scale than one might think. There are marvelous handholds. No trouble at all."

"Even with a crocodile?"

"She's not as heavy as you imagine. She held on to my back—with her claws, you know. She's very intelligent."

I could see he didn't believe a word of it.

"And why does she tick?"

So he *had* heard her incessant timekeeping.

"She swallowed a watch."

"I see." Which he obviously didn't. He was mulling something over now, then stood and headed for the bathroom door. "While you're getting dressed let me bring you some tea and scones." He stepped out of the room.

I rose from the now-tepid water and grabbed a towel hanging on a nearby rack. No sooner was I dried and in my new underclothes than he was back, bearing a tray with teapot, cup, and plate of currant scones fresh from the oven.

Apparently he had anticipated this meal, and now the aroma of yeasty buttery fruity bread filled the room. Half-naked as I was (I no longer had any body shame since swimming with Josephine), I stepped to his side and popped an entire scone into my mouth. Heaven! I chewed, gulping tea at the same time to wash it down.

"I have a favor to ask of you," he said.

I continued to chew and drink as I dressed.

"Anything," I answered, my mouth still full.

"I want your crocodile."

I stopped dressing midsock. "Daisy? Why?"

"I've never opened one before." He sounded as if he were speaking of a package or a drawer.

"You mean . . . vivisect her?"

"She won't feel a thing."

"No. No. Absolutely not. That's impossible." I continued with the first sock, then moved on to the other.

"It's the ticking, to be honest. It fascinates me. How can the watch be impervious to the digestive juices? Not that it would dissolve, of course, but the mechanical workings would surely be affected. And it's so *loud*! I mean, this is a scientific mystery—a miracle perhaps!"

"But cutting her open won't solve anything. Clearly the watch hasn't been affected by digestion, and opening her stomach will not get you any satisfying answer, let alone a commendation from the *Journal of Science and Medicine*!"

"Yes, but it *will* give me a great deal of pleasure. Solving the puzzle, I mean, not the vivisection itself. My intentions are noble and pure."

I was beginning to doubt his pure, noble intentions.

"Besides, dear boy, what are you going to do with a crocodile in London? You can't possibly *live* with it, there isn't a landlord in all of England who would allow such a thing. Nor does the London Zoo have any need of another one. They have enough."

"She's . . . my pet." I was becoming emotional, and could not wrap my brain around any logical answer. I pulled on the shirt. It fit me perfectly.

"She has no *affection* for you. She's a reptile! Their brains are quite primitive."

"But *I . . . I* have affection for *her*."

"Yes, of course, but— Look, dear boy, I've given you clothes and a bed and a bath. Do you have money? Certainly not English pounds, I imagine. I'll give you as much as you need. You're welcome to stay with me for as long as you like. I'll buy you a new wardrobe. I'll introduce you to prospective employers. You have nothing but a crocodile to your name and I have everything to offer."

"But I named her for my mother." Good Lord, I thought, logic has fled me entirely. "My mother's dead and Daisy, I'm *her* mother." I was becoming quite silly from lack of food. "I fed her. She was raised on my blood." Tears sprang to my eyes. What was happening to me? I pulled on my shoes. "No, no, I can't give her up, it's simply not possible. Simply—not. No, no, no no no." Fully dressed, with shoes unfastened, I grabbed the valise and headed for the bathroom door.

"Do think it over."

"I have, I have, thank you, Doctor Slinque, for your kindness and generosity, and for answering my questions, but it's time Daisy and I, Daisy and I, Daisy and I were . . ." The bathroom was spinning around me. ". . . going."

And then the room stopped spinning as its walls collapsed, burying me in darkness.

By the time I opened my eyes again the sky above was pinking with twilight.

I lay on a cast-iron bench in Slinque's backyard. I sat up and my head exploded. My shoes remained undone. My valise was no longer beside me. Slinque had drugged me, as surely as he had drugged my mother, and for all I knew he was at this very moment slicing open my baby to study the contents of her ticking stomach.

I staggered to his rear door and pounded. There was no answer. I walked around the side of the house and climbed the stoop to the front entrance. I pounded again. Again, no answer. I looked up, examining the exterior wall, hoping to find the ready handholds that I had told Slinque made the facade so easy to climb. It was smooth stucco.

"SLINQUE!" I shouted. "YOU BA——RD! GIVE ME BACK MY DAISY!"

The only response this elicited was from a London bobby who happened to be patrolling the street.

"Here, here, that's enough of that."

"This man has kidnapped my child!"

He looked at me as if I were on leave from Bedlam.

"Don't be absurd," he said, taking me firmly by the arm. "I know Doctor Slinque. He's a good fellow. Gives me lemon sweets for my little boy. He would no sooner harm a child than—than the Queen herself. Now get along with you, or I'll call some friends of mine to help you home."

I had no choice. Hours had passed since Slinque had drugged me. Daisy, no doubt, was already jarred and spec-imened.

I wandered the streets, trying to decide to whom I might turn. Reaching into my jacket pocket at some point, I found it stuffed with ten-pound notes and a dozen or so lemon sweets.

I entered a pub and gorged myself on chips and ale. (I could not bear to touch the kidney pie, or even the fish—they reminded me too much of Daisy's fate. Since that hour I have remained, dear reader, a strict vegetarian.) I then ordered a glass of rum, which went straight to my head, and when the idea struck me—and I made my request to the barman for a London Directory—it was with blurred vision that I strained to find a certain name. But find it I did. His residence was quite close: Number 14, Kensington Park Gardens in Notting Hill.

It was late, far too late to go visiting a stranger, and so I remained at the pub until closing, then wandered the streets waiting for my third day in England to begin.

At some point during the night I studied myself in a men's washroom mirror. I did not appear to have aged beyond thirty. The clothes that Slinque gave me fit me well, and since he was something of a dapper man, I too seemed respectable enough so that no one would run in the opposite direction if I approached them. As dawn broke I made my way to Number 14 and waited patiently nearby until the man I was looking for left the house and headed off to the nearest bus stop. I knew him at once to be the person I sought: he looked very much like me.

*   *   *

"Mr. Darling? Mr. George Darling?"

"Yes?" The man turned in my direction as I approached him.

"Might I have a word with you?"

He cocked his head slightly at the sight of me.

"Do I know you? You look familiar."

"You *do* know me in a certain way, and then again you don't. I believe I'm your half brother."

I might have been gazing again into Slinque's bathroom mirror. That is why, I explained to myself, I experienced such an odd feeling of déjà vu at the sight of him. He was slightly heavier than I, and his coloring a tad paler, but anyone seeing us side by side would know at once we were brothers. (This is one thing that wretched play got right: by a remarkable coincidence the conceited actor playing the Pirate Moi decided that the leading part of Villain was not enough for him; he demanded he play the children's father too.)

Whatever I was seeing in him, George Darling was likewise seeing in me.

"My God," he whispered and turned even paler. It would not do to question my claim; the evidence was standing before him.

We breakfasted at a club not far from his Fleet Street office. He sent a message to his secretary saying he would be delayed indefinitely due to an unexpected client meeting. Both of us ordered the same meal—tomato omelet, dry toast, fried onions, no potatoes—and both our orders sat untouched before us as we talked.

My existence, though surprising, was not altogether unexpected. He knew the circumstances of his mother Angela's death, and as an adolescent had found a series of love letters written to her by our mutual father. George knew he looked nothing like his legal father. As a child he had been told over and over how much he resembled his late mother, Angela, with no mention ever being made of George Darling Senior—and when he found the love letters he fell upon the truth. This was more a relief than not—he respected George Senior, but did not care very much for him, as they had little in common. George Junior entertained fantasies of his birth father's identity, but he never knew the man's full name—the letters were signed only "Your loving James"—so it was with great excitement that he listened to my story.

I illustrated our relationship on the back of an envelope as I explained it. "It's quite simple, really. Two sisters, Angela and Margaret, met and fell in love with two brothers, James and Arthur Cook. Margaret married Arthur, but Angela was already married, to George Darling Senior. James too had commitments; namely, my mother and myself. Still, he and Angela loved each other, and you were the happy outcome."

I admitted that I had learned of his existence only days before. I told him that our father was captain of a ship that had been lost at sea, and that we were quite possibly direct descendants of the explorer James Cook. I said that I too was a sea captain, and my visits to London were rare. He was astonished to learn that we were nearly the same age.

We parted with a hearty handshake, and he left me with an invitation to dine with him and his wife that evening. His daughter, he added, would be thrilled to meet her new uncle.

I arrived at Number 14 with flowers for his wife and a smaller bouquet for his little girl. She was three, and a lovelier child I have never seen. She was so delighted with her nosegay that when I presented it to her, once we were seated in the parlor, she danced around my chair and *under* it and *over me*. She called me her "new friend," but her lisping vocabulary could not yet make sense of the word *friend* and so I became her new "fwendy." I in turn called her my Wendy. The name, fortunately, stuck.

They had acquired a Newfoundland puppy the previous Christmas, an intelligent creature whom they named Nana. She was in training, they joked, to become their daughter's nursemaid, and if successful would act in this capacity to the newest addition to the family once he or she arrived. (Mrs. Darling—who insisted I call her Mary—was expecting another child quite soon.) The dog put me in mind of my own dear pet, and when tears sprang to my eyes Little Wendy asked what had made me so sad. I told her that I had recently lost my own Nana, and she climbed onto my lap and embraced me in consolation.

Once Wendy (and Nana) were put to bed, George and I had a frank discussion about our father. Mary, I must admit, did not express wholehearted approval of the man, but she did not condemn him either, since his womanizing had resulted in the fellow she loved most in this life, not to mention Wendy's new half uncle (me). I felt welcomed and appreciated by both of them. I must remark here that George's character was much warmer than eventually depicted by that gullible Scotsman, but I suppose the fictional George's infantile blustering was created by the author in order to justify certain preposterous plot developments. Feeding the dog his medicine indeed! The real George Darling was a delightful human being who took his medicine without complaint, and I am proud to think that we resembled each other in so many important ways.

The dinner was exquisite, the company charming, the evening unforgettable. I can't say if My Plan was born that night, but I'm sure the seeds of it took root, even though it was some time before it blossomed into what would be my revenge on the murderous Peter.

I left Number 14 around ten o'clock and only then realized I had no place to go. I returned to the Slinque residence, which stood a dark and foreboding silhouette against the night sky. From there I walked to the Kensington town house where I was raised, but I could not remain for long; looking at it brought back so much sadness. Eventually I walked to London Paddington, where I secured a cab to take me—for an enormous sum—to Eton. On my arrival I headed straight to the Eton Wall, which I had found so oddly comforting as a student. I hoisted myself onto it, and remained there for several hours.

I tried to think of happy things, which meant I could not think of Tiger Lily, or of Daisy, or of my mother, or of my grandfather and Aunt Margaret. I could think only of George and his charming wife and his sweet little girl. I marveled again at how familiar George looked, even though I had gazed at my adult self but briefly in Slinque's bathroom mirror, and then later in the men's washroom. That's when the truth of it struck me like a shot. Tears sprang to my eyes, I hugged myself tight, and my new body was racked with sobs.

I now began to understand the lies I had been told, and the secret that lay behind them. I suspected the identity of the Great White Father. I understood why I had found the watch and how it had come to be there. I knew at last that, in order to move forward with my life, I had to return to my past.

What, dear reader, was that realization that struck me so vividly on the Wall? In time, begging your patience, all will be clear. Suffice it to say that, from that moment onward, my mind was made up: I must revisit the Never-Isles. But the only way I could manage that was with the Flying Sand, tucked away in my father's valise—which valise remained with Slinque—unless, of course, he had tossed it in the rubbish, seeing that it contained only some ragged clothes and a pouch of grainy dirt. Never mind—I had to secure it somehow.

I caught the first train back to London.

Slinque's house was dark and silent. I knocked at the front entrance. No one answered. I walked around to the rear and pounded on the back door. Nothing. Useless. I considered moving the cast-iron bench beneath a back window and smashing the glass to gain entrance. The sound, however, might alert neighbors who would call the police. And then I wondered if there might be a way inside via the basement.

I circled the house again, looking for a door or a window leading below, and found nothing. I *did* discover, however, a garden shed under the backyard stairs. In the rear of the shed was a door—opening, I hoped, into the basement. It was locked, but I already knew that Slinque's locks were no match for my determination. With a few well-placed kicks the door flew open.

The room was dark, low-ceilinged. There was a stench of decay, and the earthen floor was soft and damp. In one corner rose a mound of loose dirt—humped as one finds on a freshly filled grave—and I began to fear that Slinque's experiments with vivisection may not have been limited to the lower primates. (I have since come to suspect that he may have been involved in the Whitechapel affair.) As my eyes adjusted to the dim light, I noticed several other grave-like mounds scattered around the basement. But I could not dwell on this discovery. I was on a mission.

I felt my way to a set of stairs. I mounted as silently as I could, wincing whenever a creak in a tread announced my presence. At the top of the staircase I pushed open the cellar door and entered the ground floor proper. I found myself in a kitchen, spotlessly clean, *too* clean. Whoever cooked here needed to be certain that there was no trace left of whatever he had eaten. I walked from here to a hallway, to the stair-way leading to the first floor. I mounted the steps slowly, rounded the banister, and continued my careful ascent. I still heard not a sound. On reaching the next level I tiptoed into Slinque's bedroom, fearful I might find him awake in bed, waiting for me with his pistol. But his bed was empty and had not been slept in. My valise was nowhere to be seen. I walked to the bathroom, expecting to find it there. Again I was disappointed.

The only other place for me to look was the surgery. I braced myself: the last thing I wanted to find was Daisy's corpse, freshly dissected—or worse, sliced open and splayed, like the frog of my childhood. I paused at the bottom of the dreaded stairs. I heard a sound now: someone was above, moving slowly. Slinque knew of my presence, and was waiting, with gun or scalpel. There was no weapon of defense in sight; all I had to protect myself were words. I would thank him for the clothes and the money. I would express forgiveness (falsely) for what he did to Daisy. I would humbly ask for my father's valise, and I would leave. Revenge, if it were to come, would arrive on some future date.

I climbed the stairs, making no attempt to conceal my presence. I opened the surgery door. The sight that greeted me was the worst I had ever seen, far outstripping the murder of the Never-Isle leviathan or the carnage of my recent sea battle.

The attack must have been swift. I have imagined it in countless nightmares, envisioned it again and again in fantasies of horror. What really happened I'll never know; what I see in my mind's eye is quite sufficient.

As he prepared the chloroform, she seized his ankle and dragged him to the floor. From there the consumption was slow and inevitable. First the foot, or possibly as much as a leg below the knee. Then, while he screamed in horror, she moved on to the other foot, followed by the other leg in its entirety. Once the femoral arteries were severed, blood spurted everywhere, coating walls, floor, even spattering the ceiling. After the legs had been consumed, and the man I knew was but half of his former self, he tried to drag himself away. It was then that she took hold of his middle parts and shook him like a puppy bothering a stuffed toy, after which she opened her maw in an attempt to swallow him whole. He must have died *before* she bit off his torso at the neck, leaving his head and one arm uneaten. Even a crocodile can devour only so much of a man, wicked as he might be.

She gave me a ROAR of greeting, and—I swear to you, dear reader—actually wagged her tail. I fell to my hands and knees, crying out with joy, and hugged her close, or as close as one can hug a crocodile. She was full size now, and quite as big as her mother had been. When we were done cuddling, I searched the surgery for some kind of rope to tether her to me for our journey. Oddly enough I found several dog leashes—it seemed that Slinque may have been guilty of canine-napping (the least of his many crimes, I later learned)—and I figured out a way to fasten them together into a kind of crocodile collar. Another leash stretched from this collar to my wrist. I peppered us both with Sand—yes, dear reader, my valise was in the surgery and only slightly bloodied, standing next to a jar labeled HALF A HUMAN KIDNEY—and ascended the stairs to the roof. As the sun rose I aimed us both toward the second star to starboard and headed far, far away.

PART THREE

PETER AND WENDY

Chapter Eight

—◁∞▷—

We found the *Roger* anchored between Silly and the Other One, and as we swooped down from the sky I could see that there was trouble aboard. Originally I intended to wait until nightfall before I made my way onto the ship, thinking that were I to arrive by daylight, my old shipmates—once they saw it was no bird descending but a strange man tethered to a flying crocodile— would point Long Tom at me and fire away. But I could see from a distance that they were otherwise occupied, and could hear from that same distance the clank of swords, the shouts of attack, the cries of agony, and the lonely howls of death. Daisy and I settled into the crow's nest without anyone being the wiser. Below me the men of the *Roger* and the crew from the *Princess Alice* were fighting fiercely among themselves, but it was unclear to me exactly who was trying to murder whom.

Captain Starkey and Edward Teynte, for example, sworn enemies the last time I had seen them, now seemed to be fighting side by side against Black Murphy (of the *Roger*) and Charles Turley (of the *Alice*). Cecco was screaming unintelligible words at Bloody Pete as they crossed swords, while Smee was darting everywhere sticking everyone with needles and pins whenever he got the chance. At the center of it all was Arthur Raleigh, shouting orders and waving his scythe, though as he stood alone it was difficult to learn for which side he was cheering. A few representatives of both ships lay dead or dying, and nearly everyone else (with the sole exception of Bloody Pete, to my surprise) was streaked with gore, much of it seeping from wounds (their own) both major and minor. In short, it appeared that the conflict had been raging for some time and, unlike legendary battles of fiction and folklore that burned hot for hours at a stretch, this one was decidedly flagging. Swords were dropped by exhausted seamen, and their opponents simply allowed the enemy to stoop and retrieve them while they caught their breath in the blessed respite. Those coups that succeeded in finding their targets were inflicted with the flat of the weapon, not the point—slaps of admonishment rather than thrusts of deadly intent—killing someone takes such a lot of energy, most of which had long since been expended. In short, it was plain that no one wanted the fight to last much longer; it was Honor alone that kept them at it.

Being fond of several of these men and not wanting to see them suffer, I allowed sentiment to get the better of me. Tugging Daisy along, I stepped from the crow's nest into the air and slowly descended to alight gracefully (in dancer's first position) on the roof of the Captain's Quarters. Those who saw me stopped their fight midswipe and -swoop. Those whose backs were to me, on seeing the wide eyes and gawping maws of their opponents, turned to look for themselves.

Everyone gasped, like a group of ladies at a tea party when an elephant enters the room. In less than a minute all fighting ceased and silence, but for a few weak moans from the dying, fell over all.

"Greetings," I announced, and Daisy let out a terrible ROAR.

Unfortunately that was all that was needed to send Bloody Pete, overweight and absolutely gasping for breath, into the arms of Death. His heart exploded at the shock of my unconventional entrance into the scene, and he crashed face-forward, landing at Cecco's feet. Poor Pete would bleed no more.

"What manner of thing art thou?" Gentleman Starkey asked.

"An angel, are you an angel?" Smee exclaimed.

"With a devil on leash," Charles Turley muttered.

"We are neither, good Smee, Mr. Turley." Both were astonished that I knew their names. "We are James Cook, once a friend to some of you and soon, I pray, a friend to *all*—and Daisy, who can be very sweet as long as she's fed."

No one said a word.

"So—Captain Starkey—what's all this about? When I last saw you, you left me bound to the mainmast on a burning ship. Following my demise, you intended to hang the crew of the *Princess Alice*, or at least most of them. Your mind was changed, it seems. Please explain."

Starkey was as surprised as any of them were at the sight of me. "Begging your pardon, sir—Mr. Cook—*that* man pleaded for mercy." He pointed at Arthur Raleigh. "We needed the extra hands, he said, since many of ours were lost in the *Alice*'s midnight attack. In addition, he reminded me that since our attackers were sailing under Her Majesty's colors, it was Bad Form to murder them. Being a Christian man, who sheds blood only when it is in *Good* Form to do so, I pardoned them all."

"I see," I said calmly, "but that hardly explains where we are today."

"Yes, well, in short, I could tell that some of them did not trust him," he continued, still referring to Raleigh, "but were not in a position to complain since he had saved their lives. He then proceeded to work among them, whispering mutiny to those of the *Alice* who had his sympathy, as well as to those crewmen of our own dear *Roger* who might be supportive of his cause."

"Which was?"

"Captaincy," Raleigh announced with conviction. "I declare myself the new captain of this ship. You, dear James, may be my first mate."

"I don't think I'm equipped for that," I told him, adding, "but we'll discuss that later. What do you intend to do with those who *oppose* you, once you're captain?"

"Hang them," he said. "I don't give a d—n about Bad Form."

There was muttering now among those whom he summarily condemned; at last I could identify the various sides of the conflict.

"Captain Starkey," I said, turning back to the good Gentleman, "I was present when you first laid eyes on Raleigh here, and couldn't help but notice that you drew back in alarm, as if you recognized him."

"I thought I did," Starkey answered, "from the cricket fields of England, though this man seems a bit young to have been at school when *I* was. Perhaps it was his older brother. We played against each other in a public school match, and he cheated abominably. How could I forget such *monstrously* Bad Form?"

"Did his team win?"

"Yes, d—n them!" Starkey loudly cursed.

"Smee!" I called, seeking him out in the crowd.

"Yes, Cap'n?" the little round man shouted back.

I couldn't help but smile at this familiar moniker. "What do *you* make of all this?"

"Bloody business, 'tis, sir, and I pray it won't be bloodier."

"Who should live and who die?"

"No one should die, Cap'n. It's sad and far too messy."

"Who should be captain then?"

The little man paused, chewing his lower lip.

"Come, come, now. I want an honest answer from an honest man. You're the honest-est one I know."

A few of the men chuckled at this.

"Well, Cap'n, if ye're askin' me, I'd say Cap'n Starkey has done a fine job but he's not gotten us home, or to the Carib, or to wherever we're supposed to be goin'. Mr. Raleigh, on t'other hand, is a strong brave fella who survived isolation and abandonment and he's a nice young man to boot and if he were to say he could get us home and that I might be seein' my dear Rosie again, then I'd vote for *him*."

More than a few of the men cheered.

"I'll get you home to Rosie, Mr. Smee," Raleigh promised. "You'll be kissing her lips before winter."

"I don't wish to be kissin' her lips, good sir. I wish to be *milkin'* her."

Nearly everyone laughed at this.

Smee blushed and protested, "I raised her from a calf and it's her I miss most in this world."

Now everyone *did* laugh, everyone but Starkey. As the laughter died, I addressed Raleigh.

"Mr. Raleigh, if we were to name you captain, on the condition that you would pardon everyone and hang only Her Majesty's flag, would you agree?"

"Heartily, so long as I can choose the positions I wish each man to hold, and so long as each will swear his loyalty to me. I do so agree."

"Hip-hip-hooray!" Cecco cheered (the first words from his mouth I ever understood). And everyone followed suit—but for Starkey and Teynte.

"Mister Teynte," I said to my old enemy, observing his reluctance. "You seem as disgruntled as good Captain Starkey. May I ask why?"

All eyes turned to Teynte. Everyone fell silent.

"He led us once before," he said very quietly. "He's not to be trusted, with liquor around."

No one said a word, until at length Raleigh spoke. "Mr. Teynte, I promise you," he called out, "I am now a sober man."

There were mumblings of assent, murmurings of doubt, and the problem at hand remained unresolved.

"I think we need to sleep on this," I finally said. "Bury the dead, tend the wounded, and put aside all grudges for twelve hours. We'll meet again on deck in the morning and put it to a vote. There's been enough bloodshed for the day, I'm sure you all agree on *that* at least. You need a good meal and a night's rest. Alcohol, I'm sorry to say, will not help matters, so I ask you, on your honor as gentlemen of the high seas, to abstain for this one night. Any dissenters?"

No one said another word.

I dismissed them all, then leapt from the roof (where Daisy had fallen asleep in the sun) and strode across the deck to Arthur Raleigh.

"I think we need to have a word, you and I," I said.

"It's good to see you, James. You've grown." He smiled.

"Yes, indeed I have. It's good to see you too. Father."

His smile wavered, just a little.

Anticipating the morrow's vote in Raleigh's favor, we settled across from each other in the Captain's Quarters, a dining table between us.

"How did you guess?" he asked once we were seated.

"I met your *other* son. George."

He was puzzled for a moment, until he remembered that second son. "It's a boy? He's healthy?"

"And grown and happily married. In fact you're a grandfather."

"My, my. Time has certainly flown in England." For a moment he looked confused. "Speaking of flying, is that how you returned? I figured that would be the best way. I never quite got the hang of it, mind—the boy wouldn't show me and I never learned where he kept the—whatchamacallit—sand."

His statement satisfied another suspicion I had, but more of that later.

"So," he said, coming back to his original query, "how did you ever guess?"

"When I first met George, I couldn't help but notice how familiar he looked to me. I thought at first it was myself I was recognizing, but then I realized I had seen my *older* self only once or twice in a mirror. It was *you* I saw in his face. How could George look so much like Raleigh? I asked myself. And then of course the obvious answer arrived."

"My dear boy," he said as he stretched his hand across the table to touch mine. I firmly pulled away.

"Why didn't you tell me when we first spoke?" I demanded.

"You wouldn't have understood. You were a boy. *I* didn't understand at first—about—you know—Time and all. I'd been absent from England but a few months—or so I thought. How could you be my son? And then, when I learned the truth—about Time and your mother's passing, well—it was upsetting and rather complicated. I needed to think things out."

"You lied."

"Not in everything."

"Mostly, yes, you did."

He took a deep breath. "Then I intend to set things straight. Where shall we begin?"

"It's always best to begin at the beginning."

"But which beginning? There were so many."

I waited for him to continue.

"My mother, as I *truthfully* told you, died birthing my younger brother, Arthur. My father was a stern man who hadn't a clue how to raise two motherless boys. You were either with him—which is the path Arthur chose—or you were a rebel."

"Like you."

"Like me. Much more gratifying and quite a lot of fun.

He sent me to Eton for improvement—useless, though I did leave my mark there." Inwardly I winced at the pain his past had caused me. "Then he tried to set things right with money, thinking he could *buy* my good behavior; I gambled it away. Finally he bought me a position in the Royal Navy, praying it would give me discipline. The discipline it enforced was all at sea; in port the Navy didn't give a d—n if I drank and gambled and wooed beautiful women. I met your mother, I met George's mother, I met a number of other women, and I loved them all."

"But you *lived* with my mother. You loved her *best*." I sounded like a needy child.

A careful silence. "I—saved her. From a terrible disease—"

"I met Slinque. I know the story."

"—and as a consequence I felt a deep . . . obligation to provide for her welfare. When I learned she was expecting, I asked my father to care for her and her child if something were to happen to me at sea."

"Which he did. He didn't *approve* of my mother, but he wasn't niggardly in his financial support. He was rather fond of you, I think, in spite of your profligacy."

"Well, bully for him. At the same time there was Angela, who was expecting my *other* child. She was married, so I felt *less* . . . obliged. Her husband knew nothing about me. Still"—he looked away, reliving his quandary—"I was terrified. Of fatherhood. Of the promises I'd made. And I owed a lot of money. I therefore did what any red-blooded Englishman would do—I ran away. Seeking adventure, of course, and— Well, I wasn't sure *what* that map would lead me to but hopefully to *some* solution to my problems."

This brought me to my second topic of conversation.

"A dying sailor, you said you got it from a dying sailor?" He nodded. "Did you kill him for it?"

"No, someone else did. I was celebrating my new captaincy at the Admiral Benbow Inn in Penzance, near my home. My father had bought the position for me; he knew the ship's owner and he paid him quite well. The inn was a sailors' haunt—disreputable to say the least—but there was one old fellow there I took a liking to, so I stood him a few rounds. He was even drunker than I was. He'd found something, he told me, that would make his fortune. I went outside to take a piss and he followed shortly after—with a knife in his back. He handed me a key as he died, telling me to wait until his murderer had been there first. I had no idea what he was talking about. He was staying at the inn, so I went up to his room and found the door partly ajar. I pushed it wide and discovered a man kneeling before a seaman's chest he was trying to open. He didn't hear me. He was busy prying the lock loose with a *scythe* of all things. He succeeded at last, lifted the lid, and a very large black snake reared up and bit his hand. He started screaming. He saw me and begged me to save him. I seized the scythe and chopped off the hand. He died anyway—of blood loss. I looked around—no snake in sight. I peered into the chest, and the only thing left inside was the map. And there you have it."

It struck me that the man's death from loss of blood may not have been the *whole* truth. I suspect it resulted from a delay on my father's part in applying a tourniquet or calling for help. Quite possibly it resulted from an *additional* amputation—of a head, most likely. The map was all.

"So you sailed . . ."

"To the map's location. A storm came, and here we are. My crew was desperate. Teynte in particular wanted to return to England or India or wherever our Duty demanded. I just wanted the treasure. I told them about it, promising a rich reward once it was found, but they didn't believe me. We sailed around, no luck, they mutinied, put me in a dinghy, and cast me off."

"Was that before or after the incident on Long Tom?"

He looked a bit sheepish, I must admit. "Oh, yes, *that*, well—" He cleared his throat.

"The truth, Father," I reminded him.

"The truth. Very well. I'd been drinking a bit more than I should—Teynte was correct in his comment about my liquid habits at the time—and when we spotted the island you call Long Tom I was certain that that was where the treasure lay buried. I took a bottle, a brace of pistols, two shovels, and six men, intending to disinter the entire island, if need be. The men dug, I drank, the sun grew hot, they refused to continue, and I shot them all. I could expand on the details but I don't think that's necessary."

"It was kind of the mutineers not to hang you for that."

"Teynte's an honest fellow, I must admit. They put me out to sea instead, most likely to certain death . . ."

"But you landed . . ."

"Not on the island where you found me, no. I didn't land at *all*, really. I sailed for several days, nearly died of dehydration, and then one morning I heard a cock crow."

At last he arrived where I was expecting he would. "Peter," I stated.

"Yes. He picked me up and flew me to the island."

"He never mentioned you when *I* was with him."

"I'm not surprised. I was a bit old for his fun. We never hit it off, really. He had a mind like a sieve. He probably forgot all about me by the time you arrived. I asked him if he knew of the treasure. He had no idea what I was talking about. There was, however, this little fairy he spoke to . . ."

"Tink?"

"Yes, that's her name."

"Did you see her?"

"Of course not. There's no such thing as fairies. The boy was quite mad. At any rate, his invisible friend told him that the tribe—whatever they're called—might have hidden it somewhere. He took me to their village, and having read several British treatises on colonization, I announced that I was the Great White Father bringing them God, Sovereignty, and Civilization."

"That was *you* then?"

"Yes! I told them they should give me all their pearls and yellow gold and I in exchange would give them a Religion and a Parliament and put them under the protection of Her Majesty Victoria. It didn't go over well."

"I don't think they *have* pearls and yellow gold."

"Well, I know that *now*," he snapped. "Unfortunately, I had developed a very bad cold. I think I caught it in the storm that swept us here, and all that burning sun and thirst at sea didn't improve my health in the slightest. My nose was running, I was sneezing five times a minute, it was bloody awful. At any rate, it seems they don't *have* the common cold on these islands, and, as so often happens when we whites mingle with brown and black and red savages, some of them caught it and died."

"How terrible!"

"For me especially. They had a trial and condemned me to something they called the Deep Well. I went down it, and oh, it was disgusting. Rotting carcasses everywhere. But the god who they said was awaiting me—"

"The Great-God-Below-Who-Is-Death."

"Yes, that's right. You've heard of him."

"Her."

"Really? Well, she wasn't there."

"She was probably off laying eggs. You were fortunate not to meet her."

"You have?"

"Oh yes."

"You were down the Well too? What did *you* do that set them off?"

There were many details he didn't need to know.

"It's a long story, but when I was down there, I found your watch."

His eyes lit up. "So *that's* where I lost it."

"On the little island in the middle of the underground lake. Where you were digging."

"For the treasure, yes. It was a perfect place to hide one. But there was nothing there but sand. Do you have it? The watch, I mean. I was quite fond of it."

"Daisy has it in safekeeping."

"Oh. Good. I'll get it from her later."

Best change the subject. "How did you escape?" I asked.

"I eventually found a pathway leading out of the cavern."

This, I assumed, was the very pathway I had followed *in*. "I took it to the end, following a stream which eventually disappeared under the rock. But there looked to be light coming from the other end, so I took a deep breath, dove in, and chanced it. It led me to the most beautiful blue lagoon."

"The Mermaids' Lagoon."

"Oh, you've been there too. You do get around." He seemed a tad resentful that *he* wasn't the only Englishman who had visited. "As you know, the ladies had very attractive bosoms but hideous tails. I'm a sailor—I know the dangers of mermaids—so I kept my distance. Nevertheless, I was quite exhausted from swimming and happily discovered, in the center of the lagoon, a very large rock."

"Marooner's Rock, I believe they call it."

"Yes, well, the only thing marooned there was a bird's nest. It was quite densely matted with sticks and mud and shells and things, and big enough to hold a man. So I took a chance, pulled it off the rock, and to my great good fortune it floated. I climbed in. There were two eggs inside. And the mother soon was screaming at me from the air above, diving and swooping to defend her babies. She came close enough for me to grab her, I wrung her neck and dined on her and the eggs for the next several days. Eventually I floated to another island, where I proceeded to live for many months in the cave where you found me."

"It was *years,* not months."

"Well, it *seemed* months. It was only after I boarded the *Roger* that I learned it was 1874. Astonishing. Fourteen years since I had disappeared in the storm!"

"Now it's even longer. Time is very odd here."

"What do you mean 'longer'? What year is it now?"

"In England? Eighteen eighty-eight. Possibly '89. I mean I *have* been back here for several *hours*."

I meant it as a joke, but it was more than he could fathom.

"I *do* miss the old country," he said. "What did you find there? Were things very different?"

"Yes and no. I met your father, who was still alive until a few days ago."

He became very quiet. After a short while he spoke, but softly: "Sorry I didn't see him again. He would have *hated* that, my turning up and still defiant." He gave a wry smile. "I suppose my brother's in charge now."

"His widow, perhaps."

He looked at me. I didn't explain.

"And I met up with Slinque," I added.

"Uriah! How *is* the old fellow?"

"I didn't care for him, frankly, but Daisy grew quite fond of him. I think she found him a man of excellent taste."

He smiled at the memory of his dear old friend.

The following morning the crew met and voted for captain. Raleigh—or should I say Father?—or should I say James Cook the Second?—won handily. (He now admitted his true name, by which those who had served on the *Alice* knew him. Consequently, to some he was Captain Cook, to others Captain Raleigh. To avoid confusion, everyone simply called him the Cap.)

As his first mate he appointed a Scotsman from the *Alice* by the name of Alsatian Foggerty, a sailor so inky with tattoos that from a distance one might mistake him for Black Murphy. Charles Turley (a sober, religious fellow whom I found an absolute bore) was named quartermaster, and Cecco was allowed to keep his position as chief gunner.

Black Murphy replaced the late Bloody Pete as carpenter and smithy, while Jukes remained in the galley. Assisted by a generous supply of dried apples, which had been found on the *Alice*, he now added apples to *everything*.

Smee was officially appointed ship's physician and seamstress. As promised, Father assigned him the job of sewing a Union Jack to replace the skull and crossbones we currently flew, but Smee was so busy sewing up wounds that that task was put on hold and, quite frankly, was never completed. Smee, by the way, wished henceforth to be called *Doctor* Smee, but needless to say nobody bothered.

The remaining crew consisted of

1. Sylvester Skylights, a towering paragon of muscle who suffered from an unfortunate lisp; when things got dull a crewman had but to ask him his name and the resulting "Thylvethter Thkylighth" kept the ship entertained for hours;
2. Jeb Cookson, American-born and hailing from the Wild West, or so he said;
3. Bob Mullins and Alf Mason, two friends so close they might have been joined at the hip; they even shared a sleeping hammock, as well as the redolent musky odor of sweat mixed with rum; and finally
4. Young George Scourie, who, appropriate to his name, was in charge of keeping everything clean and tidy.

Teynte and Starkey, as Father promised, were not hanged, but put in charge of emptying slops, cleaning fish, disposing of garbage, and performing any other job that might be deemed unhealthy and/or beneath their station. Father, I believe, was actively encouraging them to mutiny, which would give him a second chance to see them decorating the yardarm.

As for me, my relationship with Father was difficult, to say the least. When I was fourteen and he was Raleigh, I could look up to him and try to emulate his courageous self; if only we had been father and son *then*! But now I was twenty-eight and he thirty-four (at least in appearance). I had uncovered his ungallant behavior toward my mother and Angela Darling, not to mention his pompous colonial attitudes toward Tiger Lily's people. As a consequence, I found him rather despicable. True, he was a leader of men and not a bad captain at all; he had in truth saved my life more than once; why did I not love him? Perhaps I was merely the ungrateful son of an ungrateful son—I'm sure that's how *he* would characterize it. Nevertheless the man who was my father was too easily reduced to a pirate cliché: he wanted to find the treasure, all else be d—ned!

And so we set sail, exploring and reexploring the rest of the archipelago. He told the crew he was seeking a passage home, and if we happened to come across any gold or doubloons the discovery would be shared equally by all. This kept them quiet, for a time. Meanwhile, I served as his amanuensis, his right-hand man. I recorded everything in the ship's log and kept a personal diary of our explorations. This was perhaps the job I was best fit for: my penmanship, after all, was exquisite.

Before I continue, I feel the need to clarify, dear reader, a point which might cause confusion among those of a logical bent: how did the crew of the *Roger* come to accept that the *older* me was the same me as the *younger* me? They had tied a fourteen-year-old boy to the mainmast of a burning ship, and when next he appeared he was approaching thirty and fully mature. Do not forget, however, the superstitious character of most men of the sea. Once my mates saw me floating in the air with a fully grown flying crocodile on leash, the sudden shift in my age became a minor issue.

We began our archipelagic exploration by revisiting Long Tom, where we left Daisy lying in the sun and gobbling the occasional bird that mistook her for a log. We continued on to map Starkland, which island I now realized resembled an enormous skull. Sailing east, we discovered several new islands (new, at least, to me), one of which contained aspects of civilization that Gulliver himself had described, another of which solved the puzzle of the mysterious Gunn, who left his mark in the Starkland eye socket—but my adventures there I will save for another book as they have little to do with the matter at hand. Suffice it to say that on none of these little worlds did we find any real treasure.

I, of course, knew where the treasure was located and of what it consisted. I debated back and forth with myself as to whether I should reveal its whereabouts to Father. Then something happened which decided me, and changed my life forever.

You may recall, dear reader, my mentioning in an earlier chapter the Nights of Talent and Entertainment that were held on occasion under our late Captain Styles. These nights were extremely popular with the crew, and not merely because they involved the distribution of a great quantity of rum. They truly were enjoyable, even to a teetotaling boy of fourteen; the sailors sang and danced and mocked and mimicked each other in a spirit of generous fun and good humor. We had held none of these nights since our transportation to the Never-Archipelago, and—due to the supplies we absconded with from the *Princess Alice*—we now had an overabundance of rum. As a result, seeing that our crew was in need of both alcohol and entertainment, I prevailed upon Father to allow one of these delightful evenings to take place. And so it was, under a clear starry sky and surrounded by the vastness of the calm Never-Ocean, that we celebrated our Family-at-Sea once again.

The performance was held on deck, and since we expected no trouble from any alien source, vigilance was relaxed so that all men could partake. The celebration began, of course, with a barrel of liquor. Smee started the Talent portion of the evening with a tune on his "squeeze-box"; his musical talents were quite limited but he could at least hold to a rhythm, and young George Scourie took center stage and danced a jig. This was heartily enjoyed, and the applause was well deserved.

Jeb Cookson then sang several "authentic American cowboy songs" that mostly had to do with young men who were unnaturally fond of their "little dogies" and who, once they bade farewell to "Old Paint," were eventually riddled with bullets and left to die "on the lone prairie," where they were found by total strangers whom they begged for a decent burial.

The entire manner of living seemed to me utterly absurd and unnecessary, leaving me little doubt as to why Cookson had left his Yellow Rose of Texas to sail on the Ocean Blue.

Bill Jukes performed next, repeating jokes we had all heard before but which we thoroughly enjoyed hearing again. Few were in good taste, and so I shall not reproduce them here. The same was true of the music hall routine performed by Noodler to a few uncharacteristic blushes and uproarious laughter. Then Black Murphy stood and recited Portia's Mercy speech from the Bard, though he did so in the lisping voice of Skylights. "The quality of merthy ith not thtrained," he intoned, and everyone screamed with laughter, Skylights among them.

Cecco followed, singing an aria from some Italian opera in an exquisite tenor that left us all in tears.

During it all, Father stood in the back, sipping his rum and laughing as heartily as any one of us. Still, I could sense that something was amiss; he had been spending an inordinate amount of time in his cabin of late, and whenever I entered after our evening meal I could smell the alcohol on his breath and observe the unsteadiness of his gait. In other words, he had begun his drinking again and was showing signs—in deference to Slinque's assessment of his younger self—of being anything but a "cheerful drunkard." More than once he snapped at me over some trifle—my blotting a drop of ink with my sleeve as I wrote, or my asking him to repeat himself during the evening's dictation into the ship's log. I was becoming more sympathetic to my grandfather's irritation with his son, and less admiring of my father's spirit of defiance.

Bob Mullins began by introducing himself as Cap'n Crook. This brought gales of laughter led by Father, who laughed loudest and longest. Mullins followed this by saying that what he missed most aboard the *Roger* was not "the drink, which was adequate." (This was greeted with many a raised glass and roar of approval.) Nor was it good meals that he mourned, for he "adored the flavor of apple and could not imagine a dish without it." (More cheers and raised glasses, all in Bill Jukes's honor.) No, what he missed most on the *Roger* was "the rogering." (This, dear reader, is a colloquial phrase common at sea, and refers to one's enjoyment of the pleasant company of women. Bob's last statement, by the way, elicited more cheers, toasts, hoots, and whistles than anything spoken thus far in the evening; it seemed that Mullins was quite the popular entertainer.) Mullins then said that the girl he most longed for was his "dear Daisy," at which point a slim hand appeared round the corner of the poop deck, waving a lacy handkerchief and calling "yoo-hoo" in a high soprano. The hand was followed by a long tattooed arm, which in turn was followed by the appearance of a lovely lass, bonneted and rouged, whose tresses bore an unfortunate resemblance to the head of a mop. This was, of course, none other than Alf Mason wearing clothes that he had brought with him for just such an occasion; he delighted, it seems, in putting on women's clothing and unabashedly flirting with his fellow seamen. His bosom, on this night, was nearly as big as Josephine's.

Let me acknowledge at this point, dear reader, that I now understood that the Cap'n Crook whom Mullins was parodying was myself. Smee always referred to me as Cap'n; furthermore, the crew knew of, and shook their heads in amusement over, my devotion to Daisy. More than once I had overheard some seaman chuckling with his mates about the "danger of kissing a croc." This bothered me not in the least; it was nothing compared to the cruelties I had suffered at Eton, for I knew these men were fond of me, despite their teasing jibes. I laughed and applauded at "Daisy's" appearance, and threw her kisses, along with everyone else.

Everyone, that is, except Father.

Mullins and Mason, naturally, knew nothing of Father's history. True, our names were identical, but James Cook was not an uncommon one. We certainly could never be father and son—I now appeared to be close to him in age, and other than making a few passing comments on our near-identical noses, no one believed we were the least bit related. (Father had grown his beard long again, thus masking many of our facial similarities.) Nor did anyone know my mother's name, or anything of Father's relationship to her. In all innocence Mullins and Mason were mocking *me and my crocodile*, not Father and his mistress. Had Father been sober, I daresay he would have seen this too. But he wasn't and he didn't.

Mullins flirted boldly with "Daisy" Mason and squeezed one corpulent breast. When he did so a stream of rum squirted out, wetting the faces of a few men seated in the front row. Amid howls of laughter these men opened their mouths wide; Mullins now squeezed both breasts and the milk of island liquor arced through the air to fill these gaping targets. If laughter could kill, the entire crew would be dead.

"ENOUGH!" a voice boomed, and all turned to see Father striding boldly through their midst toward Mullins and

Mason. Both men took a step back, sensing the ire they had inadvertently aroused. Father stopped before Mason, slapped him across the face, then tore wide his dress, exposing the bladders in his false bosom. "How dare you, sir?" he muttered, then seized the bladders and ripped them from Mason's chest. Mason covered his own breast now with the modesty of a maid and lowered his eyes. "We meant nothin', sir," Mullins muttered, but Father simply turned and stared him down. Then he shouted again: "Cecco! Bring the cat!"

I was on my feet now, and hurried to Father's side. "They were joshing *me*, not *you*," I whispered, but I might have been pleading with a wall. He pushed me aside and grabbed the bag as Cecco presented it. From out of it he pulled the nine-tailed horror. He handed the weapon to Mullins. "Strip him," he instructed, "and whip him." "Please, sir," Mullins began, but Father interrupted. "If you don't, I will," Father told him, "only I'll see him *dead*."

All hands were silent. Cecco meekly bound Mason to the mast, then opened the back of the dress to expose his mate's shoulders and midriff. Father, furious, tore the dress wider, pulling it down to bare Mason's hindquarters. Then he nodded to Mullins. "Twenty lashes," he ordered. Mullins stood back, and began.

All of us knew of the close friendship that existed between these two men, and it broke our hearts to see one bloodying the other in a public display of humiliation. Clearly it broke Mullins's heart too; he was soon weeping as he swung the cat through the air, again and again, opening up Mason's back and buttocks. But even this, in Father's opinion, was not enough. After fifteen lashes Father seized the weapon from Mullins and inflicted the final five himself. The whip cracked, Mason screamed (and Mullins along with him), and the poor man was sliced to the bone.

Mason was unconscious by the end. As soon as Father turned and strode to his cabin, Mullins ran forward to catch his dear Alf as Cecco untied him from the mast. Cookson and Black Murphy carried him gently belowdecks, where Smee would tend him with his miracle salve. As for myself, I turned and followed Father to his cabin.

"How could you?" I began, as angry as Father had been, but he didn't seem to hear me. He opened the bottom drawer of his desk, pulled out a bottle, and proceeded to pour himself a mug of his private stock of poison. "They were mocking *me*, not you!" I continued as he did this. "They know nothing of who you are and what you've done! But even if they did, even if they *had* been mocking you, you had no right to interfere! That's the point of these evenings! To let go and have fun, with no consequences! You heard Black Murphy, lisping like Skylights, and Skylights was *loving* it! You were wrong! You should be ashamed! You need to apologize to everyone and you need to do it *now*!"

He lowered his mug and looked me square in the eye. "You're beginning to sound like *my* father," he said.

"I *hope* I'm sounding like your *conscience*, giving you some good common sense."

"I'd suggest you shut up about it."

I walked straight to him and grabbed the mug from his hand. He glared at me, then in defiance raised the bottle to his lips and guzzled. I smacked it away, and it sailed across the room, shattering against the wall above his bed. He struck me with the back of his hand; I in turn punched him in the face, then wrestled him to the floor. We were flailing now like a pair of schoolboys, but I was relatively sober. I pinned him to the cabin's deck and spat out words of fury.

"You should have stayed!" I shouted in his face. "You should have married Mother! You should have made her happy, which I *never* could do! You left her, you left me, you ran away because you're nothing but a bloody d—ned coward!"

"And she was nothing but a bloody d—ned whore! You are nothing but a bloody d—ned ba——rd!" he screamed back at me.

I struck him again, once, twice, bloodying his lip. He was too drunk now to fight back with anything but words. Instead, after a moment's pause, he chose another weapon: he began to cry.

"I couldn't save her, James. No one could. Don't you understand? She was in love with the *drug*, not me. Slinque warned me but I didn't listen."

"He killed her," I pronounced simply, saying aloud for the first time the thought that had been festering in my brain since I last met with him. "He put her back on the drugs. He used her for God knows what fell purpose. And in the end he slit her throat." His eyes blinked with surprise. "He knocked her out, Father, then he put her in a bathtub, put a razor in her hand, and cut her open."

"Why? Why would he do that?" Father's voice was but a hoarse whisper.

"I don't know, Father. Perhaps he wanted to see what made her . . . tick."

I released him now, and stood. He lay very still, absorbing my words. Then he sat up and wiped his eyes. Without looking at me he raised a hand, indicating that I should help him. I did, lifting him to his feet. Then I shouldered him to his bed, pulled off his boots, and left him to his nightmares.

The following morning he remained in his Quarters. The crew was sullen and sad; their anger had yet to vent itself. Mason lay suffering in the sick bay. Mullins never left his side.

I too stayed by my bed, in the tiny cabin I shared with Quartermaster Turley. As I mentioned earlier, I had begun to keep a diary of my day-to-day experiences in the Never-Archipelago, and I spent the morning writing down the terrible incidents of the previous night. I kept this diary hidden from everyone, not that most of my mates could read. Nevertheless I tucked the volume under my mattress whenever I was not making an entry, but on this particular day, just as I was concluding my personal comments, I heard the cry of "Land ho!"

Since leaving Long Tom, we had continued to sail east, and now—as many of us had feared might happen—we returned to Long Tom, arriving from the west. Once again we had circled the globe of this mysterious archipelago. I rushed on deck only to hear the delighted roar of Daisy's greeting, hallooing us from the island's shoreline. She started into the water, and in my enthusiasm to greet her properly I jumped overboard and swam to her side, where I climbed onto her back and allowed her to paddle me to the beach. We spent a relaxing afternoon in each other's company.

My father's watch continued its pleasant ticking inside her. She felt quite at home here; it was, after all, the island of her gestation.

As the sun began to set I said my goodbyes, promising to visit her again on the morrow. I waded into the water and began a lazy swim back to the ship. She sweetly accompanied me. Teynte lowered a rope ladder to assist my ascent to the deck, and as soon as I had set foot on board he nodded in the direction of the Captain's Quarters. "He wants to see you," he said.

I ducked below to my own cabin first in order to change into dry clothes. In addition, before I paid a visit to Father, I wished to make a notation in my diary regarding the afternoon spent with Daisy, and so I lifted my mattress to retrieve the book. It was not there. I then remembered that I had left it that very morning on my pillow, when I had raced above to say hello to my reptilian friend. I looked everywhere, and it was nowhere.

Father was standing by his bed, looking out of a porthole, when I arrived in his cabin. "You took your time about it" was all he said. The air was redolent of rum, and I knew at once that he had succumbed again to that terrible vice.

"Sorry, Father, but I was wet," I said. "You asked to see me?"

"Yes, I want to dictate an entry into the ship's log. I know I usually do that *after* dining but I wish to do it *now*."

I sat at the desk and took up a quill, then opened the log. I wrote the date—a completely convenient one that bore no relationship to any *actual* date—and waited for him to begin.

"You're not a bad writer, you know," he said.

"Thank you," I answered, unsure where this was heading.

"I reread the log most mornings and I'm always quite impressed. Your entries are accurate, correctly spelled, and occasionally quite entertaining."

"Thank you. I do my best, Father."

"I stopped by your cabin earlier to pay you this compliment, and to apologize for the outrageous behavior on my part that took place last night."

"I'm sorry I wasn't there. I was off ship with Daisy."

"Yes. Quite. I found this lying on your bed." He held up my diary. "As I said, your writing can be very entertaining. Not as accurate in this little volume as it is in the ship's log, but then again, what does Truth have to do with a good yarn?"

"I beg your pardon?"

"Your description of last night was filled with lies and innuendos."

"I'm sorry, Father, but that's how I saw it."

"Indeed most of the contents of your diary are pure fiction. What you say about me. What you say about my behavior toward your mother."

"That was not meant for anyone's eyes but my own."

"Then why write it down if you didn't intend to *show* it to someone? Quite possibly to *publish* it."

"And where, in these blessed isles, will I find a publisher?" I was getting angry now too.

He threw the book at me with all his might. Its corner struck me in the forehead, leaving a nasty gash. I felt the blood from it creeping down my temple. I was very still.

"'On the day after the Entertainment,'" he began, then paused and looked at me. "I'm dictating. Write. 'On the day after the Entertainment—'"

I turned back to the log and began writing. The explosion was apparently over.

"Yes. Go on," I prompted.

"'—I paid a visit to my secretary's cabin—'"

I wrote the words just as he said them.

"'—and there I found, much to my surprise—'"

I wrote, though my hand was trembling.

"'—a scurrilous document in his handwriting.'"

"Father, I don't think—"

"Write the words exactly as I say them!"

I took a breath. I followed his instruction.

"'It was with great sadness—'"

I wrote. I could not meet his eyes.

"'—that later in the day—'"

I wrote. I could hear him behind me, opening up his sea chest. As I finished writing his words, I heard its lid slam shut with finality. "Yes. Go on," I prompted again, dipping the nib into the inkwell and waiting for him to continue.

"'—I meted out my punishment.'"

I snapped my head around to look at him, but I was too late. The scythe swished through the air, severing my right hand, pen poised in my fingers, from my wrist.

I screamed. I clutched my forearm to my chest as the blood shot forth. He seized me by my collar, hoisted me to my feet, and dragged me from his cabin. Everyone on deck had heard my scream and now watched in horror as he hauled me to the ship's rail. I feared he was about to toss me into the waters below; one-handed, I would surely drown. What I failed to notice was that, in grasping me, he had also grasped my newly severed hand. It was *this*—its fingers still clutching the quill tightly in a kind of rigor mortis while my mother's gold wedding band twinkled in the setting sun—it was this and not myself that he flung over the side.

Below lay Daisy, waiting where I had left her, and as the hand plummeted toward her, she opened wide her jaws, caught it in her mouth, and swallowed.

Chapter Nine

━━━━·◦∞◦·━━━━

Why, dear reader, do you always insist on believing that sad little Scotsman, who only heard the story third-hand, instead of believing one who lived it? His purpose, you must remember, was to paint the boy in a heroic light. As a novelist, he should be praised: Peter cuts off the hand of his would-be assassin; Peter saves Tiger Lily from her incipient murderer; Peter rescues a passel of innocent children from the villain's dastardly scheme. Brilliant! For *fiction*, that is. I, on the other hand—which other hand, by the way, I am forced to use now to *write*, since my *right* one was under*hand*edly removed, leaving me but my *sinister* side to express my feelings—I on the other hand am writing a *memoir*, and cannot use the conveniences of fiction to paint a nicer, cleaner, simpler picture of how things happened. I am stuck with the Truth, and the Truth is neither nice, clean, nor simple.

Allow me to pass through the unpleasantness subsequent to the amputation as quickly as possible. After seeing Daisy lunch on my extremity, I fainted like a Victorian ingenue and was carried below (or so I was told) to the sick bay, where Smee immediately applied a tourniquet, stopped the bleeding, and then sent me on to Black Murphy in the smithy. Murphy heated the blade of a dagger and proceeded to cauterize the stump. Drifting back to some kind of awareness as the knife seared my wound, I screamed bloody murder and lost my tenuous grip on reality a second time, after which I was returned to the sick bay, where Smee applied his miracle salve and bandaged me clean and tight. I remained under Smee's tender care for several days, drifting in and out of delirium, and it was then, dear reader, that I devised the first part of my, well, of my dastardly scheme.

Once Father was sober, he visited me in the sick bay and offered his sincere apologies. He swore never to touch "that foul liquor" again, and in addition publicly expressed his regret to all of the *Roger*'s crew, and to Mullins and Mason in particular, for their having to suffer the consequences of his dreadful habit. "Some men can resist Demon Alcohol's nefarious seduction," he told them, "but I obviously am not one of them." He intended to ban liquor entirely and to dump the ship's rum supply overboard, but when I heard of this I cautioned him against it if he wanted to avoid another mutiny. I urged him instead to dispose of his own personal collection of inebriating refreshment, which he did. Then, as soon as I was sufficiently recovered and could bear the pain reasonably well, I asked to meet with him privately in his cabin.

On entering the room I inhaled deeply; indeed the portholes were open and all aroma of rum, gin, or any other form of spirits had been wafted away by the ocean breeze. Father rose from his desk, warmly took my hand (the remaining one), and kissed my cheek.

"My boy," he said, "how can you ever forgive me?"

"No, no, Father, I deserved this. I truly did," I told him.

He was not expecting such a reply. "What do you mean? Don't be absurd, boy."

"What I mean is—I have not been completely forthcoming with you about my time in these isles."

"What are you talking about?"

"I have something to confess and I"—I nodded to the dining table—"I think we'd best be seated first."

Once we were comfortably ensconced across from each other, I continued, haltingly. "I know, sir, you are anxious to find the treasure that was indicated on the map."

He sat up a little straighter. "You know where it is?"

I nodded.

I could see him restrain his anger at my withholding this information for so long, but he knew harsh words would not help in this case, and he now placed his hand gently on top of mine.

"Where?" was all he said.

"Not so much 'where,' Father, but 'what.'"

He tilted his head at a slight angle, as if he were trying to figure me out.

"Not gold?"

"Nor diamonds, doubloons, pearls, silver, none of that."

"What then?"

In answer I reached into my pocket and produced a tiny quantity of Sand.

"I don't understand," he commented.

I peppered the sand onto the crown of my head. In a matter of seconds I was hovering in the air before him.

"This, Father, is worth more than all the pirate treasure in the world."

"The Flying stuff?"

"Think what Her Majesty could do if she ruled the air. Travel would be transformed—just imagine it—locomotives in the ether! International commerce would be controlled by England—'Hail, Britannia! Britannia rules the sky!' Our flying cannons could rain down punishment on anyone who opposed us! We would no longer be the Empire; we would be the *World!*"

I floated back down to my seat.

He began to understand my meaning. His eyes gleamed at the thought of World Domination, and he now clutched my remaining hand tightly and squeezed with excitement.

"Of course. How foolish of me. All for England! We'll make a fortune! Where is it, where's the source?" he asked. "Where can it be mined?"

"I can't tell you that, Father. Not yet."

"What do you mean? Why not?" Anger stuck its head out of the mouse hole.

"Because I can no longer trust you, Father."

I could sense the blood running colder in his veins.

"Of course you can," he answered flippantly, then adjusted his remark. "What I mean is, I'll *prove* to you that you can. Tell me how; how do I regain your trust? Name it; if it's in my power to do it, I shall."

"Come fly with me."

"What?"

"Back to England. I'll be the guide but you must be the salesman. I have no head for business matters; *you do*." I had no idea whether this was true or not, but he embraced the compliment. I explained: "I know someone you can talk to, someone who has connections with the Prime Minister. He'll arrange a meeting where you will demonstrate what we have—to Parliament, to Victoria herself. Once a deal is struck—so long as I'm part of that deal—I will reveal to you all that I know."

He was quivering now; were I to insist on leaving at that very moment, he would have leapt to his feet and begun packing.

"Tonight," I announced. "Once the sun is set, we're off."

The night sky, as it always is in the Never-Archipelago, was clear, and the second star in Peter's Liana winked at us like a beacon. I had retained Daisy's croc collar, and I now put it to use again with Father, tethering him to myself lest he get lost. He had never flown before, and that was the tricky part, but since we were anchored off Long Tom's shore—where there were no trees or rocks or cliffs for him to bang into—I figured that the worst that could happen would be that he would fly back to England topsy-turvy. But he learned the art of flight quicker than I had, and after only a little bit of practice with balance and weight distribution, we headed to London.

I had retained enough of the Flying Sand from my first voyage to allow me to make another round-trip. My only worry was that it would not be enough to carry *two* of us back and forth. Still, once we took flight, the single problem we encountered was that, for a man whose stomach was accustomed to the sea, Father could not handle the air: he lost his dinner somewhere between the Never-Archipelago and Jupiter. The sun was beginning to rise as we settled down onto the Embankment, with only a charwoman and a pair of inebriates witness to our descent. The inebriates thought nothing of it; the charwoman uttered an unprintable exclamation and promptly fainted; we walked to the Savoy for breakfast.

I still had some of Slinque's money stuffed in my pockets; expenditures, therefore, were not a problem. As soon as we entered the hotel restaurant, I made a generous gift to the maître d', who ignored my one-handedness and Father's outmoded dress and showed us to a table by the window. "Would you kindly tell me," I asked him as he held my chair, "what is the current year?"

If he were astonished by the question, he did not show it. "Year of our Lord 1891, good sir," he said, unwavering. It had been thirty-one years since Father last set foot in England.

His appetite had not fully returned, and he nibbled on toast while I enjoyed a full English breakfast. We both ordered coffee, and I mentioned that—in this one instance—a tiny drop of rum in the hot beverage might be warranted, if only to give him back his stomach. He agreed. After breakfast we walked in the direction of Fleet Street, and since the hour was still quite early, we popped into a tavern that was open for business and shared another toddy—or two. Come nine o'clock I provided him with a small packet of Sand for demonstration purposes and told him the name of the man he was to meet.

"George Darling," I said to him. "Your other son."

He was shocked at this, naturally, but I soothed his nerves as best I could by handing him a tiny flask filled with for-tification that I had purchased in the tavern, and assuring him that George was expecting his imminent arrival, though getting past his secretary could prove a bit of a challenge.

"You're not coming with me?" he asked nervously.

"No, no, it wouldn't do. You are, after all, a *captain* in Her Majesty's Royal Navy. I'm still, officially, a *cabin boy*. Besides, I need to make a luncheon appointment with an investor, to secure sufficient funds for the initial mining operation. You'll do fine on your own."

I gave him some of Slinque's cash, told him I would meet him at one o'clock that afternoon on this very spot and left him to lunch with the investor. I wished him luck.

Once I dropped Father off at George's office, I spent the morning walking from Fleet Street through St. James's Park and then on to Notting Hill. I called at the Darling house-hold on the off chance that I would find someone at home, and I was fortunate to discover not only Mary Darling but six-year-old Wendy, who remembered me quite clearly and expressed her delight at my return. Nana barked and jumped and covered me in dog hair, and I barked back at her, which sent Wendy into a paroxysm of giggles. On noticing my empty cuff, the little girl asked what had happened to my hand, and I told her that I had given it to a flying crocodile,

which she found immensely funny. She then introduced me
to her three-year-old brother, Jack, who was napping when
I first arrived, after which all five of us—Mary, Wendy, Jack,
Nana, and myself—went for a lovely stroll in the Kensington
Gardens, where I made up a story about a baby named Peter
who lived with the birds on an island in the middle of the
Serpentine.

At the Round Pond, Wendy and Jack wandered off after
some ducks, and Mary had the opportunity to ask me further
about my hand. She was terribly concerned, but I explained
that it was lost in an industrial accident which was far too te-
dious to go on about. She said nothing more about it, sensing
that this was a sensitive topic, but I could tell she mourned
for it almost as deeply as did I.

Mary insisted that I stay for an early dinner, and I agreed.
By the time George arrived home, I had put Wendy and Jack
to bed—telling them of the Further Adventures of Peter in
the Gardens—decanted a lovely bottle of Bordeaux that I had
purchased on our earlier stroll, and set the table for three.
George was astonished at the sight of me. "Good Lord," he
exclaimed, "what happened to your hand?" Mary shook her
head, and he quickly changed the subject. "Your name came
up today in conversation."

"Oh really?" I feigned surprise. "With whom?"

"With the maddest man I have ever had the bad fortune
to meet."

"What happened, George?" Mary asked with concern.

I poured the wine as I listened.

"He was waiting in my outer office when I arrived," George
said, "screaming at my secretary that he had an appointment.

Poor Marjorie was beside herself. She couldn't get rid of him, so I agreed to meet with him in my inner sanctum. Well, as soon as the man passed me on the threshold I could tell he was higher than a kite. The smell of rum nearly knocked me off my feet! And no sooner were we sequestered than he insisted that *he* was my *father*!"

"Oh, good heavens," I gasped. "Incredible!"

"To say the least! There was a tiny resemblance, I admit, but he couldn't have been more than ten years older than *I* was. And then he said that *you* had sent him to me because I could get him a meeting with the Prime Minister!"

Mary laughed out loud. "I don't believe it!" she shouted with glee.

George started laughing too. "Yes, it's true, and when I asked why he wanted to meet the man, he said he had—he had"—George was laughing so hard he could hardly contain himself—"he had acquired the rights to mine a seam of very valuable Flying Sand!" I was roaring now too, and all three of us were soon wiping tears of laughter from our eyes. "I told him that he needed to leave at once or that I would summon the police and *he* said"—once again George could hardly speak for laughing—"he said that he had brought some of the sand for a demonstration. He then reached into his pocket—did I mention that his clothes were at least thirty years out of date? Anyway, he reached into his pocket, pulled out a handful of sand—I'm not joking, Mary!—and he threw it on the both of us! He then began jumping up and down and encouraged me to do the same! 'Think lovely thoughts!' he shouted." (I had added this fiction to our initial takeoff, hoping he would repeat it at the first inopportune moment.)

"Well," George concluded, "by this time Marjorie had called the police and they arrived and hauled him off, screaming at the top of his lungs, 'I can fly! I flew here! I can *fly!*'"

The next five minutes were spent in uncontrollable laughter and tears, after which we ate a delicious meal accompanied by a second bottle of Bordeaux.

It was past nine at night when I posted Father's bail at the Fleet Street constabulary. The policeman retired to the holding cells and returned with a man I scarcely recognized. He was now matured to his full age of sixty-five and looked considerably older. (I, by the way, had aged too, advancing to the deliciously ripe age of thirty-one, which suited me rather well.) Whatever bacteria had found a foothold in his body in 1860 (and I hate to speculate on the nature of the diseases they carried), they had so ravaged his muscles and mind in the last twelve hours that what was presented to me was a very thin man with little hair, half a mouthful of teeth, a wandering brain, and more than a bit of palsy. I thanked the policeman, took Father by the hand, and returned with him to the Embankment. There I tethered him to my wrist, peppered us both with the Proper Sand (the sand I had given him for "demonstration" was from the beach at Long Tom and had no special properties whatsoever), and sailed with him into the night sky. Of course I could have left him in London, but even *I* could not be so cruel.

I said not a word to him, nor he to me. He was lost in a world of madness and senility, and we never spoke again.

We arrived back at the *Roger* just after dawn. I presented

the crew with their duly elected captain and returned to my cabin.

I had taken my revenge, and I felt terrible.

I played a nasty trick on my father. Was it fair payback for the loss of a hand? Most would say so. Most would say he got his share of the pie. But I had never been so cruel to another human being in my life, and I was not proud.

I felt as I had felt at Eton after Mother died: alone, unwanted, undeserving of anyone's love.

What hurt the most, I realized on reflection, was Daisy's betrayal. How could she eat my hand as if it were a fish or a seagull? True, *I* had eaten her *mother*. And she *was* a reptile—consuming meat was part of her nature. But she had devoured the hand so readily. Perhaps dining on my blood from birth had given her a taste for me. It was almost as if she relished it, had been waiting for this five-fingered morsel since hatching.

I knew that the only way to resolve the issue was to confront her directly.

I asked Teynte and Starkey to lower a boat and row me to Long Tom.

Wading onto the beach, I looked around but could see nothing of her. Then, all at once, I heard a ROAR and she hastened toward me, as quick as a seven-hundred-pound crocodile could, from behind the clump of palms on the far side of the island. Had she been lying in wait for my arrival? It seemed so. Was she about to attack me? I braced myself for the slaughter. Was I soon to follow Slinque's fate and join my father's watch in her belly? She roared again, and slid to an abrupt halt at my feet. Then she opened her jaws wide, coughed, and spat out my hand.

She had swallowed it—not for sustenance, but for preservation! She had retrieved something of mine that had gone missing, and was waiting for me to visit her in order to proudly return the lost prize!

It was, unfortunately, in a condition that made it unreturnable. Only the stub of the quill remained, and her digestive juices had done their work on the body of the prize, reducing skin and muscle to a black rotting sinewy mush of bone. One thing, however, remained unaffected by her internal acids. The gold of my mother's wedding ring shone brighter than ever.

I knelt and kissed her snout, thanking her for her thoughtfulness. I picked up the mess, disgusting as it was, and returned with it to the longboat, where Teynte and Starkey were waiting. I wrapped the amputation in my shirttails so, though they undoubtedly smelled the decay, they remained ignorant of the source of the odor. As we rowed back toward the *Roger*, I surreptitiously removed my mother's ring and consigned, with little regret, Daisy's glutinous prize to the sea.

Once on board I went directly to Father's Quarters. He was not inside. I opened his sea chest, took out his scythe, and nearly skipping with excitement hurried belowdecks, where I presented sword and ring to Black Murphy. I gave him specific instructions, he took measurements, and went to work at once. I returned topside, and it was then that I discovered Father.

Skylights's cry alerted me that something was amiss. "Thee! Thee!" he lisped, pointing high. "He'th in the crowth netht!"

Father had climbed the rigging to the top of the mainmast. He was sprinkling an invisible something over himself. "I can fly!" he shouted. "Watch, boy!"

He stepped into the ether. His body weighed nearly nothing. His mind was light as a bubble. Still, the air could not hold him.

That night Black Murphy presented me with my new hand. Sharp as a razor on its edge, deadly as an arrow at its tip, it had the weight of Father's scythe and the words *To My Eternal Love*, bright as gold, inscribed on the arc of its claw. Death and Devotion, melded together.

The crew was gathered on deck when I arrived. I was late. Turley concluded the funeral service, and Father's body was cast into the sea. Wrapped in a dark cloak, like the villain in some music hall melodrama, I quietly entered behind them—and as the waves swallowed his corpse, I flew to the roof of the Captain's Quarters and held my new hand high for all to see. "Your captain is dead!" I shouted. *"Who shall rule in his place?"*

"HOOK!" was the resounding answer. "HOOK! HOOK! HOOK!"

Chapter Ten

————◆◆◆————

*A*h, mortality! What a terrible wonderful thing it is! Like a tiger biding its time until the unsuspecting prey draws near, the longer it waits the hungrier it grows. When it pounces, as it did with Father, it strikes with lightning horror. He had no chance to savor his life; he was young forever, and then he wasn't.

In deifying youth, the Never-Archipelago frees us from the unknown—how marvelous! At the same time it delivers a tedium of predictable sameness. "You will never grow old" promises delight; "You will never be different" sounds like a punishment.

If Peter were to age, I wondered, how old would he become? Would he wither to senility quicker than Father? Would he stand in defiance against Time, cock-crowing his eternal boyhood? Or would he disintegrate to dust in an instant, once the sun melted his frozen youth?

I could not learn the answer until I lured him to London. But how?

Alas, I knew how.

I prepared my hook with the tenderest of temptations. I baited it with children.

No sooner did I assume the mantle of captain than I ordered the men to set sail in a northwesterly direction. I made some adjustments among the crew: Teynte was now quartermaster (replacing Turley, whom I found too confoundedly dull), and I appointed Gentleman Starkey my first mate (taking the place of Foggerty, who was simply too d—ned Scots). We reached the Never-Isle after three and a half days, and anchored in a cove on the eastern shore.

I decided not to arrive at Peter's Underground Home by air: not only did I want to conserve my supply of Flying Sand, but I wanted Peter to be forewarned of my arrival—he might be less suspicious that way. I had Black Murphy row me to the beach, and I headed off alone into the jungle.

Things had changed ever so slightly. There was now an atmosphere of—how shall I describe it? Distrust. At one point during my hike I passed Barnaby and his cubs; as soon as they sniffed my presence they were off like a shot.

I don't believe it was only *me* that they wished to avoid; I later learned that Tiger Lily's death had left Panther and his people angry, and out for blood. This led, naturally, to blood-*shed*, and sadly the most common victims were the animals. True, it may have been my newly sinister self that caused alarm, but whatever the cause there was nothing I could do about it.

I arrived at the Underground Home tree in the late afternoon. "Peter?" I called down his ladder. There was no response. I sat on the ground, leaned my back against the tree trunk, and waited. After about twenty minutes I heard a rustling in the brush: Peter was returning from a visit to the lagoon. He stopped in his tracks at the sight of me and drew his blunt stick in defense.

"Who are you?" he asked, wary.

"You don't recognize me? I'm not surprised—I've grown some. It's James."

He squished his face up like he was trying to pry something from his memory. "James?"

"The boy you rescued from the burning ship. We swam with the Mermaids, and I fought Lone Wolf on the savanna."

His eyes lit up. "James! I haven't seen you since yesterday! What happened? You've—" And then a terribly sad look came over his face. "You're old."

"Yes. I'm sorry, Peter. But ever since Tiger Lily died, well, I became a different fellow. I ran away, and Time caught up with me."

"*Who* died?" he asked.

"Tiger Lily."

"Who's that?"

He had forgotten her completely.

I shook my head. "It doesn't really matter. What matters is that I've come back, to play."

"But I can't play with *you*. You're a *man*."

"I'm still a boy at heart."

"You can't be. You're too tall. You have whiskers and everything."

I rubbed my cheeks—I'd forgotten to shave that morning, and the shadow of a beard (the only shadow I had about me) had made its appearance.

"What's that?" he asked, curiosity changing the subject for him.

"It's a hook."

"That looks like fun. I bet it helps you climb trees and cliffs and things. Where do *I* get one?"

"You'd have to lose a hand first."

He looked at one of his hands, as if he were trying to figure out exactly *how* to lose it.

"Peter," I interrupted, "if *I* can't play with you, who *will*?"

He looked back at me, and tears sprang to his eyes.

"I don't know. Barnaby won't play anymore and I don't know why. The lions and tigers won't even let me *pet* them and the natives have forbidden me to enter the village. The mermaids are all right but—they're *girls*. Did I do something wrong?"

Oh, the stupid innocence of youth.

"I'll tell you what. I know a place that's *filled* with boys, just your age or younger. You could go there, and play all day long and have the best of times. What do you say?"

"James, that's brilliant! Where? Let's go now!"

"We have to wait until nightfall. And we'll need to fly. Do you have enough Sand for both of us to travel a long, long way?"

"Tink does. She has *tons* of it."

"Ask her if we can take some."

"She won't mind. She won't even *miss* it."

He entered the tree and slid down his ladder, out of sight. I moved to my old entrance, and could barely fit. It took some maneuvering, but eventually I arrived at the bottom. Peter was preparing a pipe and asked me if I wished to share.

"No, thank you, Peter, I don't do that anymore. I only smoke cigars since I've grown up."

"But they stink!"

"Yes, they do. That's why I like them."

He found that very funny, and I laughed along with him.

The remarkable thing about revenge is that it doesn't pretend to be anything other than what it really is. There's no false altruism involved, no lessons to be taught, no fortune to be gained, and, more often than not, it has terrible consequences for those who seek it out. It's a complete mystery to me why it is so attractive. Yet it is. I admit it. I was drawn to it as if it were a lovely lady (as it sometimes is).

We stood on the beach waiting for the stars to pop out. As soon as the Liana appeared we peppered ourselves with Sand. I wanted to ensure that we would not be separated, and so just before we launched I reached out my hand to take his. He pulled back at once. "You must not touch me!" he exclaimed. "No one must ever touch me!" Peter, who had been so tactile when we first met, had indeed changed: was it because, when last we were together, I struck him repeatedly and then tried to stab him? Was he like this now with everyone, both human and animal? Had I asked him for a reason, I knew he would say that he had *always* been this way, and so I said nothing.

I pointed the star out to Peter to show him the way. "We head in that general direction and continue straight on till morning," I explained. But we arrived in London long before morning dawned, and as we circled the Kensington Gardens I pointed out the Round Pond and told him that, if he were to wait here long enough, dozens of boys would appear.

He swooped down on it without even a word of thanks. As he alighted on a park bench I waved my farewell and headed back to the Never-Isle and the *Roger*. I had no idea whether or not I would see him again. Once the sun nipped the tips of the treetops, Peter would begin to grow.

What I failed to reckon on was his impatience. I told him to wait, and the one thing that boys cannot do is wait.

He began to explore, I later learned, and his explorations took him into Holland Park, where he found an open bedroom window and a sleepless boy who said that his name was Tootles. Peter asked him if he wanted to play and Tootles said he did, and so Peter peppered him with Sand and flew him back to the Never-Isle.

Tootles was the first but not the final abduction. Nibs and Slightly and Curly and the Twins soon followed, and Peter made up some story about their falling out of their perambulators in order to justify his criminal behavior. Nobody minded except their parents, I expect, who grieved and worried and may have even taken to drink or divorce as a result of the disappearances. I like to think that some of the boys could have been orphans, or victims of frequent whippings at the hands of stepfathers who did not want them, and thus Peter's thievery was something of a rescue. I like to think that, but I very much doubt it.

And the worst part of it was, of course, that Peter always flew to London and back before daylight. The sun never touched him, and so he remained as carefree and heartless as ever.

What I needed, I realized now, was something to keep Peter in London for at least a day. I needed a temptation, a lure beyond the realm of "playmate." It was then that I came up with a second scheme, which was perhaps the most terrible mistake of my life.

Those of you familiar with the Scotsman's tale may recall an incident involving a cake cooked by the pirates and given to the boys so that they might eat it and die from sugar consumption. Now anyone with any knowledge of the kitchen, or better yet anyone with small children about them, knows very well that sugar will not kill, at least not in the same way that a nice dose of strychnine will. Even *I*, blessed with no culinary talent whatsoever and, sadly, no children to my name, know this much: what sugar will do is make the child who eats enough of it wildly insane for a brief period of time, after which that child will collapse into a sleep so deep that the world's end will not wake him. The Scotsman, as usual, got it all wrong, first by placing that incident *after* the arrival of Wendy, and second by saying that I did not succeed in my sugar poisoning.

I did, dear reader, I most assuredly did.

Jukes baked a lovely apple cake, mixing the fruit with as much molasses and brown sugar as we could spare. To tell the truth, I don't believe there was much flour in the cake at all; it was mostly sweetness held together by a few slices of apple. I placed it early one morning in the vicinity of the tree, hoping the boys would discover it before any flies did. Nibs exited the Underground Home to relieve himself and nearly stumbled over the prize. He swiped one finger across the top of it to taste; he fancied that if it *was* poisonous he would die a hero never to be forgotten, and if it was just a cake he would have a little bit of it all to himself before having to share it with the others. Well, he found it delicious, sounded an immediate alarm, and before long the cake was happily settling into the stomachs of all the other boys, including Peter.

The next few hours found them running around creating all sorts of havoc on the island, fueled as they were by sugary energy. They shimmied up the palm trees and commenced to swing from the hanging lianas; they ran to the savanna and pulled all the lions' tails before scampering back into the bushes; they tried to fly without the help of any Sand, but their attempts mostly involved jumping off stumps and flapping their arms, so no one was injured. At length, once they were well exercised, they simply collapsed around the base of the Underground Home tree without even bothering to descend to their beds, and became like ones dead.

I had retired to the ship and returned just before noon to find them all quite unconscious. I even kicked the Twins none too gently to see if they would awake; their snores continued unabated. I moved directly to Peter.

He was lying half in and half out of his tree hole, his head and upper arms draped over the top rung of the ladder while his feet dragged in the dust. It was his feet that I wanted, or rather what they held. I knelt before him, seized an ankle, and lay the sharp edge of my claw against his starboard sole. I cut.

I needed to move quickly, I realized, lest he awake from

the pain; but the pain, if there was any, he slept through. He had attached the prize, as I mentioned earlier, with some sort of tree sap, and though it was well stuck, its removal involved just as much pulling and yanking as it did cutting. At one point I had to seize the prize with my *teeth*, arcing backward with all my might while at the same time holding his foot with my good hand and sawing away with the other. The sap stretched like a band of rubber, and as soon as I cut it from Peter's foot my prize slapped me in the face and stuck. Once I managed to pull it free, it adhered to my hand, and then to my hook, and then to my trouser leg, so that it took as much effort to untangle *myself* from its clutches as it did to remove it from Peter.

Nevertheless, in the end, it was mine again. It even smelled of me, of my boyhood and my London home. My shadow brought with it so many wonderful, terrible memories. I would have embraced it, if I could.

I returned to the ship and spread it out on the floor of my cabin in order to remove any trace of sap. Once I had succeeded (with a mixture of turpentine and water), I stood back to survey the whole. Inexplicably I began to cry. There he was, the boy I used to be, fully equipped with two hands. The shadow-hand was smaller, of course, than the one that had been removed, and in some ways less practical than the claw I had now. But it could never be mine again, no more than the shadow could be mine: I had outgrown them both.

I wasted no time and flew that very night. It was 1896 in London now, and as soon as the sun struck the Thames, I began to age five more years. I didn't care; I had a mission, and I could not complete it alone. I needed an accomplice, but I wasn't sure how to go about recruiting her.

I waited until George had left for the office before I rang the bell. Mary answered, infant in arm. His name was Michael, she told me after giving me a warm, welcoming embrace. Wendy and Jack were both at school, he attending my Wilkinson's alma mater, and Wendy well placed in an excellent school for girls. I was sorry to miss them, I said, but I had come on other matters. Mary looked concerned. "Is everything all right, James?" she asked.

"Not really. Is there someplace where we can talk?"

She ushered me into the drawing room. Their maid, Liza, brought us morning tea and left with the baby, and as soon as we were alone I got to the point at once.

"Do you know what this is?" I asked her as I unrolled the prize.

"Why it's—it looks like—a shadow!" She was utterly surprised. "Who does it belong to? Not—not *you*. It's much too small."

"It belonged to me once, when I was a boy. But another boy took it, and I've only just retrieved it."

"Would you like me to sew it back on?"

"No; thank you, Mary, but I'm afraid that would be absurd. As you said it's too small. What I *would* like, though, is for you to hold on to it."

"Why?"

"Don't tell George—he'll only be alarmed—but the boy who took it from me will come to retrieve it."

"How will he know where it is?"

"I intend to tell him, Mary. And when he comes, which will most likely be in the night, I need you to keep him here for a short period of time."

"But won't his mother be worried?"

"He has no mother. He doesn't even know what that word means."

"He's an orphan? How sad."

"He's *more* than an orphan. He's a fly-by-night, a runaway."

"Oh dear."

"He lives by no rules. He has no discipline. He *needs* a mother to give some structure to his life. Which is why I came to *you*."

"You want us to adopt him?" She was most alarmed.

"No, no, that won't be necessary. I ask only that you keep him here for a morning at least. Wendy and Jack will be off to school. Liza can watch over Michael."

"But *how* can I keep him here if he's a thief? Shouldn't I call the police?"

To be honest this option had not occurred to me. "I don't think that will be necessary. Distract him. Give him some of Jack's toys. Or if you must, sew the shadow back on him. But during that time, teach him the Commandments. He needs to learn about right and wrong. Most especially he needs to learn the one that says 'Thou shalt not kill.'"

"I don't understand, James." She looked, and *was*, bewildered.

"And I can't explain. Suffice it to say that the boy needs to embrace Responsibility, which can only be learned at the foot of a good English mother. You're the best one I know." I leaned close and took her hand. "Mary, you are a remarkable woman. George is very lucky, and I daresay, had George never found you, I would have been blessed to have been chosen to take his place." Nervousness made the phrasing awkward, but she understood what I meant. I kissed her hand, then rose, and handed her the shadow. "Put it in a drawer in your bedroom—a drawer that squeaks so it will wake you. George, if he's like me, will sleep through anything." She smiled and shook her head, acknowledging the truth of this. "The boy will find it, don't worry about that. Then it's up to you."

She invited me to dinner, but I declined. I took my leave of her, and never saw her again.

Whether or not Mary succeeded in teaching Peter the Commandments made little difference to me. I only hoped that Peter would be occupied in London when the sun rose. Senility or Dust was my end for him, and though I regretted the trick I played on Mary, and the shock she would receive when this beautiful boy disintegrated before her eyes, I was sure that there would be some way to make it up to her later. Revenge, dear reader, can be so focused it blinds one to consequences. And there were many.

I spent the rest of the day in the British Museum, marveling at the items collected since my last visit, at age twelve, and illuminated now by electric light! As soon as night fell I peppered, flew, and instead of returning to the ship I landed outside Peter's Underground Home. The sun was just rising.

Mimicking Peter, I crowed like a cock, and before long Slightly poked his head out of the tree to see what was what.

"Is Peter still abed? Wake him. I have some alarming news for him," I told the boy.

Slightly descended with the message, and moments later a sleepy Peter climbed out of the tree.

"James, you look different," he said.

"Unhappily I've grown a little more."

"Oh, that's terrible. Do you want me to kill you? If you don't stop growing you'll be dead before long, and that will be terrible. But if I kill you now—in a duel or something—you'll die a hero, which should be an awfully big adventure."

"Thank you, Peter, perhaps another day. I come on more urgent business."

"Oh good. I like urgency. Will someone die if I don't act at once to save them?"

For a boy destined to live forever, he certainly thought a lot about Death.

"Have you noticed anything missing?" I asked.

He looked at his hands, expecting to find one gone. "I don't think so. I slept nearly all of yesterday. We had the most delicious cake and then we ran around and became unbelievably tired and snoozed all afternoon. And then we had the crumbs for dinner and slept even longer."

"Look at your feet."

He did. "My shadow!"

"Yes, I *thought* it was yours. I was strolling the deck of my ship last evening when it flew overhead. I asked it where it was going and it said it was going to London, Number 14, Kensington Park Gardens."

"But why?" He was astonished.

"I don't know. I think it grew tired of you and wanted some different adventures. It knew the way to London, I suppose, because you've flown there so often of late, collecting the boys. But why Number 14, Kensington Park Gardens, I haven't a clue."

"Oh dear." Peter sank down onto a tree root and sat with his head in his fists. I had never seen him so discouraged, and for a moment I feared he would let the shadow have its freedom.

"You might lure it home, of course," I suggested. "Shadows can be like fickle women. They disappear without a moment's notice and you need to woo them back."

"How?"

"Oh, with . . . with determination, I should think. It needs to know that you miss it. You should fly to London, locate your shadow, demonstrate how thrilled you are to find it again, and then wait around a bit until the sun comes up to make sure it's properly attached."

"But how will I attach it? There's not the right sort of sap in London. At least I don't think there is."

My mind was racing. "There's a woman who lives at Number 14, Kensington Park Gardens, who's very good with a needle and thread. If you were to ask her to *sew* your shadow back on, well, the problem will be solved."

Stupid, stupid, stupid man. I should have thought like Peter thought, not like a vengeful naval captain drooling to get even.

First of all, I should have taken into account the passage of Time.

He flew that night. A London year had nearly passed in our twenty-four hours, and in those months Wendy had come across the shadow in her mother's sewing box and, fascinated, moved it to her own dresser drawer. (Mary had assumed that the boy would arrive shortly, and when that did not happen, she must have thought the thief would never come and so put it out of her mind.) Peter arrived ten months later than expected, sniffed out the prize, and not knowing the difference between woman and girl, he asked Wendy to sew it back on for him. She did, her brothers awoke, Peter peppered the boys with Sand, and because Wendy wouldn't allow them to travel alone, Peter peppered her too. He kidnapped all three and was gone before the sun could wither him.

This child abduction was the latest of a long series (beginning with Tootles), and the London newspapers made much of it. THREE MORE!!! the headlines blared. (I saw a copy of the paper years later.) The police were at their wit's end. Scotland Yard was brought onto the case, and a few unsavory men and several Gypsies were questioned. All were released. The great Sherlock Holmes was brought out of retirement to get to the bottom of it, but he was passionately involved with cocaine and bees by that point, and the mystery remains unsolved to this day.

Mary Darling, deprived of three children in an instant, was driven to the care of an alienist, who urged her to reexamine her life and become more independent. George was indeed alienated and eventually they separated, but remained friends.

I learned of this much later, of course. But even at the time I sensed that it had all gone terribly wrong. Once I was told of the children's arrival on the Never-Isle, I indulged in a good amount of denial ("Not my fault!") followed by an even greater amount of conscience salving ("You couldn't have foreseen *these* consequences!"). But in the end I realized that I, who had gone on and on about Peter's Lack of Responsibility, needed to embrace Responsibility myself. Poor Mary! Poor George! Most of all, poor Wendy! (The boys, I figured, would have a grand time, no matter what the outcome.) And it was all my fault! The Agony of Blame culminated in a sort of Dark Night of the Soul, which involved, I admit, a great deal of alcohol. (I suffered terribly for it the next morning, and would not advise its use, especially in cases of moral confusion.) During the night I was visited by visions of my mother, of my father, even of Tink (for heaven's sake!), all of whom filled me with such thoughts of self-loathing that dawn found me on my knees, praying fervently for forgiveness. God could not forgive me, of course, until I had forgiven everyone else, and so I formally pardoned Peter for Tiger Lily's murder and all manner of other things that irritated me so. I pardoned Scroff, I pardoned Slinque, I pardoned every master and boy at Eton whose names I could recall, and when I arose from my knees I was a new man, Born Again. The grappling hooks of Revenge had loosed their grip on me.

But God's forgiveness bestowed on James Hook né Cook did not mean I bore no further responsibility. No, no, my good reader, I needed to make amends.

I needed to rescue the children.

I felt for the parents, George and Mary in particular, but even the thought of Tootles's grieving father and mother broke my heart. I felt for Wendy, who I knew missed her home. I felt for the children themselves. I felt for *my*self, and all the experiences of growing older that I had missed. And so I concocted a plan.

By this time Peter was, of course, aware of the presence of a ship anchored off the Never-Isle's eastern shore. I admit we had yet to remove the skull-and-crossbones flag and replace it with Her Majesty's colors (Smee was a very busy man), and so Peter told his boys (and Wendy) that we were pirates, captained by the notorious Hook. I daresay he had nothing against us; it was all part of his game of adventure.

Still, his boys took it all too much to heart, and so they feared us. In truth they had nothing to fear: Black Murphy, who perhaps looked the fiercest of us all (pointy teeth, wagging earlobes), *adored* children. This made the rescue all the more of a challenge. The fear-addled boys would not accept our invitation to visit the ship.

Logic was not an option. Bribery might have worked, but we had nothing with which to bribe them: we were grown men with few possessions who didn't smell very good. I was at a loss. I finally decided that my only option was to do what *Peter* had done: kidnap them.

I began with an on-deck meeting with my crew. I was very forthcoming. First of all, I explained that the Never-Archipelago was so far from England that it was nearly impossible for them to return. This announcement was met with such wailing and weeping that Niobe herself would have been put to shame. I then said that, should they stay here in this wonderful place, where the weather was always lovely, they would never age and might live forever, barring someone stabbing them or hanging them or such. They now became very quiet and seemed to reconsider their predicament. I then ordered a ration of rum to be distributed, and after that they were with me.

I next told them that there were some children on the island who had been kidnapped from their loving parents, and that it was our heroic task to rescue them and send them home. The rum had had its effect by now, and so no one asked any difficult questions. I explained that I intended with their help to bring the children to the *Roger*, but that this would require some force, as their kidnapper had mesmerized the innocent babes into believing that they *belonged* here. On no account, I emphasized, was any blood to be shed. The men grumbled a bit at this, but finally agreed.

Some of what the Scotsman wrote regarding what followed was accurate, though most was convenient fiction. I ordered Jukes to bake a covered-dish compote of cinnamon and apples and cloves, from which wafted an indescribably delicious aroma, reminiscent of Christmas. The entire crew but Noodler and Turley traveled with me to the Isle (it was all I could do to keep them from devouring Jukes's culinary masterpiece), and together we made our way to the Underground Home. I knew the boys would be frightened, so I brought along some potato sacks and rope. We arrived at the tree at dinnertime, and Jukes uncovered the compote while Smee fanned its scent into the tree holes.

It wasn't long before Nibs (who since the last adventure had appointed himself the Official Taster) popped out of the tree. Starkey seized him, plopped him into a potato sack, and that was that. Others followed one by one, thinking that Nibs was devouring the entire deliciousness all by himself.

We got them all without a hitch. (I had, by the way, put a few molasses sweets in the bottom of each sack to give them something with which to occupy themselves during the journey.) Wendy was the last to leave, and rather than give her over to the ignominy of sackdom, I trusted that she would recognize me (or at least my hook) and allow me to explain. As soon as she emerged, Gentleman Starkey cupped his hand over her mouth in a gentlemanly fashion, and I reintroduced myself. She was delighted to see me. I nodded for Starkey to release her, and she embraced me as if I were her long-lost uncle (which, in a half way, I was).

"Thank goodness you've come," she said. "Mother and Father must be beside themselves with worry, and that terrible boy does nothing but encourage us all to do whatever we wish, so long as he approves. He's like a little dictator. Oh, Uncle James, won't you *please* take us home?"

I told her that was my intention, and so Wendy, accompanied by my crew carrying sacks of boys happily munching molasses sweets, headed for the ship.

I waited behind, for Peter. I DID NOT, I repeat, DID NOT descend underground to poison him, or Tink, or any such nonsense. I merely waited, and when he finally emerged, I hit him over the head and tied him up with *very* loose knots, after which I descended (with some trouble) into the Home to do *the one bit of pirating I have ever done in my life*! I stole Tink's Cotswold Cottage, tucked it into a final sack, and at last ascended. I apologized to Peter and left.

* * *

Once on board the ship the boys were desacked and given some apple pie. Each sailor was assigned to one boy, and before long Mullins and Mason were playing tag with the Twins, Jeb Cookson was teaching Tootles how to "lasso a dogie," and Black Murphy was bouncing Michael on his knee and letting the child play with his dangling earlobes.

I brought Wendy to my Quarters, and there I told her everything. She was as sympathetic and understanding as I knew she would be, and promised to do her best to convince the boys to return with her to London, and the loving arms of their grieving parents. I explained to her about the Flying Sand (she knew the rudiments already, having flown here with Peter); I then ordered Starkey to gather the giggling boys into a group and sent her to her work. Meanwhile I removed the Cottage from the sack and carefully lifted off its roof in order to scoop out the Sand all the more easily.

It was then I saw her, a tiny winged thing no larger than my littlest toe's toenail. She was furious at me for transporting her Cottage, and demanded to know the reason why. I tried to explain, but I fear she did not listen. She flew out of the porthole in a huff and, as I later learned, whizzed directly to Peter, who by this time was nearly escaped from his ropes. She told him I was responsible for everything, and urged him to murder me at once.

Wendy, in the meantime, brought all the boys to tears, reminding them of their dear parents, whom they had, until this point, entirely forgotten. Conveniently, they had also forgotten everything else about their lives in London, and so she was able to convince them that school was a delight and church even more so. "I can't wait to learn my multiplication tables," Curly was heard to exclaim, and both the Twins expressed a fervent wish that next Sunday's sermon might be twice as long as the last one they'd heard.

I emerged from my Quarters, carrying the Cottage, which held (I hoped) enough sand to transport them every one back to England. Wendy, surrounded by the boys, met me mid-deck. But before I could begin the peppering, Peter struck.

Granted, he was a boy without education and so knew nothing of Form, Good or Bad. Nevertheless, he attacked from behind, hurtling down through the air to stab me in the back. Had he had any weapon sharper than a blunt stick, I would have been sorely wounded.

I cried out and whipped around. His eyes were ablaze with fury. I could see at once that *this* fight was serious, but the boys thought differently. Assuming this was another of Peter's adventures, they took off screaming, attacking the very sailors with whom moments ago they had been frolicking. Luckily my crew joined in on the fun, allowing themselves to be skewered by invisible swords, decapitated by tiny chopping hands, and frightened into heart failure by some imaginary something called the Doodle-Doo, which had sequestered itself in my cabin. Sadly little Michael insisted on dying himself, and was murdered again and again, collapsing in horrific screams at the feet of Black Murphy, though the poor sailor did not lay so much as a finger on the child. "Kill me one more time!" the toddler cried as soon as his blood was spilled, and Murphy had but to wag his earlobes for Michael to screech his death agony at the top of his lungs and crumple in a puddle of gore.

Peter and I, in the meantime, faced off against each other. "Peter," I pleaded, "release them! You can't give them what they really need!"

"They need fun! They need play! They need FREEDOM!" he shouted, swiping his blunt stick at me with every exclamation.

"No, Peter," I said. "They need Love."

He paused for a moment midair. "I don't really know what that word means," he said, and it was the only time I remember bitterness coloring his voice. "Except it's a lie."

"No it isn't, not always," I answered.

"How can you tell?"

"That's easy. When the people who love you change, when they leave you, when they die, it hurts more than knives, and arrows, more than Long Tom blowing you to pieces. It just hurts."

And then a coldness descended like a mask across his face. "When *you* die I won't be hurt *one bit*," he said. "I hate you, James. I wanted you to be my friend and you changed. You *grew up!*"

"I'm sorry, Peter. It happens to us all. Most of us, anyway. Besides, what you just said sounds a *bit* like Love to me."

This was the final straw. Cecco had just been disemboweled by Curly and lay on the deck in operatic agony. Peter swooped down and plucked the sword from his belt. Before I could respond he swished it through the air and cut me deep. Blood welled from my chest. "Peter, please," I begged, but he swiped again, cutting low this time, clipping my side. The wound, I feared, was mortal. It was only now, as Death approached me, that my senses grew acute. I could hear the gentle tick-tick of a watch beating like a heart smothered in cotton. She had followed me here, all the way from Long Tom, and now she was offering me sweet repose. And so it struck me: at this point in the game I was simply a pawn.

There was no other way left—I had to give Peter his victory.

I backed to the ship's rail, the tip of Peter's sword pressed against my throat.

"Prepare to die, O most terrible of men!" Peter hissed.

I uttered a prayer, for Eton and the boys and for children everywhere, then threw myself over the side.

Like a mother cradling the fall of a child tossed from a burning building, Daisy caught me in her open jaws.

What happened next is exactly what I expected. Peter crowed his triumph and ordered all the boys back to the Underground Home. (My crew, during this, were wise enough to feign death, and lay about the ship in positions of extreme rigor mortis.) Wendy protested Peter's command, and when Peter objected she began to cry and all the boys felt bad for her and agreed to fly back to London that very night, and the rest is, more or less, history. The Darling children returned to Number 14, Kensington Park Gardens, the other boys found their separate ways back to their parents, none of the children remembered anything of what had happened, and Scotland Yard declared the case closed. The one thing that no one commented on was the fact that, although the year of their return was 1898 and all the children had been missing from between two and seven years, not one of them had aged. Thus it was that five-year-old Curly was at first three years *younger* than his younger brother Fred, and so forth and so on. By the day's end, however, all had caught up with themselves and aged properly. (Tootles sprouted a silky beard and mustache in a matter of hours!) Still, everyone was happy to have the families reunited, so nobody bothered much about the details. Everyone was happy, that is, except for the Darling family, for Mary and George had separated by this point. Still, they were overjoyed to have their children again, and Michael and Jack at least had no memory of their parents having lived together, so they were happy *enough*.

I learned all of this very much after the fact, and here is how that came to be:

Daisy returned with me to Long Tom, carrying me gently in her jaws. It was a journey of days, during which time I drifted in and out of consciousness, but all of that salt water did wonders for my wounds so that, though I bear the scars to this day, Peter's attack did not prove fatal.

I rested on Long Tom for several months. Daisy saw that I was fed, bringing a daily supply of fish to me, and the occasional bird or turtle egg.

Eventually the *Roger*, once again under Starkey's command, returned to Long Tom, and, oh, the celebration that followed at our reunion! We had a glorious evening of Talent and Entertainment, held on the island itself, and even Daisy seemed to enjoy herself, especially when Skylights pretended to be her and Black Murphy pretended to be me, and Skylights picked up Black Murphy and gave him a big kiss and carried him off into the sea, from which they soon returned, soaking wet.

The next morning Starkey offered me the captaincy again, but I declined. I did not wish, I told him, to be responsible for anybody else for a long, long while, though I did have one request to make of him. I retrieved from the Captain's Quarters the Cotswold Cottage, and brought it with me back to Long Tom. After a week in their happy company, I bid my crew farewell. They were off to explore the archipelago one more time, and promised to return in a few months. But I knew that I would never see them again.

Within a week or so after they departed, I began preparing Daisy for the inevitable. I told her every day how much I would miss her, but said that she could not come with me, as pets of her size were not welcome where I was going. She lay in my arms at night (or at least as much of her as would fit, which wasn't much), and I said that I would always live inside her, a presence as real as my father's watch, and that she would forever live inside me. Finally, on a beautiful evening, as Peter's Liana winked at me from the horizon, I peppered myself with Flying Sand and held her close one last time.

"I love you," I whispered to her. I like to think that as much affection as a crocodile can have for another being, Daisy had for me.

Mortality, I decided, was far preferable to its alternative. I *wanted* to grow old, and to change, and to suffer loss, and to learn new things, and to be human once again. I longed for everything that *wasn't* Peter Pan.

The year had become 1905 by the time I returned, and *Peter Pan* was the talk of the London stage. I could not bring myself to see it, and to this day I am glad that I have not added that pain to my life. I did read the book when it came out several years later, and found it execrable. Michael, I believe, was the Scotsman's main source, and he had been barely more than an infant at the time of his transportation.

But the play did grant me one blessing in disguise: it allowed me to find Wendy again.

She had just turned twenty, and was living with her father, who was not well. George and Mary, long separated, had sold the house at Number 14, so that when I showed up at the door I was greeted by a total stranger. The publicity surrounding the play, however, allowed me to learn both of their new addresses. Mary had told the press repeatedly that the play was, of course, a fiction and nothing more, born of her sons' friendship with the author. Shortly before the play's premiere, George contracted a cancer of the jaw.

His illness was slow and debilitating, and when I appeared on the scene he was nearing the end. I sat by his bedside, holding his hand and reading to him when necessary. He could not speak, but was fully aware of who I was, and I consider it one of the great honors of my life to have been present at his deathbed. Wendy was there with me, and each of us held one of his hands, and because he could not speak his last communication was a smile that was nothing less than beatific.

Mary refused to see me, and I cannot blame her. I was the cause of the deepest sorrow of her life. She too succumbed to cancer, less than six years later. Michael died in the war. Jack, who also served and suffered terribly from shell shock, became a publisher, and has promised me that this little tome will see the light of day, once I'm finished.

I, in the meantime, found a job as a clerk. My sinister handwriting had improved with time until, if I wrote carefully, my penmanship was as much a thing of beauty as it ever was. I lived in a small rented flat in Southwark, and my income was sufficient for all my needs.

Wendy married, and mothered two lovely boys and a beautiful girl. I was godfather to all three. In my sixty-fifth year I had a minor stroke, and Wendy and her husband (James!) offered to take me in. I resisted, but another attack made me unemployable, and so I surrendered.

I have lived with them for many years now, and Wendy has kindly taken dictation during these past few months, as I reminisced.

And what of Peter? I do not know. One night, quite recently, I awoke from a sound sleep to find a boy standing over my bed, examining me closely. Was this a dream? Perhaps. Nothing came of it. I closed my eyes and opened them again, and he was gone.

Daisy, I'm confident, ticks on.

I still have the Cotswold Cottage and its precious contents, should I ever wish to visit my dear croc again. But I think not. I'm content with the regular ticking of time, and don't wish to jump around in it anymore.

And so, dear reader, I bid you farewell.

Peter's story will live on, as long as children are "gay and innocent and heartless."

Time will remedy that.

My tale is over and, like all human tales, must soon be forgotten. It must.

FINIS

Postscript

———··◆◇◆··———

$\mathcal{J}$ ames Cook, author of this manuscript, passed away in July 1940, during a bombing raid in the Battle of Britain. Only a few months earlier, according to his half-nephew Jack Darling, he had captained a small boat in the Dunkirk evacuation, in spite of his poor health. This information was gleaned from *The Times'* obituary, which, due to the war effort, was extremely brief. The manuscript itself was never published, for reasons I cannot explain. Very few individuals knew of its existence, presumably, until its rediscovery in a small American college library by myself, when I was perusing the stacks for another book. I was employed by the library at the time, and when I showed the manuscript to the professor in charge of the collection, he told me to "keep it if you find it interesting." I did. It was very worn and the handwriting faded and quite difficult to read. I therefore took it upon myself to "restore" several sections, and any resulting confusions or doubts that you, dear reader, might have, I take full responsibility for.

John Leonard Pielmeier

Where James Cook is buried I do not know. I only know that he chose Death over Eternity, Change over Certainty, and Pain over Happy Oblivion.

We all should be so fortunate.

—John Leonard Pielmeier

Acknowledgments

First and foremost, thanks must go to Hook's "little Scotsman." The good Captain may despise him; I bow to this remarkable writer. I grew up with Peter and his story; it was the first book I learned to read, though truthfully it had been read to me so often that I simply recited it word for word while turning the pages, so that what my mother took as a four-year-old's precociousness was really just a trick of memorization. My first play (age seven) was the story of a boy named Jack—who flew. (I too flew at times, though I can do this now only on very special occasions.) Then, shortly after my thirtieth birthday, I saw an eye-opening production of *What Every Woman Knows.* Immediately I went to the local library and found a *Collected Plays*, which I devoured. Following this, I spent time on an artist-colony island where I read Andrew Birkin's moving and fascinating *J. M. Barrie and the Lost Boys.* I visited Scotland and the birthplace. I wrote a play about the man. I was in literary love.

Scholars, in my opinion, often misunderstand Barrie. He

was not a boy who refused to grow up; he was a boy who grew up too quickly. There is a photo of Barrie playing Hook with the Llewelyn Davies boys: he identified not with Peter at all but with the sad, softhearted Captain.

My thanks extend to others: to my friend and one-time TV agent Brian Pike, who was so supportive both professionally and personally of the earliest draft. My good friend Tracy Strong read it next, the first person (after my wife) to understand what I was trying to accomplish. My friend Thomas Donahue followed, and my friends Richard Kollath and Ed McCann, and David Rintels and Vicki Riskin, and all appreciated the humor, and the narrative, and the crocodile. My British friend David Oakes read it hunting for Americanisms; hopefully they are as invisible as Tink. All of these good people gave me confidence in the work and belief in myself, something which all writers need, and which I seem (at times) to be particularly short of.

You would not be reading this book without the kindness of my friend George Birnbaum. Over dinner one night I complained to him that I could not find an agent to represent the book, let alone a publisher. He introduced me to his agent-friend Jeff Schmidt, who offered to read the book, and who fell in love with it in a way that all agents should fall in love with all books they agree to represent. Jeff promised me that he would find a publisher, and he did.

That publisher was Scribner, and the editor who bought it—the wonderful John Glynn—has guided me through the process of publication with the sure hand of a Pan teaching a Hook to fly.

All of these I thank. Each one is "first and foremost."

Acknowledgments

But the first and foremost—est is my wife. Irene O'Garden is the best writer I know, and I aspire to some day be as good as she is. Poor Hook never found a partner, best friend, or lover; I am fortunate to have found all three in this amazing woman. Thank you, my Darling.

And thank you, readers. You too are "first and foremost."

—John Leonard Pielmeier